THE LAST NIGHT
AT TREMORE BEACH

THE LAST NIGHT
AT TREMORE BEACH

A NOVEL

MIKEL SANTIAGO

TRANSLATED BY CARLOS FRÍAS

ATRIA BOOKS

New York   London   Toronto   Sydney   New Delhi

ATRIA BOOKS

An Imprint of Simon & Schuster, Inc.
1230 Avenue of the Americas
New York, NY 10020

First Atria Books hardcover edition February 2017

ATRIA BOOKS and colophon are trademarks of Simon & Schuster, Inc.

For information about special discounts for bulk purchases, please contact Simon & Schuster Special Sales at 1-866-506-1949 or business@simonandschuster.com.

The Simon & Schuster Speakers Bureau can bring authors to your live event. For more information, or to book an event, contact the Simon & Schuster Speakers Bureau at 1-866-248-3049 or visit our website at www.simonspeakers.com.

Interior design by Laura Levatino

Manufactured in the United States of America

10 9 8 7 6 5 4 3 2 1

Library of Congress Cataloging-in-Publication Data has been applied for.

ISBN 978-1-5011-0224-0
ISBN 978-1-5011-0227-1 (ebook)

To my father, who left us before
this book was published.
For him.

THE LAST NIGHT
AT TREMORE BEACH

PROLOGUE

I've heard some writers describe it as "the tunnel." Something that magically opens up in their heads that allows them to travel to a place where their stories, events, and characters come into crystal clear view. At that point, the writer need only act as a reporter for the events as he sees them. He writes or types as fast as possible so as not to miss a single detail before the door to the tunnel closes again. He watches his characters like a spy, observes their expressions, feels what they feel, and he tells us all about it afterward.

The nature of inspiration is similar for a musician. In my case, it's something that "comes out of the sky." Don't ask me why, but I've always felt that "It" came from above, like a revelation. A melody is something anyone in the world can follow, but few can corral. If you picture it as an elusive butterfly, we composers have a butterfly net in our minds. Some nets are bigger and better than others, but we're all out for the same thing: to capture that fleeting melody, that whisper of magic we can feel all around us, to seize it, and, as if it were a priceless antique, to try to restore it, paying careful attention to each tiny and marvelous detail that only a divine being could have designed. We are, in a way, like mediums who communicate with another world. A world of lovely and elusive phantoms. Phantoms who exist to remind us we are more than animals born of pain and destined for oblivion. Phantoms who may yet explain to us the origins of life, time, and the stars above.

—Peter Harper, *Contemporary Music Writer Magazine*

PART ONE

ONE

THE STORM, which some meteorologist with a fetish for biblical verse dubbed "Lucifer," had been expected for days before it struck. It was going to be a big one, too, even by Donegal's standards: look out for flying roof tiles and toppled streetlamps. The announcer from Coastal Radio broke in with an update every sixty minutes: "Make sure to fill up your generators with fuel. Do you have enough frozen food? Cans of baked beans? Don't forget about candles and matches. To those of you who live near the coast, make sure to tie up your vessels. Dry dock your sailboats, if you can."

That morning, they'd predicted fifty-five mile per hour winds and advised against trying to drive on the roads beyond the late afternoon. They'd said we should be ready for a powerful downpour and flash flooding inland. For everyone who lived on the coast it was going to be a night of hell on earth, they said.

I had gone to Clenhburran early that morning to run errands and to shop for some last-minute groceries. Clenhburran was a little town, the only one for miles around, which makes it significant when the only thing that ties you to the outside world is a narrow and tortuous stretch of road between rocky cliffs.

My first order of business that morning had been to take my lawn mower to be fixed at John Durran's shop.

"Got your windows all boarded up, Mr. Harper?" he asked as I walked into his store. "You live over on Tremore Beach, right? Supposed to hit hard there tonight."

Durran was one of the people in town lining his pockets thanks to the impending storm. Piled by the door on one side of his store was a stack of plywood six or eight feet high and hanging from the roof above a light-up sign cautioned his customers, "Protect your windows!"

Naturally, there were special offers on gasoline generators, candles, propane grills, and other survival gear. The few tourists or weekend residents who happened to be in town filled their shopping carts, and Durran rubbed his hands together in anticipation. Too bad—for him—we were still a month away from the official start of high season.

I told him I was hunkered down for the storm, though I hadn't as much as boarded up a single window. Neither had Leo Kogan, my only neighbor on the beach, who had counseled me against it: "I'm sure it'll amount to nothing." He's a veteran of the beach, and I'd always trusted his expertise until that morning. I confess, after witnessing the pre-apocalyptic tension at Durran's and driving past homes completely shrouded in plywood, I started to get a little nervous.

I pushed the mower into the shop and told Brendan, the mechanic, that the day before I had again—for the second time this month—smashed into the same damn hidden septic tank drain, which was only partly covered by my lawn.

"Brand-new Outils Wolf and it's already got four dozen battle scars, Mr. Harper. If you want, we can rig some kind of metal plate over that septic tank drain," he said.

I told him the rental agency was supposed to do something about it—if, in fact, they ever got to it this *millennium*—and asked him when the mower would be ready.

"Well, we've got to change the blade and check the motor," Brendan explained. "Maybe two or three days."

I told him I'd be back for it then, and set off for a stroll down to the harbor. At the end of Main Street, I watched as the fishermen battened down their ships, and even Chester, the little old man who ran the newsstand, warned "something big" was headed our way tonight.

"Notice there's not a single seagull around," he said, as he placed my usual purchase into a bag: a copy of the *Irish Times*, a carton of Marlboros, and the latest best-selling mystery novel. "A clear blue sky and not a single one out hunting for food. That's because they're running from it, you know. The storm. They've all flown inland and right about now they're probably shitting all over Barranoa or Port Laurel. If you ask me, there's something big on the way. Haven't seen anything quite like this since the big one of 1951. That night, tractors and sheep got tossed across the countryside. See that store sign over there? Wind caught it and my cousin Barry found it on the road to Dungloe a couple miles from here."

But then I thought of my neighbor, Leo, who had insisted there was nothing to worry about. Just some sand spraying up against the windows, maybe a loose roof tile or two. Nothing major. He'd been living on the beach for more than three years now. He hadn't even bothered to change his dinner plans for tonight. We'd made arrangements to have dinner together at his house more than two weeks ago and yesterday he'd called to confirm.

"You think it's a good idea to be out tonight with the Apocalypse on its way?" I had asked him.

"It's just two miles to my house, Peter," he'd said with his usual cheeriness. "What could happen in the space of two miles?"

AROUND SIX in the evening, when I awoke from a nap, the storm front had already rolled in like a carpet across the late afternoon sky. I lay on the couch watching it through the living room's large picture windows: A titanic mass of storm clouds bloomed on the horizon, as deep as an abyss and as wide as the eye could see, advancing like an implacable army. Its darkened innards crackled with lightning, threatening an epic battle with the earth below.

I stood up and the so-called best-selling mystery novel—whose first fifty pages had managed to lull me to sleep—tumbled off my lap and onto the Aztec-patterned rug. I picked my guitar up off the floor, laid it against the throw pillows, and pulled open the sliding glass door to go outside. I was met by a furious gale that whipped across my lawn and shook the bushes like baby rattles. The white picket fence around my yard was bearing the brunt of it, as well. Down on the beach, sand swirled in giant clouds and pelted my face like needles.

Watching that monstrous storm fast approaching the coast, I felt like an insect about to be squashed by a giant. I thought back on John Durran's plywood and instantly regretted not bringing home a few sheets. This goddamn storm was going to swallow the entire beach whole. *Jesus, Pete, what were you thinking?*

I ran back inside and slid the balcony door closed. The latch had never really worked, but I slammed the door hard until it was sealed tight. *Relax, Harper, it's not the end of the world.* I went upstairs and made sure every north-facing window was shut tight.

THE LAST NIGHT AT TREMORE BEACH

It was a two-bedroom house: a master bedroom, a guest room with twin beds (which, in a few weeks, would welcome their first visitors: my children), and one bathroom. Beneath the tile roof was a tiny attic filled with dusty boxes and a few old pieces of luggage. I went up there for the first time in weeks just to make sure the skylight was locked. While I was up there, I grabbed a few candles, which I would spread throughout the house in case the lights went out in the middle of the night.

I unplugged everything and came back downstairs. The kitchen had just one window facing the sea, a double-paned glass that looked strong. I went out the kitchen door to the backyard, rounded up a few loose wooden chairs, and stacked them in the shed. Inside were several tools and planks of wood that some previous resident had bought. There was also a small ax, which might have been used to split firewood. I briefly thought about trying to board up parts of the house but just as quickly dismissed the idea. I'd probably only manage to hack off a finger or worse. And with no one to come to my aid out on this desolate beach, I'd bleed out and die alone.

Back inside the house, furious gusts of wind rattled the living room windows. Would they shatter? It was best not to risk it. I dug out a plastic cover to wrap my Steinway piano and figured it would at least keep the glass and rain off of it if the windows gave way. Once I'd wrapped the piano (a baby grand that was almost seven feet long and weighed nearly eight hundred pounds), I unlocked the caster wheels and rolled it as far as possible from the window. It left an empty space in the room, surrounded by notebooks, stacks of sheet music, pencils worn to the nub, and countless wads of balled-up paper. I shut my MacBook Pro and stashed it as high as possible on a bookshelf away from the window. I did the same with the electric keyboard I used for my recordings. That done, the living room was ready to receive the mother of all house guests, this impending storm. Raindrops started to pelt the window, and you could hear distant thunder, though I couldn't see any more lightning just yet.

And then the phone rang.

I ran to answer it.

Leo said, "Evening, Harper. Looks like we're about to get under way. You coming over or what?"

"Sorry, Leo, I'd totally forgotten," I said, pacing toward the window with the phone to my ear. "Hey, so, do you still think we don't need to board up the windows?"

His laughter calmed me down just a bit.

"Durran put a scare into you, did he? Trust me, Pete. Unless a meteor hits your house, I doubt anything is going to break your windows. Still, get over here before that huge thunderhead reaches the coast. They say there's going to be a lot of lightning."

I promised I'd be there in ten minutes. I hung up and chuckled at myself. *So you wanted to live on the beach, huh, city slicker?*

I went back upstairs and took a hot shower to try to wake myself up a little more. I'd barely slept the night before after getting a late-night call from my agent, Pat Dunbar, that had tied my stomach in knots.

Pat was fifty-six years old, morbidly overweight, a walking invitation to a heart attack, who had divorced and remarried a svelte twenty-one-year-old Russian girl. He lived in London though he tended to spend months at a time in a splendid villa in the Mediterranean. He smoked less than he had before, though he still drank just as hard. We had almost a father-son relationship, except I was (or, at least, he'd hoped I'd be) a son who brought a 20-percent commission.

"So I ran into Alex Wells at the BAFTA gala," he said, after asking how I liked the desert-island life. "We talked about you a bit. He wanted to know what you were up to, if you had any availability.

Turns out they're filming a new series about Drake the pirate. Well, the Spanish called him a pirate, anyway. To the English, he was a hero or something. Anyway, it's guns and boats . . ."

"Yeah, I know who Sir Francis Drake is," I said, and felt myself tense up. I knew where Pat was going with this.

"Good, perfect. I can skip all the historical bull. So when do we start? They're looking for a composer and they need someone in place by the end of the month. I told him I'd talk to you. Would you be willing to meet him in London . . . say, next week?"

I suppose it was inevitable. Pat was my agent, not my mother.

"What, you think I'm calling to ask about your health?" he added.

"Pat, you know the deal," I said. "I'm busy with something else—at least until September. I can't leave it half-finished."

There was a brief moment of silence on the phone. I'd known Pat for years and I'd bet anything that at that very moment he was mouthing my words and making a face.

"I'm not asking you to leave anything half-finished, Peter," he tried again, softening his tone. "I respect your decision. I always have, haven't I? I'm just asking you to check back into reality for just a minute, okay? To get out of that Buddhist temple of yours for one weekend, put on a suit, and have a cup of coffee with Wells and his producer. Hear him out. I know you, you'll have the principal score written on a cocktail napkin within five minutes. What do you say?"

It was quintessential Pat Dunbar, master of the twenty-five cent psychological analysis, trying to pull off a motivational technique above his pay grade.

"Pat, there's no point in meeting with Alex Wells if my heart's not in it. You and I will both end up looking bad, and that's not good for anyone. You know I'm right. Besides, I'm already working on a project . . ."

"And how's *that* going?"

"What do you mean by that?" I asked, a little tense.

"I know you've been working on your personal project," Pat said, "an 'experimental album.' That's all I've been telling people for the last eleven months. 'Pete's taking some time for himself.' Eleven months, man! You know what can happen to a career in that amount of time? I've already turned down . . ."

"I know, Pat. You've run down the list for me a million times: two six-figure jobs for video game companies, one feature film, and this will be the third TV series I turn down."

"I'm going to be honest and tell you something you might not want to hear. People are going to forget you, Pete. You're starting to get a reputation as an eccentric, a wild card, and that's a hard stink to wash off. For all your BAFTA awards, the Golden Globes, the Oscar nomination, you're still no Elfman or Williams or Zimmer. I'm sorry to be an asshole about it, Pete, but I think you need to hear it from somebody. You're not at the point where you can take these kinds of luxuries just yet."

And there it was. This argument had been a long time coming. I'd finally worn out the patience of the ever-insistent Pat Dunbar.

The line fell silent for a few short beats. We both caught our breaths.

"Look, Pete . . . I know you've been dealing with some stuff. I've been divorced, too. I know the shit storm you're dealing with. Clem screwed you over, and now you're pissed off at the whole world. But you have to help yourself here."

"That's what I'm trying to do, Pat."

"By hiding from the world?"

"I'm not hiding. I just need some peace and quiet. To get away from it all." *To get away from you, too,* I thought. "Besides, I was only producing crap and you know it."

"It was *not* crap. You were just affected by the divorce. Call it an accident. Those jokers are always in a rush; they don't wait for anyone. You know I fought like hell to keep you onboard . . ."

Here we were again, discussing the disaster that—among other things—had caused my exile. The movie I hadn't been able to finish. FOX studios. Their lawyers. Just another tumble for Mr. Harper and his finances after the divorce from Clem.

"Listen to me, Pat," I said. "I know you're speaking as my friend. I know you mean well beyond your precious twenty percent, but I can't go back now. I feel like I'm about to take a huge step forward, about to shed this skin. The thing with Clem, this nightmare, I think it was meant to help me in some way. But I need time."

And now I could picture Pat leaning back on his couch staring at the ceiling, thinking, *Well, I tried everything.*

"Okay, Peter. I'm not going to push you. I'll break the news to Wells. I've always trusted your instinct. Keep at your album, get better, and let me know when you're ready to work again, okay?"

We hung up. His "get better" rang in my head.

IT WAS TRUE. Who was I kidding? I didn't dare meet with Alexander Wells because I wasn't sure of myself anymore. Pat knew it. FOX knew it. The BBC knew it. The whole damn world knew it. I'd compose a piece of music, listen to it, and toss the crumpled notes into the garbage. Deep down, I should be thankful to Pat for continuing to risk his reputation on me.

Over the last three months, my creative life had been a frustrating bout of agonized trial and error. A manic-depressive spiral in which one night I might think I had something brilliant, the melody that would mark the end to my creative drought, and listening to it the next morning would make me want to vomit. (Mostly figuratively, though a couple of times it did inspire dry heaves.) I'd desperately leap up from the piano and have to leave the house to keep from exploding with rage—rage that led to drinking. So I'd stalk the beach, looking for crabs as a way to distract my mind, each time childishly wishing that a massive tidal wave would crash down on me and end my suffering. Or I'd walk along the cliffs toward the ruins of the Monaghan monastery, where I'd pray that God would send me some kind of sign. Mostly I ended up in the backyard, mowing the lawn, which had become the richest form of entertainment in my monastic life.

AFTER SHOWERING and shaving, I put on a clean shirt and blazer. It felt good to get out of what had become my uniform, jeans and a T-shirt, at least for a little while. I grabbed the bottle of Chilean wine I'd bought that morning at Andy's, turned off the lights, and headed for the door. The keys hung from a hook. I grabbed them and shoved them into my pants pocket. When I took hold of the doorknob, I could feel the evening cold transmitted through the metal. It trembled lightly in my hand amid the pounding wind outside.

Then it happened. A moment I'd think back on so many times.

Don't leave the house. Not tonight, I heard a voice say.

It was a sort of disembodied voice. Like a phantom hiding behind my ears. A whisper that might easily have been the wind. *Don't open the door. Not tonight . . .* I froze with my hand on the doorknob, my feet glued to the tile floor.

I looked back into the darkened living room. In the distance, lightning flashed over the ocean and for just a moment, the entire room was flooded in cold, blue light. Of course, there was no one else there. It was no specter's voice but my own. It had risen from somewhere deep inside of me.

Until that moment, I'd only ever heard that voice once before. So sharp, so clear in its message . . .

No, it can't be. I was only frightened last time, I told myself. *Just like tonight. Don't be stupid, Peter Harper. There's no such thing as . . .*

(But wasn't the voice right *last time?)*

"Don't be a wimp," I said out loud this time, in the quiet of the living room.

I turned out the light, stepped outside, and shut the door with a slam, as if that could frighten off the spirits.

TWO

I DROVE amid the dunes through a confusing swirl of sand, wind, and rain, up to the top of the hill that separated my house from Leo and Marie's. The neighbors called this high point "Bill's Peak," in honor of a legendary local smuggler. They also say it was the beach where the Nazis landed to unload arms for the Irish Republican Army during the infamous Plan Kathleen of the last world war. Although, like every other story they told in Clenhburran, you could find no trace of it in any book to either confirm or deny it. It was simply up to you to believe it or not.

An old, twisted elm—whose branches revealed centuries of damaging winds and storms—was the only barricade for the thirty-foot drop down a small ravine onto the beach below. It was also the place where the road forked: toward Clenhburran through the marsh, or toward the only two houses on that entire beach. Peter Harper to the left. Leo and Marie Kogan to the right.

I stopped on the ridge for just a beat. Through the darkness, I could see white-crested waves crashing onto the beach. In the distance, lightning pounded the black ocean. It was a spectacular view against that darkened coast, with not a single light in sight other than the golden beam of a lighthouse on a faraway cape, occasionally sweeping over the night sky.

Five minutes later, I came upon the lights from the Kogans' house, which was built at the very edge of the beach, where a band of black shale marked the boundary between the smooth sand and the jagged and dangerous reef beyond. It was a compact little house on which they'd built an addition (illegally, Leo confessed to me later) for a garage that connected to the kitchen.

I parked my car by the fence—next to a Ford minivan I'd never seen—and walked through the driving rain that pounded me in waves, particles of sand that prickled my skin like thousands of angry needles. Leo must have seen my headlights and came to get me with an umbrella.

He was about my height with an athletic build that was enviable for someone in his sixties. Strong jaw, white hair clipped to a buzz cut, and an easy smile. He ran toward me, dodging puddles that had formed around the flagstone steps through his front yard. We met halfway, greeted each other with a clap on the back amid the deafening wind, and ran together toward the house.

"I thought you were going to back out on us," he said as soon as we reached his covered porch. "Just a couple of raindrops, is all."

"Sure," I said, "just a little sun shower."

We looked back at the horizon and squinted against the swirling sand. The imposing storm front was just five or six miles off the shore now. Lightning pounded the sea with impunity.

Leo grabbed my arm.

"Let's get inside before we end up as fried chicken."

» » »

LEO AND MARIE'S HOME was a comfortable space, not ostentatious, decorated to give it a rustic feel but for the Bang & Olufsen flat screen television, an upright piano that Marie had been learning to play over the last few years, and bookshelves packed with travel books and a fantastic photography collection. Above the doorways and against bare walls were beautiful watercolor landscapes of Ireland, signed by Marie ("M. Kogan"). I had one over my fireplace that she had given me a few months back.

Marie came to say hello the moment we were through the door. She was a tall, svelte woman who exuded elegance. I'd always thought she came from money or aristocracy until the day she told me her parents had owned some kind of wholesale business in Nevada. She was a perfect match to Leo, who looked like he'd made a deal with the devil for that physique. My friend, Judie Gallagher, had joked that maybe they were vampires because Marie had a smooth complexion that rivaled hers at twenty-nine. No doubt she was a woman who still turned heads among the men in town.

Also invited to the get-together were the O'Rourkes, Frank and Laura, who owned the flower shop and antiques gallery on Main Street. Marie had become friends with them recently, though I only knew them from seeing them around town. Leo confessed that he thought they were a little full of themselves—"they love to hear themselves talk and inveigh against the townsfolk as if they weren't one of them"—but he admitted sometimes you had to make an effort to socialize, especially in a community as small as Clenhburran, where the winter population thinned to barely one hundred fifty people.

Marie kissed me on each cheek and introduced me to the O'Rourkes, who were lounging on a couch by the fireplace, praising a brandy Leo had just poured them, a glass of which was soon in my hand as well. Laura stood up the moment I came into the room. She laced her fingers together, as if in prayer, and said it was "a real honor" to meet me: "I have all your albums and love *all* the songs. They're . . . they're . . ." she said, sighing and sitting down, patting the seat for me to sit next to her. "I have so many questions for you! Leo tells us sometimes you play for the two of them," she said, gesturing toward the piano. "Perhaps you could honor us, as well."

I shot Leo a furtive, murderous glance that he responded to with only a stonelike smile. So I dug deep and located the most magnanimous part of me to answer all of Laura's questions, waiting for her husband, Frank—a man with a thin face and glassy eyes—to play his role as social moderator and counsel his wife not to overwhelm me with all her questions. But that didn't happen. No, seated next to her with my glass filled to the brim with brandy, I received Mrs. O'Rourke's full-on barrage. "I remember seeing you on television two years ago during the BAFTA awards. You came out to get your award and were holding hands with Darren Flynn and Kate Winslet. Oh my God, and look at you now, sitting on the couch right next to me!" She put her hand on my knee and unleashed such a belly laugh that it made me laugh, too. Leo laughed along and Mr. O'Rourke downed his brandy so he could assure himself a refill. "So, Mr. Harper, tell me, what is Kate like in person . . . ?"

I did the best I could, spinning one tired anecdote after another, aware that each story belonged to my previous life from two years ago, until Marie called us to the dinner table. It couldn't have come too soon.

"It's getting ugly out there," I said, desperately changing the subject as we sat down to dinner. "I think I heard them say we'll see hundred-mile-an-hour winds."

"It's not unusual to get fifty-five-knot winds. Even a little bit more," Leo said. "But not with these kinds of fireworks. I radioed over to the Donegal weather service and they said it's going to be like this all night."

"Shortwave radio fan, huh?" Frank O'Rourke said.

"Not really. I use it every now and then to talk to the local authorities or with Donovan and the other fishermen. It's really more of an emergency thing. Phone service can be iffy out here."

"It's bad in Clenhburran," Frank agreed, "I can't even imagine how spotty it is out here."

"How do you like living in such an out-of-the-way place, Mr. Harper?" Laura jumped in to ask. "Aren't you ever afraid? Though there's really nothing to worry about. Nothing ever happens out here."

"I'm glad to hear that," I said. "Actually . . ."

"Although recently there's been some trouble," she said, taking advantage of my brief pause. "Someone broke into the Kennedys' house last year. And I also heard someone ransacked a house down near Fortown while the owners slept. Sure, they were isolated incidents. But they say nothing like that ever happened around here before. Some gang of Eastern Europeans, they say. Though Frank thinks it's a cock-and-bull story the alarm companies made up."

"And I agree with him," Leo said. "I don't think a thief would come all the way out here to steal a television. I, for one, am not worried."

"Hear, hear," I said.

"What about you, Marie?" Frank asked. She'd been quietly staring into her wineglass. "How do you like living out on this lonely little beach?"

"I hadn't thought about it, really," she said. "We've lived in far more dangerous places and nothing's ever happened to us. Well, except some minor theft or a mild scare. No, I agree with Leo. Who'd come all the way out to this deserted little corner of the world for a heist? There are plenty of better targets for a band of thieves."

OUTSIDE, THE STORM was gathering strength. Lightning seemed to strike every minute now. The lights went out for stretches inside the living room. At times, we were plunged into darkness except for the fireplace glow. Other times, thunder cracked overhead, interrupting our jokes and laughter.

But even that wasn't enough to deter Laura. No sooner had the first course ended than she resumed her interrogation. "How did you come to choose Clenhburran to get away . . . ?" "Do you think you'll stay long . . . ?"

Wine and appetizers loosened my tongue. "I grew up in Dublin," I said. "I used to come to Donegal with my parents as a boy. The place still puts me in a good mood, makes me feel protected. I guess it reminds me of happier times from my childhood."

The second I closed my mouth I knew I was in trouble. I'd touched on a dangerous topic I had no interest in discussing. Laura saw it clear as day.

"Your kids will be here in couple weeks, right Pete?" Leo said.

"Yeah, they're coming to spend the summer. I hope they like Donegal," I said.

"Oh, of course they will. They'll love it," Marie was quick to say.

Laura's face lit up like she'd struck gold. She put on her Cheshire cat grin and asked the question all of us knew she would ask.

"So, you're . . . married, or . . . ?"

"Divorced," I said, flatly.

"Oh. Oh, I'm sorry. It's terrible, especially when there are children involved, I'm sure. My cousin Beth . . ."

Leo moved quickly to serve more wine and to try to change

the subject, and as Marie brought out the second course, exquisite steaks with mashed potatoes and a side of green beans, Laura turned her attention to the Kogans. She'd heard they were from Portland, Oregon, and she had a cousin living there. *When did they decide to move to Ireland? Was it true that they'd lived in Asia for years?*

I supposed a lot of stories swirled around town about us, the "newcomers." Maybe it was a matter of survival. A community this small had to protect itself, and to do that, it has to stay informed, know who everyone was and their backstories. Laura O'Rourke was just following her instincts when she bombarded us with questions. Leo was much more generous with his answers. And with a few glasses of wine in him, he easily regaled us with stories of his life and world travels.

At twenty-five, he hung up his boxing gloves. Instead of fighting in the Nevada slums, he took a job in San Antonio in private security. Marie was already his girlfriend at the time. She'd been dancing at one of the big Las Vegas hotels on Friday nights and performing as a backing singer for headliners such as Tom Jones. They took off together and never looked back. They never lived in the United States again, except for a three-month stretch when Marie's mother died and they both officially became orphans—alone in the world but for one another. Later, when they reached the age where they "had earned the right not to have to do anything," he said, they started looking at places to retire to. "For some reason, we always came back to Ireland or Scotland or Thailand," Leo said. "I knew a lot of old folks who'd retired to Thailand. After fifty, you can get a permanent visa to live there. And with a solid pension, you could retire comfortably—if not lavishly. But Marie always talked about Europe and the ancient coasts of Ireland . . . and . . ." Leo went on into the tale of his arrival in Clenhburran, a story I'd already heard a few times, and my mind started to wander. Other thoughts rushed to occupy my mind . . . above all, that voice. The voice that had spoken to me from deep inside before leaving the house . . .

Another glass of wine?

"Still with us, Mr. Harper?"

I opened my eyes—or rather, I snapped back to reality—and saw Laura O'Rourke tipping the wine bottle toward my empty glass.

"I was asking if you'd like some more wine . . ."

"Uh . . . no," I answered, coming back to my senses. "No, thank you. I think I've had more than enough."

BY THE END of dessert, I was tired and bored of Laura O'Rourke. The five of us were having tea by the fire. Laura stood with her tea and went on and on about Marie's paintings. She asked when Marie might start offering classes for the town's women.

"Actually, I'm self-taught," she said. "Besides, I don't think I'd make a very good teacher."

Laura did not look pleased by the answer. She added that she'd love to have one of Marie's paintings and had "just the spot for it" in her living room.

"You know, Marie could paint a portrait of you," Leo added. "Aside from painting landscapes, she's an excellent portraitist."

"Is that right, Marie?" I asked. "If I'd known, I'd already have put myself on the list."

"Well, actually, I used to make a living at it," she said shyly. "In the hotels where Leo used to work, I'd paint some of the clients and . . ."

"She painted one for François Mitterrand's wives, no kidding," Leo said proud on his wife's behalf. "She painted Billy Crystal, too. Paid for half the house, it did!"

"But all the ones I see here are of Ireland," Laura said, scanning the walls. "Don't you have others from your travels?"

Marie shook her head.

"I've sold or given away most of them along the way. When I got to Ireland, I didn't have a single painting with me. And now look at this place. There isn't a place left to hang one. I'm thinking of donating some to the church."

The storm and the lightning had let up and the lights had been solidly on for a while. Laura had mentioned the piano for a second time, and though I'd managed to play dumb, I knew she wouldn't let go of it. I figured it was the perfect time to slip out and head home. I stood up from the couch and apologized for being a party-pooper on a Friday night.

The O'Rourkes said they'd host a dinner soon and would love to have me over. "Maybe when your kids arrive, we could go out on Frank's sailboat."

I accepted their offer diplomatically and thanked Marie for a stupendous dinner. I threw on my coat, and Leo saw me out.

It had stopped raining, but the wind continued to howl. Leo, who'd gotten a little tipsy, let slip his opinion on the O'Rourkes: He said he felt like he was being interrogated every time he was with them. I laughed and said I knew the feeling. Just as we got to the car, I noticed Leo staring at something in the sky. I lifted my head and saw it.

A monstrous thunderhead hung over the beach. Moonlight that managed to creep between the clouds highlighted its gigantic silhouette. It was a thick and roiling sheet of cloud more than a mile-and-a-half wide that churned and sprouted tiny tornadoes within it.

"Well, that doesn't look good," I said, staring upward.

"You'd better get going before that thing unloads, Pete," Leo said. "You sure you wouldn't rather stay a while longer?"

I stared up at that writhing thunderhead, pregnant with blackness like some angry ancient goddess about to unleash its wrath. It seemed to float on the horizon, directly over Bill's Peak—precisely my path home.

Don't go, Pete.

I wish I'd had a good reason not to leave. Maybe, if I were lucky, my car's engine wouldn't turn over. Or maybe Leo would insist I stay. Or maybe . . .

"No . . . I think if I hurry, I can make it home before it rolls in," I found myself saying as I patted Leo on the arm. "You take care. Get back in there. I'm sure your new friends have a million questions for you."

Leo laughed as I hopped down the steps into his front yard. I ran to my car and jumped in. Leo stood by the door, waiting to see me off. I slid my key in and started to turn it. Sometimes, the old Volvo stalled out and sometimes, on stormy nights, car batteries lose their charge. Then, maybe your friends will *insist* you stay over and spend the night . . .

The engine started right away.

THREE

I DROVE SLOWLY up the narrow gravel road between the dunes as the wind tossed around my three thousand pound Volvo V40 as if it were made of papier-mâché. My headlights cut into the darkness like narrow lightsabers. I kept a keen eye on the road since, as you leave Leo's house and climb toward Bill's Peak, the path narrows and twists along the edge of a cliff, with nothing to shield you from a precipitous drop but some wild shrubbery along the shoulder.

Overhead, the great Goddess of the Storm had begun to stir, roiling in labor pains.

I leaned into the gas, a bit. I didn't want to still be on the road when this mother started bearing her young, unleashing them on the earth below. But just as I crested the hill, something up ahead made me slam on the brakes.

A tree branch in the middle of the road.

It was an enormous branch, one of the four or five main ones from the lovely old elm at the top of Bill's Peak. One of the ends of the branch was charred and still smoking, and I guessed it had been severed by a bolt of lightning. The gale-force winds must have tossed it right into the middle of the road.

I ducked my head and peeked up through the front windshield. The thick blackness overhead had started to rotate directly over my car. There were flashes from deep within it and thunder that rumbled like a sleeping giant who'd been abruptly awakened.

If I had driven a Land Rover Defender like Leo's instead of a Volvo V40, I wouldn't have thought twice about it: I'd drop it into low gear and climb over the thing. I'd worry about coming back to move it tomorrow. But the domesticated underbelly of my station wagon wasn't having that. I'd bust a wheel or an axle, for sure. Plus, the O'Rourkes would be coming down the path later, and they might not see it before it was too late.

So I decided to act as quickly as I could.

I hopped out of the car and as soon as I did, I realized how dangerous this was. Everything I knew about lightning storms told me I was in exactly the wrong place: at the top of a hill, next to a tree, right below a storm cloud that was ready to burst.

Not tonight, Peter.

I remember hearing somewhere that you were safe inside a car (as in an airplane) during a lightning storm, that electricity from a lightning strike grounded itself without affecting anyone inside. I was about to sit back inside. Maybe it'd be easier to drive around it . . . dammit. *Come on, Pete. Stick your chest out and be a man.*

The wind gusted furiously. I looked up at the ancient elm, mutilated and still smoldering, and I could smell a burning in the air. But not the smokiness of a fireplace or barbecue, rather the electric char of a short circuit. It reminded me of the time my daughter, Beatrice, stuck her finger in an electric socket when she was just four years old. The lights in the entire house flickered and when we found her, her eyebrows were standing on end. That's what it smelled like tonight.

Overhead, the writhing, twisting darkness let out a powerful roar that shook the earth beneath my feet. I looked up and noticed some kind of light coming from deep within the storm. A twister of blue light.

Lightning never strikes the same place twice, I told myself.

Still, the quicker you get out of here, the better.

I grabbed one end of the branch but the damn thing weighed more than I had imagined. I started pushing it as if I were trying to move the minute hand of a giant clock, turning it toward the side of the road. Behind me, the beach was shrouded in darkness. Only the white breakwater could be seen crashing onto the shore.

I pushed until the branch was parallel to the side of the road. That should do it. I let it drop with a thud, and I dusted my hands on my jeans. I took one step toward my car, and that's when I noticed something all around me.

Light. Too much light.

At first, I thought it was the Volvo's headlights. Maybe I'd flicked on the fog lights by mistake? All I knew is that it was suddenly very bright—almost too bright.

A little dizzy, I started to walk back toward the car, and then I noticed something else. It felt like an electrical wave was running over and through my body. A tingling that snaked from my neck to my backbone, down to my fingertips. I looked down at my arms and saw the hair standing on end, perfectly straight, like the quills of a sea urchin. It was as if someone had hung a magnet directly over my head. . . .

Over my head . . . ?

I looked up one last time. The whirlwind of blue light twisted above me, picking up speed, like a record spinning at a thousand revolutions a minute. *Lightning never strikes the same place twice.*

I felt something in my temples. My car's headlights suddenly seemed too bright, hurting my eyes and becoming an all-encompassing whiteness. I had just enough time to realize what was happening. It was just a moment, and I think I even tried to run for the car, but I never made it. And that's when I felt it: something *bit* me; my face, my shoulders, my legs. It shook me like a rag doll and tossed me aside.

It felt like a thousand-pound safe had landed squarely on my head, knocked me to my knees, and exploded as if it had been filled with dynamite. My eardrums were overwhelmed. They simply shut off, faded to white. . . .

I felt I was screaming and falling in slow motion, waiting for my body to hit the ground with a thud. But it never came. I fell, and continued to fall, into an endless sea of darkness.

FOUR

I OPENED MY EYES and felt a terrible nausea. Where was I? Wherever it was, the world here was spinning.

"Look! He opened his eyes," someone said. I recognized the voice: Marie.

I was in a car racing at top speed.

"Marie . . . pull over, I need to throw up."

I felt the car screech to a halt. I reached toward the door handle, holding back the rising bile, opened the door, and let it all out.

Other doors opened. I heard footsteps. They came closer.

"There's a bottle of water in the trunk. And paper towels. Bring a few."

I felt someone patting my back.

"That's it, son. Let it all out."

Someone handed me an opened bottle of water. I sipped it. It made me feel better. Someone else handed me a paper towel. I blew my nose and wiped my mouth. I had a sickening taste in my mouth. Even so, I managed to say thank you.

I tried to open my eyes, but they felt too heavy.

"Is he conscious?" another voice said. I recognized it as Frank O'Rourke's.

"Looks like it," Leo said.

I turned my head and tried to look at them but could only make out silhouettes.

"What happened?" I asked aloud.

"You passed out, Peter, but you're doing okay. We're on the way to the hospital."

"The hospital?" I asked. "Are you kidding?"

"It's no joke, bud. We think you were struck by lightning. Now, lie back down. We'll be there in a few minutes."

I'm not sure how long we drove. I kept fading in and out, and the last thing I remember was arriving at the hospital (Dungloe Community Hospital, I'd later learn) and being carried in by Leo and Frank. A pair of nurses rushed from their station to heave me onto a gurney. Marie held my hand and told me everything was going to be all right as the gurney rushed down a hall.

You'll be fine, Pete, a voice said.

I closed my eyes and passed out again.

MY DOCTOR WAS NAMED Anita Ryan, a pretty, stout, redheaded woman with freckles who spoke quickly and assuredly. She read my pulse, listened to my heart, and checked my pupils with a penlight.

"Do you know why you're here?"

"I think I got hit by lightning."

She started by asking me a few simple questions. My name, my age. "How did this happen, Mr. Harper? Where did you feel the impact? Does it hurt anywhere?" I tried to explain what I remembered. The car, the tree branch in the middle of the road, that blinding white light. The blue whirlwind overhead. It felt like something had clocked me on the head . . . and now I had a pounding headache and nauseating dizziness. Even my skin hurt.

The doctor said I'd need a brain scan. She injected something into my arm, and I lay back down onto the hospital bed. I was wheeled down another corridor into an X-ray room. They fed me into the belly of an enormous scanner, and I lay still, listening to indistinct thumping and whirring all around me. My headache eased a bit and the tingling in my skin subsided. I figured whatever sedative they'd given me had taken effect.

An hour later, the doctor met with me again. Everything was fine, she said. They hadn't found anything I needed to worry about. My brain scan was clear. I was "lucky," she said, although she still seemed worried I'd felt the blow on my head.

"Now . . . I want to show you something," she said.

She asked me to sit up on the edge of the bed and take off my shirt. When I did, under the florescent hospital lights, I discovered something unbelievable. The left side of my body, from my neck to my chest, going down to my thigh, was flushed red and covered with a series of strange markings. The shapes looked like the leaves of a fern, and they were so perfectly shaped that it looked like someone had spent weeks tattooing red ink onto my skin.

The doctor called them "Lichtenberg figures," named after the German physicist Georg Christoph Lichtenberg who had discovered them. He hadn't been hit by lightning but had studied electrical currents. Those "tattoos" were the result of capillaries bursting as the electricity passed through my body. The good news is that they would fade in a few days. The doctor told me she'd only seen one other case, a fisherman who'd been struck and marked with the shape of a starfish on his back.

"He survived, too, thank God," she said. "Actually, despite what people often say, it's not rare to survive a lightning strike. It all depends on the amount of energy in a particular bolt, where it impacts the body, and which path it takes. There's always an entry point, a particular course it travels, and an exit point. The electricity singes everything in its path. How the bolt travels or what organs it hits determines whether it's fatal. It looks like you were lucky, but you'll still need to stay overnight for observation."

LEO AND MARIE were waiting for me when they wheeled me into my room for the night. The doctor had filled them in. They offered me their phones in case I wanted to call anyone.

"No . . ." I said. "I'll be fine. The doctor said it'll just be overnight. I don't want to alarm anyone."

"Not even Judie?" Leo insisted. "I think she'd like to come and see you."

"I'm sure," I said. "I think it's better I'm alone, what with my painkillers and this hospital smell all over me. Besides, Judie's busy at the hostel. She told me yesterday they'd just gotten a group of German backpackers in. But, before you go, tell me what happened."

It turned out the O'Rourkes had left a half hour after me, and they were the ones who found me. My car was still running with the lights on. When they saw me lying in the mud, completely drenched, they thought I was dead. Laura was so shaken that they had to give her a sedative when we arrived at the hospital, and Frank had taken her home.

"Please thank them for me when you see them."

"We will do. But get ready to be the new talk of the town," Leo said, smiling. "Leave it to Laura O'Rourke to be the town crier."

"Oh, I can only imagine . . ."

"You two are terrible!" Marie scolded us.

They insisted on staying, but I finally convinced them to go home. "I don't plan on dying tonight, don't worry. Besides, I'd never ask a friend to spend the night in one of those torture devices," I said, pointing to the uncomfortable chairs.

"I'm going to leave you my phone," Leo said, placing his cell phone on the side table. "Have a good night and don't flirt too hard with the nurses."

Marie smacked Leo on the back of the head. She kissed me on the forehead and said goodnight. "Sweet dreams, Pete."

THAT NIGHT, electricity must still have been coursing through my body, because I couldn't sleep a wink. My head started pounding again.

I lay awake imagining the hours ticking away. Beyond the door, I could hear the rumblings of the hospital: a patient whimpering, a nurse pacing, the television blabbing in some other insomniac's room. It had been a long time since I'd spent the night in a hospital. When was it? I could remember it clearly.

I'm just a little dizzy. It's nothing.

Deirdre Harper, my mother, had passed out in a shoe store and a couple of people had helped sit her up. My father had rushed her to the emergency room, and by the time I had arrived on an Amsterdam-London-Dublin connecting flight, she was in observation. "She says she's fine. That it was just a little dizziness," Dad had said. We thought we'd all be home for dinner.

It's nothing. You'll see.

She was a beautiful woman, especially for fifty-two: auburn hair and a smile that could brighten the darkest day. And that's how I remember her, flashing that smile when they told her they'd have to keep her overnight for a full workup. It was "just for a little while."

That's when I heard it. The same voice that would later speak to me the night of the storm: *Say goodbye to your mother, Peter. Remember her this way: in that very dress, carrying that very bag, in those brown shoes, with that lovely auburn hair.*

She must have seen it on my face. I remember her eyes filling with tears, but she managed not to shed a single drop. She was doing it for Dad, of course. She repeated that she'd be home that very night . . . at worst, first thing in the morning. She walked tall past the hospital doors that swung closed behind her and took her from us forever. She would be a slave to a hospital bed, wires and tubes running out of her as she lost her hair, but never that smile, until God took her from us one hard November morning two months later—shattering our happy household, turning my mother into an eternal shadow, and ripping a hole in my chest that would never heal.

Thinking about my mother brought me to tears in that lonely hospital room in the wee hours, until I finally drifted off to sleep.

I had a dream that night, and I feel like my mother was in it. She was scared and trying to warn me about something. But I couldn't understand what she was saying.

I WOKE UP the next morning with the same headache. The doctor stopped by after breakfast and asked me about the pain. Was it constant or pulsating? As if I could feel my heart beating in my temples?

"That's it exactly," I said. "A throbbing."

"Okay. Where do you feel it? Up front, in the back of your head, on one side or all over?"

I told her it hurt "inside" but more toward the left side. "Any double vision? Flashing lights? Any abdominal pain? Excessive sweating?" The doctor prescribed me some pills. "Take two in the

morning, two in the afternoon, and two just before bed, after meals.
If the pain continues for more than two weeks, come see me. You
should try not to drive the first week, unless it's absolutely necessary. No drugs, no alcohol."

"How about sex?"

"Like I said, 'Whatever is absolutely necessary,'" she said.

I noticed a missed call from Judie. I figured Marie and Leo had
brought her up to speed.

I hit redial and after a couple of rings, Judie picked up with her
unmistakable, warm, lively voice, though she sounded a little hoarse.

"Mrs. Houllihan's store, how may I help you?"

"Hey, there," I said. "I just moved into town and want to know
where I can rent a good porn flick."

Judie burst out laughing. I could picture her sitting quietly behind the counter, engrossed in some thick novel while sipping a cup
of hot tea (maybe blackberry or ginseng or some weird variety of
herbs she liked).

For months now, Mrs. Houllihan's store had stood out among
all the other buildings in Clenhburran. Pink facade with windows
trimmed in yellow, flowers and flags and little bells everywhere.
And miniature Buddhas sitting on the windowsills. On the bottom
floor was Mrs. Houllihan's store, designed with tourists in mind,
but which had served during the winter months as a pharmacy,
bookstore, toy store, and video rental store. But that was before
Mrs. Houllihan had retired two years ago and the sparky young
Judie Gallagher had taken over, starting a kind of revolution in the
store—and in the town. Now, the old building housed a yoga studio
(Judie taught two classes a week) and a massage and acupuncture
practice. The place had become the unofficial gathering place of all
the town's women, who had previously met in a back room at the
tiny Church of Saint Michael.

Judie had also renovated the living quarters on the first floor and turned it into a hostel with bunk beds. She catered to backpackers (she'd managed to get Mrs. Houllihan's listed in Ireland's Lonely Planet guide last year), as well as musicians who came to play traditional Irish tunes at Fagan's and lost tourists who hadn't managed to snag a room in Dungloe and showed up in the middle of the night, begging for a place to stay.

To top it off, Judie had the best collection of classic DVDs in all of Donegal.

"Well, we've got a fine collection of adult titles," she said. "You into bestiality? Maybe a little bondage?"

"Hmm, wow, that all sounds great. But do you have anything involving vegetables? I did grow up on a farm, you know. . . ."

"Okay, okay, enough, Pete!" she said, cackling. "How the hell are you feeling? Marie called me and told me all about it. Why didn't you call me last night?"

"I didn't want to worry you. And I knew you were busy at the hostel. Besides, it's not such a big deal."

"Jesus, Pete, are you kidding? That's like surviving a plane crash! I would have liked visiting you last night, even if I had to leave the German backpackers on their own for a little while. Well, are you feeling better? What happened?"

"Frankly, it's still hard to process," I said, thinking back. *The light. That whirlwind of blue light* . . . "It all happened so fast, but I think I'm okay. My head hurts a little, but the doctor said I should be fine in a couple of weeks."

"Marie said you were pretty unscathed except for some burn marks."

"Yeah, it's like a huge tattoo. You know what, I think I kind of like it. Maybe I'll get one after this is all over. By the way, you missed a hell of a meal last night. And the O'Rourkes."

She broke out into a wry laugh.

"Yeah, Marie told me you had a blast hanging out with them. It's a good thing I didn't go, or Laura O'Rourke would have woven together such a story about us in her mind that we would probably even have a couple of kids in secret by the end of the night. I suppose she got your whole life's story out of you?"

"Almost," I said. "I held back a little bit."

"That's what you think," she said, chuckling. "So, how can I help now? Need me to rescue you from the hospital?"

"Yes, please. The doctor gave me some pills, and they already want to kick me out of here this afternoon."

"Okay, give me a couple of hours. The Germans are showering and heading out after breakfast. As soon as they're gone, I'll be on my way. Can you survive that long?"

"I think so."

"Okay. I've got to let you go, now. I've got an actual customer and the amazing part is I think she actually wants to buy something. See you in a bit, Peter *Sparks*."

THE ROAD between Dungloe and Clenhburran was like a rally race course for Judie. We sped along the tortuous and winding forty-mile route in less than fifty minutes, and I thought how ironic it would be to survive a lightning strike only to die the next day in a car accident. We stopped at Andy's to buy some groceries for dinner and a bottle of wine. ("If you can't find it at Andy's, you don't need it," their slogan read.) We crossed through town and headed toward the beach.

An old military-access road cuts through a long stretch of meadows, bogs, and rolling hills between Clenhburran and Tremore Beach. About ten miles in, the road veers toward the cliffs, and the only path is an even narrower, treacherous gravel track lined with a stone wall. All manner of wildflowers bloom along its base throughout the year.

As we crested the last hill, the blue vastness of the ocean came into view. The scent of powdery saltpeter that was so common in this part of the countryside mingled with the smells of the livestock, and sometimes, with the smokiness of a far-off wood fire. It's just then that the small, white Tremore Beach, encrusted between formations of black shale, unfurls before you.

"This is where it happened," I told Judie as we reached Bill's Peak.

We stopped and got out of the car, and I began to piece together that night. The tree branch now lay on the side of the road, one end of it singed black. Tire tracks dead-ended at the place where I'd been struck.

"Good old Frank O'Rourke must have found me lying right here. Hell of a shock he must have gotten."

"I can imagine his wife yelling at him to run you over," Judie joked.

She hugged me, and we held still, feeling the haunting wind that today would not bring a storm.

"Jesus, Pete, didn't you ever hear of not standing under a tree during a lightning storm?" she said before leaning in to give me a long, sweet kiss.

That night, Judie cooked stuffed eggplant, and we dined by the fireplace with the bottle of Chilean wine, of which I had only a single glass. She undressed me and traced her fingers over the burns that spanned my body like branches. We made love on the rug and fell asleep in front of the fire.

A headache woke me at midnight. It was a pulsing that seemed to radiate from the very center of my skull. I went for the pills the doctor had given me, which I'd left in my coat pocket. I took them and returned to the living room.

Judie was having another one of her nightmares. I woke her with a hug and soft kisses to keep from startling her. We climbed up to the bedroom. The sheets were cold, and we held each other for warmth. We fell asleep, and I dreamed about Leo and Marie.

In the dream, we were back at the hospital in Dungloe, but I wasn't the patient this time. It was Leo. He lay in a hospital bed motionless. At some point in the dream, I realized he was dead. The sheet covering him was soaked in blood. His eyes were wide open, and his open mouth was a dark, infinite void.

FIVE

THE STORM'S AFTEREFFECTS lingered a couple of days. But when the sun finally shone, the days were so stupendous most people thought summer had come early.

I spent a few days recovering at home. My body ached, and it felt as if every muscle was exhausted, as if someone had given me a serious beating. And then there was that headache. I took the pills as the doctor ordered, kept the room dark (the light still hurt my eyes), and for hours on end listened to classical music I didn't know I'd had on my iPod.

At night, I went downstairs and turned my attention to the piano. And I mean that in the most literal sense. I'd stroke the surface, feel it, caress it, as if trying to coax a benevolent genie from inside this magical lamp. *Good afternoon, Peter. I'm here to grant you three wishes. What'll it be?*

I just have one: to be able to hear the melodies in my head again.

While I showered, while I took a stroll or read a book, they'd come to me. I'd hum them for fear of losing them, rush home, and jot the notes down on staff paper. How many times had I done that? How many beautiful melodies had come to me that way, out of nothingness, out of that magical spring I'd thought inexhaustible? Now look at me: reading other compositions and trying vaguely to plagiarize something. I'd become just another mediocre composer among the thousands and thousands of mediocre composers who spent their entire lives trying to create just a single piece of passable work. The fairy dust had worn off. The magic was gone, and it was never coming back.

Four days after the accident, I woke up with barely any pain except a remote pulsing in the back of my head. Otherwise, I felt good. I had my energy back and decided to take advantage of my mood and do some things around the house. I put on some old work jeans, a flannel shirt, and Timberland boots. I tied my hair back in a ponytail and slipped on a pair of Ray-Bans. Someone might have thought Neil Young was living on a remote beach in Ireland. I sipped a cup of Barry's Tea while listening to the Kinks sing on Coastal Radio on a tiny transistor radio I'd found in the attic when I moved in, about how fucked up it is to be a celluloid hero. With that, I hopped in the car and headed into town. I hoped to buy some paint, brushes, and sandpaper to fix up the fence, which had taken a beating during a long and harsh winter. Stupid fence. Had I known what it would come to mean in my life, I'd have torn it out that very day.

Just as Leo predicted, the story of me getting struck by lightning had spread through Clenhburran like a spring pollen. At John Durran's hardware store, I ran into half the town and everyone asked about my health. "You're alive, Mr. Harper!" "Did you buy a lottery ticket?" "You try putting a lightbulb in your mouth yet?" Durran wouldn't let me heave the lawn mower into the trunk. He called over his son Eoin, a freckle-faced kid who always had his head in the clouds, and between the two of us, we loaded the mower into my Volvo. "You ought to cover that septic tank drain, or you're just going to end up hitting it again," Durran said. "If you like, I can have Eoin swing by one day and take a look at it. Oh, and don't forget what I told you about the varnish. Give it three solid coats or the bloody salty air will eat right through it before the end of summer."

I took a stroll through town. New faces started showing up about this time of year. Clenhburran was a small community in winter. But in summertime, it swelled to more than eight hundred.

I came upon Judie at the store, meeting with Marie and a group of women who were organizing the upcoming outdoor movie night in Clenhburran. They were arguing about where to set up the projector and screen.

It all depended on the weather. You had to have a Plan B in case it rained, which it very well might even though we were having the kind of lovely summer everyone had anticipated. The old warehouse down by the port could work as a cover, but that would require switching around a host of other things, they argued.

Laura O'Rourke was there, of course. It was the first time I'd seen her since the night of the accident. She told a dramatic story about how they'd found me lying in the middle of the road, "half dead," and how she hadn't had the courage to get out of the car. "Frank kneeled down, took his pulse, and I only managed to say a prayer for poor Mr. Harper's soul," she said, as she held my hand, and her eyes filled with unspilled tears. Then she announced she wanted to ask me a favor in name of the entire organization of moviegoers.

"I think you're exactly the right person to give the opening address for movie night, Mr. Harper. Will you do it? Perhaps you could play a small piece? Oh, yes! That would be marvelous."

I thought Judie or Marie would come to my defense, but quite the opposite, they thought it was a fabulous idea.

"Maybe you could accompany a short silent film on the piano," Judie said, "although I don't know how we'd get a piano to the port."

I nodded as if to say, "Ah, too bad, it was a nice thought, but how would I ever get my Steinway to the Clenhburran port?"

"Well, it wouldn't have to be a 'real' piano, would it, Pete?" Marie said. "It could be an electric one. We could rent one for the event. I think it's a brilliant idea, Judie."

The women all clapped at once, and I could do nothing more than smile and nod and hope something went awry with their plan. I said goodbye to the ladies, and drove back to the beach with my Volvo loaded with supplies. I lowered the windows and filled my lungs with that unique mix of fresh earth and salty sea air.

My house was set up on a small promontory at the foot of the beach. It was a relatively modern two-story home (built in the seventies) with a slate roof and a wide wooden deck built right into the dunes, with stairs that led down to the beach. It was the stairs that did it for me. It's something I'd wanted since I was a boy (maybe I'd seen it somewhere?), and when my real estate agent, Imogen Fitzgerald, told me "the house has a set of stairs that leads right out to the sand," it was as if a light went on in my head. "Yes! That sounds exactly like what I'm looking for. When can we see it?"

We first came to see it in October 2009, when the sky was steel-gray and filled with strange, enormous clouds. The house shimmered like an open treasure chest in the sand. It was painted white and surrounded by a lush lawn and a cute white picket fence enclosed the property. It faced the ocean and a two-mile-long beach wedged between black cliffs. I almost said "Yes," without setting foot inside.

It was said that Tremore Beach was in the windiest area, and that's why no one built homes here. I'd also heard some say the ground was far too sandy, and the beach eroded several inches a year, which would explain the cracks along several of my walls, and why the floor of the downstairs bathroom was slanted.

"Think we could squeeze a piano in there?"

Imogen, my good friend who was looking out for me, tried to play devil's advocate.

"This isn't Amsterdam or even Dublin, Peter. There's spotty telephone reception out here, problems with the plumbing and electrical service. The house needs tons of work. You have grass to mow, a septic tank to maintain . . . not to mention the solitude. You're ten miles from a little town that itself is in the middle of nowhere. You'll have to drive everywhere. However, the next house over is occupied year-round, so that's a plus . . . ."

I said I'd take it as I stood in the living room, looking out that huge window, imagining placing a Steinway & Sons right in front of it. In spring and summer, I'd be able to play with all the windows open to an audience of one: the sea.

"Are you sure about this, Peter? You'd be all alone out here, just you and your piano. Some nights, it'll be just you and the howl of the wind."

A deafening wind that would drown out the sound of the music, of a ringing telephone, even of my desperate screams if I ever needed to call for help.

"I'm sure," I said, finally.

I WAS IN THE BACKYARD with all the supplies I'd bought at Durran's to begin painting the fence when I noticed Leo running up the shore. He saw me, too, waved, and headed toward my house.

Tremore Beach was close to two miles long, shielded on each side by huge, black rock formations, so that Leo actually could run several laps on the beach. He called it "basic training." I remember one morning I was seated at the piano when I saw him strip his clothes off at the water's edge. It was February and although it had been a mild morning, the ocean was icy with semi-frozen bergs. Leo Kogan jumped buck naked into the platinum waves of the Atlantic, and I nearly leaped up to call the police, thinking he was trying to end it all.

"Are you kidding? It's great for the circulation! You should try it sometime," he told me a few days later when we bumped into each other on the road to town.

It was that kind of thing that made me wonder whether Leo and Marie were either eccentric or just crazy when I first met them. They didn't look to have children, nor any kind of a job, and they seemed to be enjoying a fantastic quality of life. And even though they were older, they were in enviable shape. I thought they might be retired millionaires, but their humble home was evidence to the contrary.

One day, about two weeks after I'd moved in, they showed up at my door with a basket of sweets and a bottle of wine. "Welcome, neighbor!" they said, and quickly made themselves at home. I admit at first I was a little cold with them. I'd come here to find solace and to focus on my work, and I was worried these chatty neighbors were going to make a habit of showing up at my door every morning. It turned out to be quite the opposite. My first month was full of problems. The boiler stopped working, and the house got so cold I spent several nights huddled in front of the fireplace, covered in quilts and blankets. While I waited for the rental agency to send a repairman, Leo offered to take a look. He inspected the electrical panel and offered me his gasoline generator.

I got used to seeing them daily. It wasn't hard to do in that secluded place. Either I'd see Leo running along the beach in the mornings or our cars would cross paths as we headed into town. I didn't have to live in that secluded outpost for more than a month to realize just how important it is to have someone nearby. During the winter months, all the beach areas were semi-deserted. And since Tremore Beach was one of the more remote spots, Leo and Marie were the only souls for miles around. It's not that I'm scared or paranoid, but given the remoteness of that place, it suddenly didn't seem like such a bad idea to be friendly with my neighbors.

One day, about a month and a half after my arrival, I bumped into them at Fagan's, and we immediately sat together. It was one of those wonderful, interminable talks over too many drinks, and Marie had to drive Leo and me home. At their house, we polished off a bottle of Jameson and sang and laughed until I passed out on their couch. I guess that was the night we officially became friends and earned the right to pop in at one another's house whenever we liked.

"Need an extra hand with a paintbrush, neighbor?" Leo panted, running in from the beach.

"Hey, wouldn't hurt," I said. Though John Durran had given me a few pointers for fixing up and painting my fence, I knew Leo was handier than me. "I'll pay you in beer."

"Deal. Lend me a dry T-shirt, will you? I'm melting with the heat out here."

First we had to sand down the whole fence, and you had to be careful about it or the paint wouldn't adhere. He cut me a piece of sandpaper and told me to start left of the gate and he would handle everything to the right. I counted about forty picket slats and figured if we moved at a steady pace, we might finish by nightfall. Clearly I was dreaming.

As the sun turned orange and began melting into the sea, I'd only gotten through three slats. Leo, on the other hand, had sanded eight. Eight! In four hours of work! All of a sudden, mowing the lawn seemed less of an arduous task. I told Leo that was enough for today and offered him a cold one.

The surf was calm, and a warm breeze swept over us. The horizon was a canvas for wide brushstrokes in orange, red, blue, and black. I pulled a couple chairs into the yard, and brought out four bottles of Trappistes Rochefort 6 I'd bought three weeks ago from a Derry craft beer store that specialized in Belgians. We leaned back, our feet on the soft grass, and clinked bottles while watching the sunset. The doctor had said no alcohol, but what the hell? One day wasn't going to kill me. Besides, those pills weren't doing a damn thing for the pulsing in my head. Maybe a stiff drink would help them along.

The first Rochefort (at 8 percent alcohol by volume) got us in the mood to talk about everything. Leo had a lot of stories about hotels. He'd spent the majority of his life in them, all over the world. Las Vegas, Acapulco, Bangkok, Tokyo . . . the list stretched into the dozens. Just when you thought you'd heard every story, he came up with a new one. "Ugh, this pudding reminds me of the slop I had once in Shanghai," or "I only ever cried over losing a car once, and it was the day I left Buenos Aires."

He'd held a job that was as retro as it was romantic: "Hotel detective," a position that only existed at the larger hotels nowadays. Most hotels outsourced the work to private security firms that barely passed muster. But the "grand hotels," he said, still staffed their own security team.

You couldn't get enough of his stories, and he always seemed to have a new one you hadn't heard.

We polished off the other bottles of Rochefort as the sun disappeared beneath the sea. Leo said he should probably get going before Marie came over and chased him home with a broom. But before he left, he looked at me with a devilish gleam in his eye. "So since I'm drunk and technically it's your fault, mind if I ask you something?"

"Shoot," I said, laughing, "since it's my fault."

"How are things between you and Judie? Still 'friends with benefits'?"

"Yeah. Well . . . yeah," I said, rubbing my eyes.

"But, when are you going to make it, you know . . . official?"

I finished rubbing my eyes and smiled at him. It wasn't the first time he'd mentioned Judie and how back in his day, when you were interested in a woman, you didn't waste any time . . .

"I told you, Leo, we're not at that stage . . ."

"I know, I know," he said. "It's just that whenever I see the two of you together, I say to myself, 'What a great couple!' Okay, I'll shut up, now. Nosy old man that I am . . ."

"No, no, it's fine," I said. "I like to hear your opinion. It's just that right now neither one of us wants anything serious."

"I hear you, Pete. Crystal clear."

"But you're right. She's a fantastic girl."

We both fell silent for a moment. Waves broke on the shore beneath an orange sky. The ocean seemed aflame.

"Well, now I really better get going, or Marie is going to have the broom ready. Pick up where we left off with the fence tomorrow?"

"Whenever you want. I'll take all the help I can get, but I don't want to abuse the privilege."

"It's my pleasure, bud. Besides, I'm going to need help with my fence pretty soon."

"You can count on me."

Leo sauntered home by the water's edge under a darkening indigo sky, and I went back inside feeling my headache resurfacing. I went for the pills but figured I better eat something first.

I've never been a great cook, but every now and then I've been known to whip up a killer bangers and mash; anyone who's had them will tell you they're finger-licking good. I started peeling potatoes while listening to Coastal Radio. "We're expecting a warm month of July with some scattered storms but plenty of sunshine." I was happy to hear it. I wanted Jip and Beatrice to have a great summer vacation.

I dined on the bangers and mash, licked my fingers, and downed my pills. A few hours later, as I lay on the sofa reading my murder mystery, my headache had subsided but was still present. It had moved deeper inside. If I still felt like this next week, I should probably call the doctor.

SIX

I'M NOT SURE when I fell asleep or at what time I finally woke up. I never looked at the clock for some reason. But looking back—given everything that would happen—I wish I had.

Something woke me. A noise. Or was it the headache? I opened my eyes and heard a pounding. Was that the door? Everything looked blurry. Maybe I hadn't heard anything, after all. *Maybe I dreamed it? Or had something fallen over?*

I was still lying on the sofa. I'd fallen asleep while reading, like so many other times, but this time I woke up confused. The pounding in my head had grown louder.

It had started to rain. I could hear the drops pelting the glass and tile roof. Another storm? And then I heard it again: a pounding, louder this time. An urgent knocking at the door.

"Hello?" I yelled, each word a struggle. "Is someone there?"

I sat up on the sofa with my bare feet on the rug, the mystery novel rumpled beside me. No answer. *You must be hearing things*, I told myself. *Who could be way out here at this time of night?*

I closed the book and pulled off the blanket that was still draped over my lap. I waited a minute. The room was bathed in shadows. Wind shook the windowpanes, but the rest of the house was silent.

Just when I'd started to believe it was all a figment of my imagination, I heard it again: loud, clear knocks on the door. One. Two. Three. Heavy and insistent. I flipped the switch on the end table lamp, but I remained in darkness.

"What the hell . . . ?"

I got up and tried the light switches in the hallway, but it looked like the power was out. Maybe that was it, a problem with the electricity. Maybe it was Leo or Marie, or some county worker or a firefighter . . . or a goddamn Martian. It had to be three in the freaking morning.

There was no peephole on the door, but there was a small, stained-glass window that at this time of night was too dark to see through.

"Hey!" I yelled. "Who the hell is it?"

I gave whoever-it-was a few seconds to answer, but I received only silence in return. I unlocked the door, all the while thinking I was making a big mistake, and opened it.

Marie stood soaked and shivering in the doorway, my elegant and reserved neighbor who I'd just seen that afternoon in Judie's store. Earlier when I saw her in town, she had told me she'd been waiting for Leo to pick her up on his way back from running errands in Dungloe. All of it flashed through my mind in a split second. I could taste the sulfur of bad news in the air. You always can when death darkens your doorstep.

"Marie! My God, what's happened?"

She said nothing. She stood frozen in the doorway, completely soaked. She stared at some ambiguous point between my face and chest. She was completely out of it.

I helped her inside and sat her on the faux velvet sofa in the foyer. I glanced out the door and saw only my Volvo parked outside. Marie had walked here in the pounding rain in the middle of the night. I grabbed a blanket from the couch in the living room and a bottle of Jameson from the bar.

"Here, take a sip. It'll help warm you up."

"Peeete . . . Peeeete."

She was in shock. Gone. Her eyes floated in their sockets, her face a skeletal visage. Her hair was matted against her head. I stroked it, trying to calm her. She raised her eyes to meet mine. Two frightened eyes that looked lost, wild.

"Marie. Easy, now. Whatever it is, I'm here to help."

She wore soaked purple pajamas and a bathrobe caked in sand. She was barefoot. I put the blanket over her shoulders and quickly rubbed her arms and shoulders to warm her. She breathed heavily. He body was on fire, as if she'd just run a marathon. She was panting like an asthmatic. For a moment, I was scared she was going to have a heart attack on the spot.

"Help . . . me . . ."

"What's happened, Marie? Where's Leo?"

The question made something come to life in her mind, and there was no doubt something terrible had happened. At hearing her husband's name, Marie twisted her face into a pained expression.

"Leo!" she yelled.

She closed her eyes and leaned toward me, and I realized she had fainted against my chest.

"Marie! God, oh my God . . . !"

I held her up and tried to tap her face gently to wake her, but it was like touching a frozen corpse. My mind went to Leo. I realized I was wasting valuable time. If something had happened to Leo, I needed to act fast. I ran to the living room and grabbed my cell phone. I found it under a book of sheet music, but when I tried it, I discovered the battery was dead.

I calculated it would take the police at least half an hour to get here, and that's assuming Barry, Clenhburran's garda, hadn't gone to spend the night in Dungloe as he sometimes did. Same thing with the ambulance. Half an hour, at least, by the time they got here. And time wasn't on our side.

I ran back to the foyer, grabbed my keys off the hook, and ran out of the house. "I'm going to have a look," I yelled to Marie, though neither she nor anyone else could hear me. And just then, I remembered the voice from the other night.

Don't leave the house. Not tonight.

Outside, the wind raged. I sprinted toward the Volvo, but then something caught my eye that made me stop dead in my tracks. The picket fence Leo and I had spent hours sanding was broken. A stretch of about six feet near the house lay flat on the ground. I ran toward the car, drenched by raindrops that seemed to grow fatter with each passing moment. What the hell had happened? Maybe Marie broke it on her way here? Maybe it was the wind. But the wind wouldn't have snapped the slats in half. Hell, the wind wasn't this bad the night of the storm. The last thought I had before starting the car was that maybe they had been hit by lightning.

Worry about it later, I thought. *Focus on driving and not killing yourself.*

My mind was in a fog. I was nervous but managed to keep my cool. I wasn't sure what was in store that night. Something had happened at Leo and Marie's house, that much was clear. But why hadn't they called me? *Dammit, because your phone is dead, that's why.* Okay, but why had she walked the whole way when they have two perfectly good cars in their garage? Was there a simple answer to that, too?

I was reminded of Claire Madden, a neighbor in Dublin when I was still a boy. Mrs. Madden's husband would beat her when he came home stinking drunk. She or her daughter would sometimes show up on our doorstep crying because he'd kicked them out of the house. Sometimes, one of them had a bloody nose or a busted lip. When they'd show up in the middle of the night, on a rainy night just like this one, my mother would wake the local priest, Father Callahan, who lived at the church down the street. He'd come over and they'd all sit and talk for hours. I remember her sobbing that she "couldn't live without him." I'd dreamed about killing her husband as a boy. I'd dreamed about it a lot. Could Leo be one of those types? Happy-go-lucky Leo? Could he have lost his mind and . . . No. No, it couldn't be.

In no time, I'd reached Bill's Peak and was headed down the road to Leo and Marie's. My windshield wipers, turned up to top speed, started squeaking against the glass. All of a sudden, the rain stopped. I could even see stars in the sky. Where the hell did the storm go?

Leo and Marie's house was plunged in darkness. There were no cars out front and the garage door was closed. I pulled up slowly, scanning the house. It was built right up against the rocks lining Tremore Beach. Nothing looked out of place. Even the sea was calm. Waves crashed languidly against the sand about a hundred fifty feet out.

I parked by the fence, got out, and started up through the front yard. Wind chimes by the door clinked softly in the night. (*Seriously, where the hell did this storm go?*)

I tried to open the door, but it was locked. Through the nearby window, I could only make out their darkened living room.

I tried the doorbell and pounded on the wooden door.

"Leo! Leo! Are you in there? Yell if you can hear me!"

I waited a few seconds. If Leo didn't answer, I could try to get in through the door that connected the garage with the kitchen. Worst-case scenario, I could break a window.

Just then, I looked over and saw a lamp had been turned on in one of the rooms on the second floor. Shadows moved behind the curtains and a few seconds later, I heard footsteps coming down the stairs. Lights came on in the living room, and the door opened. I was standing with my fists and teeth clenched.

"Peter, Jesus! What's going on?"

It was Leo. He was wearing a black robe over his pajamas. He looked exactly how you would expect someone woken in the middle of the night to look. A little angry, maybe, but otherwise fine.

"What do you mean, 'What's going on'? I should be asking you!" I said.

There was a brief silence between us. Leo looked me up and down. Then he looked over my shoulder, scanning the yard.

"Peter, it's—" He looked at his watch. "—three-something in the morning and you're pounding on my door. I think I should be the one asking the questions."

I held his stare. He didn't know . . . that much was clear. He had no idea Marie was at my house, and I wasn't sure I should tell him that his wife was passed out, soaked and shivering from the cold and fright. That she had hiked across the beach on foot in the middle of the night to ask for my help.

I took a deep breath and held Leo by the shoulders. How to break this gently . . . ?

"Listen, Leo," I started to say, "I don't want to alarm you, but . . ."

And just as I started to tell him, a shadow moved behind him.

"Look out!" I yelled, trying to pull him toward me. Leo, a former middle-weight boxer in his youth, was no easy chess piece to move across the board. But before I could save him from whatever was coming at him from the dark, I recognized the figure behind him.

I think I lost my mind a little.

Standing in a beautiful silk robe, her brilliant hair pulled into a perfect ponytail, looking sleepy and without a scratch on her, was Marie.

"What's going on, Peter?" she asked, leaning against her husband as if this were all some kind of a joke.

"Oh, God," I said in a burst of laughter that sounded crazy even to me. "Oh my God . . ."

SEVEN

"SO WHAT HAPPENED NEXT?" Judie asked, listening literally at the edge of her seat on the leather sofa in the office at her shop. "Did you go back home?"

It was one thirty the following afternoon. I had shown up at Judie's with dark circles under my eyes and told her I desperately needed to talk to her. She tried to finish up quickly with a British tourist who seemed hell bent on knowing all the finer points of miniature lighthouse statue construction. (Judie had three figurines for sale and hadn't managed to sell a single one. This time would be no different.)

We had ducked into a back office that Judie had decorated with Buddhas, paper lanterns, and other Asian trinkets to make it feel like "a temple of good karma." It was furnished with a pair of comfortable leather couches and small tea table that Mrs. Houllihan had left behind. A kettle of fresh green tea steamed atop it. And next to it, in an ashtray with a yin and yang symbol, a small marijuana joint glowed with a red ember. (Judie guarded her supplier's name with her life, even though I thought I knew who it was: one of the three musicians who regularly stopped in.)

"We went back together," I said, sipping my tea. "At first, they tried to convince me to just stay the night. But I was so sure that I'd left the door open and that woman inside, whoever she was, laying on my couch. Leo insisted on driving me, so they threw on some clothes and we drove over together."

"And?" Judie said, her blue doe eyes open wider than usual.

I relayed the story as if reliving the moment.

"And nothing. The house was dark and silent. The door was closed, there was no one inside, not even a wet footprint. And the fence I'd seen blown down was perfectly in one piece. Even the ground was dry. There was no trace of the storm that had soaked me on the way out."

"Son of a . . . ?" Judie said as she took a hit off the joint then passed it to me. "It gives me goose bumps just to think about it."

"You're telling me," I said, slowly puffing out smoke. "I was so sure that woman was still in the house, I wanted to call the cops before going inside."

Leo considered it, but said there was no time to waste. He got out of the car, searched around the house and came back. "Did you see anything?" I asked. He said no, but that we should be careful, just in case. He'd go around through the back door and I'd come in the front. Marie would stay in the car and keep an eye out to make sure no one slipped out through a window.

"My God, it sounds like something out of *Law & Order*. Then again, Leo was a cop or something, right?"

"A detective," I said. "Still, it was a sight to see him at sixty years old still so cool under pressure."

"Okay, so then what happened?" Judie said.

"We went in and met up in the living room. The foyer was empty, not so much as a muddy footprint on the floor. The sofa where I'd fallen asleep was messy and unmade, and the sheet music on the piano showed the last notes I'd made before falling asleep. We searched the rest of the house. Nothing. A woman hadn't been there at all."

"Well, not it the real world, at least," Judie said.

"We made tea, sat down, and Leo and Marie had me tell them all about the 'nightmare' again. Marie had this strange look on her face the entire time I told the story. 'It's a little disturbing to hear yourself the subject of some high-definition bad dream,' she'd said. But she ended by cracking a joke about the whole thing. 'It's not every day you find out your neighbor dreamed about you in nothing but your nightgown.'"

"What about Leo?" Judie said. "What did he have to say?"

"Well, you know Leo. He had a good sense of humor about it. Told me about a guy who was sleepwalking and broke both his legs after falling from a third-story window at one of his hotels. That's what he figured, that I was sleepwalking."

"You think that's true? I don't know, Peter, you sleep like a log. You don't even talk in your sleep."

"Clem never said she heard anything in ten years of marriage either. I did have an uncle Edwin who was a sleepwalker. One night he pissed into the refrigerator like it was a urinal, but he never remembered any of it the next day. On the other hand, I can remember every single thing I did. Not just that, I remember why I did it. I drove my car, and that's as real as it gets."

"I don't think you were sleepwalking, either," she said. "What you're describing sounds more like a delusion or a lucid dream."

She saw the quizzical look on my face.

"It's rare," she said, pouring more tea into cups decorated with Chinese dragons, "but it does happen. Some people wake up in the middle of a dream and realize they're still dreaming. It happens more often during childhood or adolescence, but there have been some cases in adults. There are even some people who continue to do it throughout their adult lives."

She was quiet for a moment. "What's the matter? Why are you looking at me like that?"

"It's nothing," I said, smiling. "I just remembered the girl who teaches yoga out of the store that sells incense is also a licensed psychologist."

"Idiot . . ."

"You think that's what's happening to me?" I said. "Some kind of dream? But if it was really a dream, when did I wake up?"

"That's the part of your story I can't make sense of," she said. "Maybe you woke up once you left the house and got in your car. Maybe later. You did say the storm 'disappeared' suddenly. Maybe that's when it happened. I've heard of cases of sleepwalkers who drove for miles, bought a hamburger, and drove home. But your case is something different altogether. It could have something to do with the lightning strike."

The same thing had occurred to me that morning. My headache was still there, despite the fact I'd already gone through half the blister pack of pills. After breakfast, I'd spent the morning scouring the Internet and found several cases like mine. Nightmares, suddenly waking at night, even epilepsy were some symptoms people reported after being struck by lightning. All of the possible effects could fill a book or two.

But why did I have that particular delusion? Why not, say, a sea lion sex orgy on the beach? Better yet, why not a bus full of lost *Playboy* models? Why didn't I end up down the rabbit hole like *Alice in Wonderland*?

"You think I should go back to the hospital and talk to the doctor about it?"

"I think you should wait," Judie said. "They're just going to give you more pills. Maybe antipsychotics or even something stronger. Poison to dull your mind. Give it a few days. Maybe it'll go away. In the meantime, if it happens again . . ." She got up and went to her desk. She came back with a notebook and a pen attached. "Try writing them down. They say it helps."

The Frames CD playing on the old stereo had ended a while ago. Judie placed the joint in the ashtray and said to wait for her while she went out to run a quick errand. "I want you to stay here tonight, Pete. I don't have any guests, and I don't think you should spend the night at home alone after everything that's happened."

I HAD FALLEN ASLEEP on the sofa, and when I woke up, it was almost eight. A series of rings woke me. I heard Judie speaking to someone at the door. She returned to find me awake on her couch.

"I'm sorry," she said. "I'd hoped to have the place all to ourselves tonight. But I've just had some unexpected guests."

It was the musicians from Belfast who'd come into town to play at Fagan's this weekend, and they needed a room. The musicians (five guys and their girlfriends) would take up every bed. I told Judie not to worry about it.

"It's okay, I'll go back to Tremore. No big deal."

"Oh, no you don't. I'm telling them to go find a hotel in Dungloe."

I told her not to. I knew she needed the money, although she'd never admit it. Even with the store sales, the yoga classes, and the hostel rentals, some months she barely covered her expenses. Sometimes, you'd open her fridge and find bread, milk, and a single apple. But she was too proud to accept a handout.

"We still have the couch, don't we?" I said.

"It's too narrow. And you know you always complain that it makes your butt sore to sleep on it."

"Okay, I have an idea. Let's go get drunk and by the time I get home, I won't care that my ass hurts."

So that's exactly what we did.

WHEN I WALKED into Fagan's, Chester came up to shake my hand and pretended to get electrocuted. Adrian Cahill, the kid from the shoe store (which sometimes turned into an impromptu watering hole), wanted to screw a pair of lightbulbs into my ears to see if they'd light up. I'd endure months of Peter Sparks jokes. It's the kind of thing that was inevitable in a small town where nothing ever happened.

Donovan the fisherman and his friends were a bit more serious when they talked about my scars—they were fading fast—and asked if I was feeling better. I told them about the headaches. Donovan diagnosed me right away. "What you need, Mr. Harper, is a pint of the black stuff. A Guinness a day keeps the doctor away."

Indeed. The doctor had said to stay away from alcohol, and this was the second time I was thumbing my nose at her orders. But I really needed that drink. To feel the beer's silky smoothness against my lips, to smoke a Gauloises by the front door and chat with everyone walking by. The traveling musicians arrived a little later and sat at a table near the fireplace. Soon, music filled the pub.

Leo and Marie showed up around ten and it was packed by then. There was no such thing as closing time in Clenhburran on Friday nights. The only rule was you drank until the wood-burning fireplace burned to embers or the last keg of black gold kicked.

Leo bought a round and brought it to the small corner table where they joined Judie and me. Marie toasted my health.

"Mental health," I added, and we all laughed. I guess we all needed it.

Surrounded by all that body heat, and with the musicians feverishly leaning into their flutes and violins, a sweet drunkenness soon fell over me like a spell. I hadn't eaten much so the alcohol quickly went to my head, where the dull pain persisted, ticking away like a tightly wound watch. People danced in step in the center of the pub, and we swayed in rhythm with our drinks in hand.

Marie came over to snap me out of it. She grabbed my hand and pulled me onto the dance floor.

"Come on, Mr. Harper. Let's see what you can do with those two wobbly legs."

I made the mistake of taking her up on her offer. The second I staggered to my feet, the guitar player played the first few chords of "Cotton Eyed Joe," and I was soon surrounded by a crowd that started whirling around me. I somehow survived the initial chaos and Marie's merciful hands were there to hold me up and spin me like a top. But the inertia was too much and so was my drunken stupor. I slipped out of her hands, tumbled into a nearby table, and spilled several beautiful pints onto three young men. I landed flat on my ass and the entire pub broke out into one collective burst of laughter.

It was around three or four in the morning when Judie and I stumbled out of Fagan's.

We returned to the dreaded couch and the recalcitrant springs dug into my ass, as I knew they would. We kissed and caressed one another passionately, but I was too tired and fell asleep before it got any further.

In the middle of the night, I felt a shudder next to me. It was Judie. Again.

"No, please . . ." she muttered. "No . . . no . . . no . . ." she said, and she moved her hands beneath the covers. She was trying to defend herself against something. Against someone.

I held her and waited for it to pass. Sometimes, it took her a minute to calm down.

It hurt to see her like this, but she herself had told me, "Let it pass. They're panic attacks. Anxiety. It'll pass. It always does."

I felt her slender body trembling in my arms. Who trembles like this over a panic attack? *What about that scar, Judie?* She had a long scar that started on her hip and snaked its way up to her spine. I'd noticed it while stroking her side on one of our first nights together. "Wow . . . this is some scar," I'd said, and she quickly turned around in bed and said, "It was a motorcycle accident. I don't like to talk about it." She immediately got up to make breakfast, and I learned something that day about Judie: She had a deep dark secret she would never feel comfortable discussing.

Judie started to calm down, and I stroked her face and kissed her sweetly until she stopped shivering. She relaxed her hands. Her body was still again. She muttered an unintelligible phrase and finally drifted off into a deep sleep.

It took me longer to fall back to sleep. The image of Marie, standing at my door like a phantom, wouldn't let me rest. I remembered the dream where Leo was covered in blood. I remembered the voice that urged me, "Don't leave the house" the night of the storm. And now Judie and her terrible nightmares . . . For a moment, it occurred to me that all these things might be connected. But I dismissed the idea.

THAT WEEKEND, Leo and I finished sanding down the fence and started painting it. The weather was ideal for it. It hadn't rained in days, and there was very little wind, so we were determined to lay down at least one coat before the weather changed. Sunday afternoon, Marie showed up with a quiche she'd cooked the day before, and we ate lunch in the yard, chatting quietly. They must have noticed me rubbing my head and eyes.

I confessed that the headaches were beginning to worry me. I took the pills religiously after breakfast, lunch, and dinner, but the pain never subsided for more than a few hours. I woke up with vertigo at night, and it took me a long time to get back to sleep. The doctor had wanted to see me in two weeks, but Leo and Marie insisted that I see her sooner. I decided to take their advice, and the following Tuesday, I visited Dungloe Community Hospital.

Dr. Anita Ryan greeted me with a glowing smile playing across bright, red lips and she asked me to take a seat.

"So, Mr. Harper, how are we feeling?"

"The pain is still there," I said, "deep inside my head."

The doctor read over my chart while I told her about my episodes. When I'd finished, she folded her hands, which had perfectly manicured, gold-painted nails.

"Did you suffer from migraines before the accident?"

"No," I said, "other than your run-of-the-mill headache after a long day at work. But they always went away the next day. I've also gotten kinks in my neck, thanks to my profession."

"Ah, yes, your profession," she said, rifling through her papers, "which is . . ."

"Musician. Composer."

She looked at me differently this time with those green eyes. It was a look I'd grown accustomed to.

"Oh, how interesting. What type of music do you compose?"

"Contemporary scores. Film soundtracks. Musicals, sometimes."

For a moment, Dr. Ryan forgot about her paperwork. Her eyes widened, her lush red lips curved into a smile.

"Anything I'd recognize? I'm a bit of a music buff."

I went for the answer people usually recognized. I asked her if she'd seen *The Cure*, with Helen Beaumont and Mark Hammond. It was the biggest hit on the BBC a few years ago, a TV series about nurses and soldiers during World War I. It was on its third season.

"Don't tell me that's your music. I love the melody of the opening credits. The one that starts with that piano. I didn't know you lived around here."

"Just here for a few months. Finishing a project."

"Well, that makes sense. Quite typical for a musician, isn't it?" She turned back to my chart. "Well, let's see here. Yours is a pretty unique case. The throbbing headaches you're describing are typical of migraines. But migraines aren't very common to cerebral necrosis injuries, like the one you suffered in the lightning strike. More common is a persistent pain that grows until it keeps you from sleeping or something similar. But a headache that comes and goes, that disappears during the day . . . that's strange. I think we're going to have to take another peek at what's going on in there."

She started by examining my eyes with a light, and followed with more questions about the pain (to which she got the same answers as just after the accident). And then it was back to my favorite piece of hospital torture equipment: the giant MRI donut. More noise and claustrophobia. I felt like a pizza inside a microwave.

Dr. Ryan said she'd study the results and call me in a few days. Until then, more pills. This time it was a beta-blocker three times a day to stave off the headaches and anti-migraine medication to dull the pain.

While she was writing the prescriptions, I took the opportunity to tell her about the visions and the sleepwalking episode I'd had a few days ago. I didn't get into all the details, but just told her about what I *thought* had happened.

Dr. Ryan looked more serious now.

"Nightmares and hallucinations are pretty common after a lightning strike. Though I've never heard of a case of sleepwalking quite like this one. But it could be a result of shock."

"I don't think you get it . . ." I said before realizing how arrogant I must sound.

But she took the critique with an easy smile.

"It's not all simple equations when you're dealing with the human brain, Mr. Harper. But I do understand your concern. If you like, you can get a second opinion."

"No, I'm sorry, I didn't mean to insinuate . . ."

"I understand, don't worry. No doctor could say with one hundred percent certainty she knows exactly what's going on with this case. Hold on just a second . . ."

She walked over to a bookshelf, pulled out a small date book, and started flipping through.

"There's a doctor in Belfast, a renowned sleep expert. His name is Kauffman. He has published extensively on the treatment of sleepwalking and other sleep disorders through hypnosis. He's the foremost authority on the subject. Maybe it'd be worth a visit."

Dr. Ryan wrote down his name and telephone number and handed it to me along with the prescriptions.

"Although, honestly, I think your headaches will disappear by themselves in a matter of time."

I nodded in agreement, trying to make up for my lapse in manners. I left her office and remembered what Judie had told me earlier: *They're just going to give you more pills.* And I decided I'd probably wait before taking any more pills or calling that doctor in Belfast. Maybe Dr. Ryan was right, and it'd all go away on its own.

» » »

I DIDN'T WANT to be alone that afternoon, but Judie was busy at the hostel, and when I reached the crossroads at Bill's Peak, I thought about heading to Leo and Marie's. But at the last minute, I turned the wheel in the other direction.

When I pulled up to my house, the ocean was lapping gently onto the beach, and a pair of clouds floated over the horizon. I took off my shoes and walked barefoot over the grass. I'd just mowed the lawn two days ago, but maybe I'd give it another trim. I had no desire to be inside with the piano. I knew there was no point in risking another bout of anxiety.

I ended up standing in front of the wood fence. Leo and I had managed to give about half the slats one coat of white paint, which stood out against the verdant lawn.

I kneeled down and felt the ground around the bottom of the fence; it was flat and solid. The grass was thick and lush. Not a single sign of being disturbed or dug up. I grabbed the fence and tried to shake it, but it was solid as an oak.

I recalled how I'd seen it a few nights ago, knocked to the ground, split in two. The dirt all around it had been dug up as if something had knocked it clean out of the ground. I sat on the grass and stayed there a long time, thinking. What had happened that night? Something inside me told me it was a sign. A message.

After sitting there awhile, I had an idea. I went inside and rifled through my files and magazines until I found my address book.

I called my friend Imogen Fitzgerald, who worked for the property management company. She was busy at work. Her voice was bright and cheerful.

"How's it going, Pete?"

I'd been meaning to call her for two weeks about the issue with the septic tank grate, so I used that as the excuse for my call. I told her about the problem, and she said they'd send someone out ASAP (which I know would mean a month). In the meantime, she suggested covering it up so I wouldn't wreck my lawn mower again. After that, I ran out of things to say.

"So, how's everything over there? Adjusting well to your new life?"

I didn't know how put my question to her, so in the end I just had to come out with it. I asked her how long her company had been managing my property and whether anything "strange" or noteworthy had ever happened there.

"We've been managing the property for about five years. It belongs to an American family from Chicago. You know, Irish descendants. They visited the motherland one summer, fell in love, bought a house, but never came back. It's been rented only three times since then. An American family three summers ago. Two years ago, a German student spent a spring and summer there studying migratory birds. And I know it was also occupied in February of 2007. Weird though, I don't have a lot of details about that one. Why, is there something wrong, Pete? You didn't find a body in the attic did you? Buried treasure in the yard?"

"The person who rented the house in February. Was it a woman?"

"The paperwork I have doesn't say. Sorry. It could've been someone within the company. They do that sometimes. It was paid for in advance by wire transfer. I could look into it. But only if you tell me what the hell is going on."

"It's stupid, Imogen. You're going to laugh, actually. The other day a friend came by and said she felt some kind of . . . 'presence' in the house. We'd been drinking a little bit. She said she's always had a sixth sense for these kinds of things and she felt the presence of a woman."

"What, a ghost, Pete? Don't tell me . . ."

"I didn't take it seriously," I said, stopping her, "but I'm curious whether there might be something to it."

"Okay. I'll look into it, Pete. But don't go spreading it around. That house is hard enough to rent as it is."

"Fair enough. Thanks, Imogen."

I hung up feeling a bit like an idiot. There was a note of sarcasm in her voice and why not? It was a ridiculous request. I tried to put it out of my mind by going into the shed, starting up the lawn mower, and giving the yard a once over. The engine noise rattled the quiet afternoon like thunder.

PART TWO

ONE

JIP AND BEATRICE had to fly into Dublin so that we could visit my father, who hadn't seen his grandchildren in nearly a year.

I Skyped with Clem a week before the trip and she was on-board with the idea. She offered to pay for half the airfare, but I insisted on taking care of all their expenses for their stay in Ireland. Sure, it was a stupid pride thing, and God knows my finances weren't as stable as I'd like them to be. But I hated the idea of Niels—Clem's new boyfriend—and his money having an iota of influence on our idyllic vacation time together.

I could see her perfectly on the video chat. She wore her hair short and wavy now—it looked good on her—and she looked to have gotten some sun. I imagined she and Niels had recently taken one of their trips to yet another exotic location. She was the same smart and attractive woman she'd always been, except now our conversations were more strained. I tried to make the old jokes to get her to laugh, maybe even to flirt with her a little. But all my best intentions bumped up against a cold, hard reality: She was with someone else now. And she was no longer in love with me.

She mentioned Niels would be traveling to Turkey on a business trip during the kids' vacation with me, and she was thinking of joining him. A trip through Cappadocia and the interior of the country. I said it sounded *very* impressive, with a note of sarcasm and poorly hidden jealousy.

"You seem a little under the weather," she said. "Is everything okay?"

"Yeah. It's nothing . . ."

I just got struck by a little lightning, and since then, I've been having macabre visions, but other than that, I'm totally fine.

"I was up late playing. You know how it is. There's not much else to do around here," I said.

"I'm glad to hear it. How's the work coming along?"

I knew Clem was asking with the best intentions, but coming out of her mouth, everything sounded like an accusation. *What do you want to know? Why bother asking, since you already know, don't you? I wasn't up all night playing. I was tossing and turning in bed dwelling on the river of shit my life has become. I came downstairs, downed a glass of warm milk and whiskey, and managed to sleep for an hour before waking up again. THAT's my life . . .*

"It's coming along slowly but surely," I managed to say. "I think I'm about to turn a corner, to start a new . . ."

Just then, I heard another voice reverberating in their grand apartment in the Netherlands: Niels. Clem turned her head for a second, and I missed out on telling her about the new creative and spiritual phase I was entering (mowing the lawn and painting the fence like in *The Karate Kid*). She turned back to look at me with a pitiful smile. She said she had to go. Niels was waiting for her, probably to do something magnificent. A big social event, a highbrow lunch in Concertgebouw, something else equally out of my reach.

"Don't forget to get the kids' paperwork ready for when you pick them up at the airport, okay? I'll call you next week."

JIP AND BEATRICE arrived on July 10 on an Aer Lingus flight from Amsterdam to Dublin.

I got up early that morning. I was one of the first customers at Andy's that day. I fueled up the Volvo, bought a huge caffè latte, two candy bars, and a pair of CDs for the trip: Neil Young's *Harvest,* and an album of Fleetwood Mac's greatest hits.

I drove all day, stopping only once in Ballygawley to eat some fish and chips and use the restroom. I reached Dublin in the mid-afternoon to find it packed with traffic. I eventually reached the new-and-improved international airport, a sleek and futuristic port that was far different from the old shoe box of an airport I'd left from all those years ago, in search of a new life. I arrived with enough time to finish the paperwork to pick up the kids and down a second cup of coffee.

At five-thirty, after only a twenty-minute delay due to some issue with high winds, Aer Lingus flight EI611 landed without incident. Twenty minutes later, Jip and Beatrice followed a gate agent among a multitude of passengers to the arrivals area. They held hands and wore the serious expressions of children who were flying alone for the first time. Thirteen-year-old Beatrice pulled along a pink carry-on case. Eight-year-old Jip toted his Ninja Turtles backpack. My heart leaped at seeing them for the first time in three months. They both looked like they'd grown six inches.

They didn't spot me right away. They stood next to the gate agent, looking around with their brows furrowed and an expression that said, "Where's Dad?" Jip was the first one to pick me out. He dropped his bag and ran to me, jumping into my arms. Then Beatrice came running and jumped on my back, and we almost tumbled to the ground. They complained that my new beard was itchy and Beatrice poked fun at my ponytail. I told her it was better than letting my mane run wild; I hadn't been to the barber in a couple of months, and I didn't want the cops to arrest me for looking like a nut.

"They'd never arrest you, Dad," Jip said. He turned to the smiling gate agent. "That's 'cause my Dad's famous, you know."

I signed off on the "unaccompanied minors" form, and the agent did the same. She checked in with her supervisor over a walkie-talkie, and my children were officially mine again.

"They behaved really well during the whole flight," she said, stroking Jip's hair. "They're two very brave children."

We arrived in Dublin at about six-thirty. The city was just as I remembered it. A line of taxis up Dame Street. The Olympia Theatre. Tourists gathering like lemmings at the Temple Bar. Traditional music wafted in the air and mixed with the scent of the breweries. My fun, old, dirty blackguard of a city, Dublin.

My father, Old Patrick Harper—still built like an ox, with a strong jaw, clean-shaven and groomed, and redolent of Old Spice—greeted us with the best you can expect from an Irish widower: beef stew, oven-roasted potatoes, and an ice cream cake from Tesco for dessert.

We ate while the children spoke and filled the silence between us.

Dad asked them how school was and, of course, they answered just "fine." They always were bad liars. I knew Jip got good grades, but he didn't have many friends—basically, zero. Beatrice, on the other hand, was going from bad to worse in all aspects. She said she "didn't give a flip" about school because she was going to be a musician, like me, and I hadn't been good at school either. "Right, Dad?" Brilliant decision to tell them about all my high school troubles.

The start of her teen years had been a challenge: a divorce and an exiled father; it was no wonder she didn't give a shit about school. Clem paid a child psychologist a thousand euros to tell us what we already knew: that the divorce was the reason for all their troubles. That's when we decided they'd spend at least the first few weeks of the summer with me, away from everything. Tremore Beach would be our refuge.

I set the kids up upstairs in my old room. My posters of Thin Lizzy, Led Zeppelin, and Queen were still up, as well as a flyer for a gig for one of my first childhood bands: *Punzi and the Walking Zombies, in the BomBom Room on Parnell Street. May 26, 1990.*

"This was your room, Dad? You actually slept right here?"

"Every night," I said, "until I turned eighteen."

"And then you met Mum and left to live in Amsterdam, right?"

"Yep. That's how it happened."

My God, how time flies, I thought, looking at the Punzi poster. Of our original four, only Paul Madden, the drummer, was still into music, playing "Sweet Caroline" at weddings and baptisms, and covers of Thin Lizzy, Led Zeppelin, the Stones and Creedence at Mother Reilly's in Rathmines. The rest had gotten married, had children, started careers, and forgotten all about music. I was the only one to make a living at it, and it hadn't been exactly easy. Every generation is like a giant orgasm, and I'd been the lucky sperm cell to make it all the way to the ovum of musicians who made a living with their music. Hooray, for me. But if I didn't get my head in the game soon, I'd end up like Paul, playing for peanuts at weddings and baptisms.

Dust gathered on my diplomas from the Royal Conservatory along with a couple of sports trophies (one for hurling, the other for track and field, where I was never better than mediocre). After tucking in the kids, I tiptoed out of the room and back downstairs.

Dad was on his comfy couch by the windows facing Liberty Street, watching TV. This must be a freeze frame of what his life looks like nowadays—sitting alone in the dark, merely surviving. He hadn't lost or gained weight, but his hair had gone totally white, and he dressed neatly in clothes he'd probably bought back when Mom was still alive. I cried inside; outside, I tried to smile.

I sat on a chair by the dinner table and offered him a cigarette, but he said he'd stopped smoking and drinking at home. "Ma never liked it," he said. I respected his rule and left the smokes in my coat pocket. But he did take me up on my offer to make tea. I went into the kitchen and set the kettle to boil. Meanwhile, I nosed into his fridge and cupboards and didn't find anything too frightening. Your basic food, some canned, some fresh fruit. No alcohol to speak of, and everything looked neat and orderly. His mind was still sharp, and I thanked God for that. As an only child, I'd felt guilty about leaving him alone after Mom died and thought I should live closer. But when things went to hell with Clem, and I returned to Dublin, I realized that living back home with my dad, in that city, would've shredded my last bits of self-respect.

I came back into the living room with the old pink teapot and a couple of teacups with images of Amsterdam on them. They were souvenirs my mother and father had bought when they came out for Beatrice's baptism, the only grandchild my mother ever met. When Jip was born, Dad settled for pictures and listening to him cooing over the phone until we finally made a trip out here. Nothing in the world could make him leave Dublin—hell, he barely left this house—since Mom died.

We sipped tea and made small talk for a while. Eventually, he asked me about Clem, the divorce, and how I was holding up. I told him about Clenhburran, about the friends I'd made, and about the house. I left out all references to Judie. I started to tell him about my creative problems, but Dad never was too interested in any of that (or maybe it was just too boring a topic for a former Irish railroad worker.). "How are the kids holding up?" he asked. "They're the big losers in all this, remember that, Peter. Never use them against each other. Christ, I'd never forgive you."

The last time I was there, after a visit to Amsterdam, I'd told him about the problems with Beatrice and her new school and how I'd been against starting her at a new school during a year in which she'd already endured so much. (Although, I saw Clem's point. The neighborhood school had become a haven for drugs and fist-fights.) I'd asked him how he was doing, and he asked me whether I really needed to ask. *Look around you, lad,* his eyes seemed to say. *I haven't so much as moved a picture frame. Everything is where your mother left it. Including me. I spend all afternoon sitting on this couch. Sometimes, I go to the pub, numb my brain with a couple of pints, and manage to have a bit of a laugh. Then, I come home and open the door. . . . Sometimes, I imagine there's a light on, and it's your Ma who's here. I imagine that she hears me come in, and she calls out to me with that voice that was music to my ears. I dream that she hugs me and flashes that radiant smile—because she was always in a good mood. And she shoos away all the demons in my head. I imagine her sitting beside me, quietly knitting a scarf while I watch television, one of the thousand boring and happy evenings we spent together. You really want to know how I'm doing? I'd rip out my own goddamn heart, if I had the guts; jump in front of a train. Stick my head in an oven. But I can't do that. She made me promise I'd push forward, but I can't do that either. And so I sit here in my little cave, waiting to breathe my last breath. Does that paint a clear enough picture?*

We sat quietly for a while, as the television droned in the background. Some show about the Chieftains on RTE 1.

"I had an accident," I said, finally. "Nothing major, though. I got hit by lightning out by the house, near the beach."

Well, that succeeded in getting Dad to turn away from the television.

"Jesus, Mary, and Joseph . . . Are you . . . ?"

"I'm fine, Dad. Just a little bit of a headache, but the doctor says that's normal. Went in and out clean, like a bullet."

"Thank goodness, Pete," he said, clapping me on the shoulder, a gesture I appreciated. "You should buy a lottery ticket."

"Yeah, that's what people keep telling me," I said, sipping my tea. "But you want to hear something strange? That night before I left the house, I had sort of a bad omen. A kind of a premonition. Like something inside me was saying, *Don't go out tonight . . .*"

My words hung in the air. Paddy Moloney's flute from the television filled the silence between us. My father sat stiffly, staring ahead at the television, but his eyes were looking somewhere beyond it.

"Dad . . . did you hear what I said?"

"Yes," he said, without turning away from the television. "A premonition. Like the ones your mother had, isn't that so?"

"Well, yeah," I answered. "I mean, I think so. Although, I know you never believed . . ."

"It was true," he said, cutting me off. "Ma had the gift. I guess you do, too. A sixth sense, or whatever it's called."

I blinked, incredulously. I couldn't believe my ears. I looked closely at my father and noticed his eyes filling with tears. My cheeks flushed, and I felt my throat tighten. It was the price we paid for remembering Mom.

"I always played it off when your mother talked about those things," he said. "Someone in the family had to be the realist, to counterbalance the crazy talk. And, sure, at first, I didn't believe any of it. But when that thing happened with the flight from Cork, the accident . . . Do you remember that?"

"Yes," I said.

"It happened just like your mother said. She woke up crying that morning and hugged me. She told me she'd seen it. The funerals. And then, that afternoon, the news came out over the radio. I was working down at the station, and I had to get out of there to get some air. I was scared, you know? Scared that your mother was . . . sick or something. That's why I hated talking about it. But it was true. So when I hear you speak about it, I figure you must have it, too. That 'gift.' After all, her mother had it and so did she. It ran on her side of the family. It must be something that's passed down."

His words kept ringing in my ears. I felt a shiver run down my spine. *Passed down? What if Jip or Beatrice . . . ?*

We continued watching TV in silence. A half hour later, he got up, and announced he was going to bed.

"I left you two blankets," he said, pointing to the oversized sofa by the fireplace. "If it gets too cold, light a fire or come and get another blanket. You know how much your mother loved to stockpile them. I still have forty pounds of blankets collecting moths in the closet."

"Have a good night, Dad."

He ruffled my hair as he passed.

"You too, son. And, listen, the local barber needs to eat, too, okay?"

"Did you just make an actual joke?"

I lay down on the couch, covered myself in a wool blanket and closed my eyes. I figured after a long day of driving, I'd fall fast asleep, but my body resisted. Even though I'd taken my new pills after dinner, my headache was pounding. God, it was driving me crazy. Dr. Ryan couldn't do anything else for me. Not even the most vile drug could manage to yank this railroad spike out of my head. There *was* that doctor in Belfast she suggested, Kauffman. I'd thought about calling him a few times, but I didn't want to mess with the kids' vacation. Dammit. Nothing left but to grin and bear it.

I grabbed the cigarettes out of my coat, threw the blanket over my shoulders, and went out to the yard for a smoke. It was a clear night with a full moon, and I smoked looking out at the old Dublin houses silhouetted against a starry sky. When I eventually walked back inside, I found myself lingering by my old upright piano. I sat on the stool and opened up the keyboard. A scent of old wood and marble wafted up to my nose and filled me with memories.

A musician? Get those ridiculous ideas out of your head, Peter Harper. You're the son of a seamstress and a railroad man, you get it? Not an aristocratic bone in our bodies. Our people work with our hands; it's what's in your blood. No use fighting your destiny. Learn a trade and forget about fairy tales. This is all your fault, Ma, for putting those ideas in his head.

I found an old notebook of musical scores in the bench compartment. It was full of hastily written melodies. Ideas plucked out of the air.

He was right, Mom, I thought, caressing those old pages and feeling tears well up. *This was all your doing.*

Maybe it was the cigarette or the mental distraction, but the pain in my head eased. I lay on the sofa, turned a couple of times to get comfortable despite the ornery old springs, and closed my eyes at last.

SOMETHING WOKE ME a little while later. Moonlight shone into the living room. And a strong scent of burning tobacco was in the air.

I looked over and saw an ashtray filled with butts smoking in the darkness. I remember putting out my own cigarette in one of the pots in the backyard, so it must have been Dad. *But didn't Dad say he gave up smoking in the house . . . ?*

I sat up on the couch and noticed something next to the ashtray. It was enough to make me get up and walk over. Sitting on the table was a bottle of whiskey and a half-finished glass. And next to it was a newspaper, its pages open.

Now I was worried. Had Dad gotten up in the middle of the night for a nip of whiskey and forgotten I was asleep in the living room?

But something in the newspaper caught my eye. It was a copy of the *Irish Times*, which Dad usually bought, and it was open to a center section. Inside, was a headline in huge typeface. By the hazy moonlight, I read it to myself:

TRAGEDY IN DONEGAL

Vicious crime spree ends in the deaths of four in the quiet town of Clenhburran

---

A single cigarette butt smoked in the ashtray, casting a fine and twisting column of smoke into the darkness. And then I noticed the whiskey bottle was completely empty.

Please, let this be a dream.

It was dark, but in the photograph just below the headline I could make out a police officer standing guard. It was somewhere along the coast. It could've been any place; it was hard to tell in this light. What you could see clearly, however, were the shapes of four bodies under a white sheet at an officer's feet behind a line of police tape.

I squinted but couldn't make out the caption under the picture. Same thing with the rest of the article. The letters were too small and fuzzy in the faded moonlight. I looked back at the picture and something rang so familiar about it. Wasn't that the same tile roof as on Leo's house? I felt a horrible wail ready to rise in my throat, enough to fill the house, the neighborhood, the entire city. I ran to the doorway, looking for a light switch. I needed to read this. Though I knew (I *feared*) what I might learn. That it was Leo, Marie . . . and maybe even Judie?

But why hadn't Dad said anything to me? Didn't he know I lived there? Had it only happened that night?

I flipped the switch and electric light flooded the room. The light disoriented me for a moment and I felt a sharp stab from deep inside my head. I held on to the wall to steady myself a moment until I could fully open my eyes.

And just then, I noticed something was different.

I staggered over to the table to read the paper. But the table was empty. There was no newspaper. No whiskey. No cigarettes. Nothing but the old polka dot tablecloth and napkin holder that had always been there.

TWO

"MOM SAID we had to share!"

"Beatrice, *please* . . . !"

We were on the road heading north. Fleetwood Mac filled the Volvo's cabin. In the backseat, my kids fought over ownership of an iPad. But up front, I drove in silence, deep in thought, my eyes glued to the road.

It was all in your head. There was nothing there. It's the damn lightning strike, that's all it was. What did the doctor say? "Hallucinations are normal. They go away in time." You're an adult, Peter. Act like one. Do you want to ruin Jip and Beatrice's vacation because of a couple of bad dreams?

But even Dad admitted it. He said Mom really did have visions. Premonitions. And I know that voice told me not to leave the house. Maybe all these visions are . . . are . . .

By the time we'd left Louth County, I had nearly rationalized away the newspaper nightmare at Dad's house. An hour later, when we reached Fermanagh, I'd filed it away deep in my mind. *Hyper-*

realistic nightmares caused by the electric shock, I told myself. *I need to start taking the new medication. Maybe I'll even go and see that psychologist, Kauffman. I'll make an appointment after the kids go back. For right now, concentrate on driving and getting your kids to the house and giving them the best vacation you can. They deserve it. They've had a horrible year.*

We arrived at the beach house at about six, and the view was spectacular. Several elliptical clouds floated over the ocean like UFOs, painted in the last rays of a dying sun. The sea was a deep green that appeared illuminated from within, and the sand glowed in pink hues. And there, in the foreground of this picturesque scenery, was my little house on the hill, surrounded by a (very) manicured lawn.

"Oh, my goodness, Daddy," Beatrice said. "It's like a fairy tale!"

"Yes it is, my love," I said, stroking her face.

The children immediately wanted to go down to the water for a swim. It was windy, but after being locked up in the car for so many hours, it was only normal that they'd want to stretch their legs. I parked, and we walked down the wooden staircase toward the beach. Jip ran into the wind, opening up his jacket so the breeze would carry him like a kite. Beatrice started doing it, too. "Look, Dad, I can fly!"

Maybe it was their playful, childlike imagination that inspired me to join them. I ran as fast as I could, leaped into the air, and opened my Windbreaker to the powerful wind. The wind tossed me, and I fell to the sand in a pile. Gravity quickly reminded me I was no longer a child, but a forty-two-year-old, two-hundred–pound adult. But Jip and Beatrice came to the rescue. They each grabbed me by a hand and helped me up, and together we headed back toward the house, arm in arm.

» » »

MARIE REALLY WENT all out in cooking dinner for us that night. The second we walked through her door, the delicious scents of her labor mingled in the air: fresh-baked bread, pie . . . Jip and Beatrice were a bit shy and followed me in, trying to be invisible. But Leo met us at the door with outstretched arms. "These must be the famous Jip and Beatrice I've heard so much about," he said. Beatrice responded, "It's a pleasure to meet you," and Jip copied her answer. "My, what well-mannered children!" Leo said, winking at me.

Marie appeared a few minutes later, perfectly dressed for the occasion, as always. She'd prepared two "welcome bags" for the kids. Each contained a sketch pad, a box of colored pencils, and a large eraser. They said thank you timidly. And after asking permission (something they only did when they were at someone else's house), they quickly tore open the packages, spread their contents over the coffee table, and started drawing.

"Careful not to color on the furniture, okay?" I said, while Marie cleared out some picture frames and ashtrays to make room.

Judie arrived a few minutes later. I heard her old Vauxhall pull up to the house, and I started to feel a little nervous. The kids had heard me mention Judie, but only in the same way I mentioned Marie or Leo. They thought she was just another person I'd met in my new neighborhood, but nothing more. I'd planned to tell them about her during our drive up. To explain to them subtly that she was Dad's "special" friend, something like a girlfriend. But I never found the right moment to bring it up.

I think Leo sensed some tension building, and he disappeared into the kitchen to "help Marie."

"Will you get the door?" Leo said.

Come back here, you coward! I thought, as I nodded and he left the room.

Judie looked a little nervous, too, when I opened the door. Neither one of us made to kiss the other, and we almost broke out laughing. "Should we shake hands?" I noticed she was wearing makeup and had dressed for a special occasion, with a black skirt and lilac top that made her look like a nice school teacher. The only thing she was missing were the professorial glasses.

She approached the coffee table by the fireplace where the children were absorbed in their drawings and squatted down next to them.

"Hello," she said, stretching out her hand. "I'm Judie."

"Hi, Judie," Jip said, giving her a quick and unexpected peck on the cheek. "My name's Jip."

"And I'm Beatrice," my daughter added. "I love your braids," she said, gesturing to Judie's hair. Her braids were like twin vines that started at her forehead and stretched back into a bun twisted into a flower shape.

"If you like, I can do it to your hair, too," Judie said. "You have such pretty hair."

"So do you," Beatrice said. "Do you live here?"

Was it just an innocent question? Maybe she thought Judie could have been Leo and Marie's daughter. (*You'd be surprised how keen a child's instincts are.*)

"No," Judie said, "but Leo, Marie, and your dad are friends of mine, and they asked me to join you for dinner. I live in town. You probably drove through it on your way here. I work in a store."

"A clothing store?" Beatrice answered.

"Well, there are some vintage outfits, but we really sell a little bit of everything. Books, movies, souvenirs . . ."

Marie called us to the dinner table, and we all sat down. Jip and

Beatrice sat on either side of me, and Beatrice wanted Judie to sit next to her.

Okay, not a bad start, I thought to myself. Judie gave me a complicit smile and I noticed Leo and Marie sharing one themselves.

The first course was fried calamari with a Caprese salad. The children, who'd only had a gas-station sandwich and a bag of chips, had to resist digging in with both hands.

Marie asked them how their flight had been. Had it been exciting to fly alone for the first time?

"The flight attendants gave us toys," Jip said.

Leo had leaned over and was talking man-to-man with Jip.

"You'll love this place, son. It's full of cool, interesting spots. Has your dad already told you about the Monaghan monastery? It's on the other side of the cliffs. In ancient times, the Vikings attacked it two or three times a year but were never able to take it. The monks were tough guys in those days. Legend has it they buried treasure near the castle in case the Vikings ever succeeded, and that the loot is still out there, somewhere."

"Really, Dad?" Jip turned to ask me wide-eyed.

The Monaghan monastery was little more than ruins, three semi-upright walls that scarcely recalled their past splendor.

"Well, son, if someone did bury treasure there, I'm sure it'd be hard to find. They must have stashed it a thousand feet below ground."

Leo and Judie entertained the kids while I helped Marie clear the table. I carried a pile of plates into the kitchen, and she asked me to set them next to the sink. Theirs was a square kitchen with a window that overlooked the dunes and a door that led to the garage. The kitchen cabinets were all light wood and the newer black refrigerator had no fewer than a dozen souvenir magnets on it from Vienna, Amsterdam, London. . . .

"Just leave them. I'll toss them in the dishwasher later," she said when she saw me pick up a sponge. "How'd it go in Dublin? How's your dad?"

"He's alive," I said. "Not much more than that. But I do think it did him a lot of good to see the kids. I saw him laugh for the first time in a long time."

Marie was usually a woman of few words who kept a formal distance from people. So it caught me a bit off guard when she took me by the shoulder and smiled at me warmly.

"I'm sorry about your dad. But maybe there's still another chapter waiting to be written for him, something really good . . . once he stops mourning."

"Yeah . . . maybe," I said. "Thanks, Marie."

"Still having those weird dreams?" She meant to ask breezily, but there was a disturbing silence after the question.

I smiled stiffly.

"I've had some nightmares," I said, "but nothing like the other time. Nothing to make me drive over here in the middle of the night. God, I'm really sorry about that."

Marie smiled as she pressed a steak into a sizzling pan.

"I'm glad to hear it. Honestly, I was worried, Pete. I'm not like Leo. I believe in those kinds of things, dreams. I think it all comes from somewhere. . . ." She poked the steak to check it. "This one's ready. Hand me a plate, would you?"

There were six plates on the table, already served with salad and a baked potato. I put one of them next to the stove. Marie speared the steak and carefully laid it in the place of honor.

"You mean, you think this dream of mine means something?"

Another steak hit the searing pan. Marie watched it sizzle without looking away.

"If it were a recurring dream, maybe. But, if it was just that one time, I guess it's nothing. . . ."

I thought of the newspaper on Dad's dining room table. And of the dream where Leo was covered in blood.

"Right," I stammered. But I fell silent and readied a plate for Marie.

"If it were something you were seeing over and over, it might be some kind of message. Know what I mean? That'd be something you'd want to decipher."

I remained quiet, staring at Marie, trying to read between the lines. *What are you trying to tell me?*

"Ready," she said, placing the second steak on a plate. She looked at me right in the eye, and I didn't look away. And we stared at one another for a long moment. "You can talk to me if you need to, Pete. Always."

"Thank you, Marie."

"Now, go serve these steaks before they get cold. And tell them not to wait. Dig right in."

The conversation at the dinner table was lively. Beatrice was recounting a couple of anecdotes from her trip to the south of Spain recently. Jip had brought his new sketch pad and pencils to the table and had asked Leo to draw him a couple of dinosaurs. Jip was deep into his dinosaur phase.

WE FINISHED the second course and all agreed Marie had outdone herself that night. As we awaited dessert, I noticed Jip had been quiet for a while. I started to suspect what was going on and was proven right when he got up and came over to whisper in my ear.

"Dad . . ." he said, blushing. "I have to go. You know."

"Bathroom, sport?"

He nodded, embarrassed. It was bad enough having an unpredictable digestive tract and worse when it decided on its own it was time to move in a stranger's house.

The bathroom was upstairs at the end of the hall. We excused ourselves just as Beatrice was telling a story about Amsterdam's houseboats, and we slipped out relatively unnoticed.

When we got to the bathroom, I had one of those moments that happens to divorced parents who have to miss long stretches of their children's lives. As I went to unbuckle his pants, Jip said, "I can do it by myself, Dad," as he lowered his pants and sat on the throne.

"Okay. I'll wait for you outside. Good luck."

I stepped out and closed the door behind me, chuckling silently.

The hallway led to three rooms: Marie and Leo's room—a comfortable master bedroom with a double bed and an *en suite*, a guest room, and a bedroom they used as a catch-all room, where Leo kept his weights and where Marie played solitaire on her Windows PC. I paced the hall quietly with my hands behind my back, listening to the conversation and laughter coming from downstairs. I was glad the children's first meeting with Judie had gone so well and that Marie and Leo were wonderful neighbors. What a meal! And they'd even thought to buy the kids gift bags! Best of all, I'd gone the better part of a day without even thinking about my headache. Not that it went away altogether. I could still feel a mild pulsating in the center of my head, but it hadn't gotten any worse all day. It's like my entire body decided it was going to get better for Jip and Beatrice's sake.

I paced up the hallway, passing a bookcase that jutted out halfway into the hall, and paced back. I rapped against the bathroom door.

"Everything okay in there, champ?"

A second or two passed before Jip said, "Yeah, Dad," with the voice of someone carefully trying to pluck a splinter. Poor kid had the same problem as his mother. Bea and I were the exact opposite.

I paced up the hall again, and this time stopped in front of the bookcase. It was a narrow piece of furniture that fit right between the guest room and the office. Its shelves were filled with books, movies, and CDs. There were some old photos of Leo and Marie taped to the inside of one shelf. Pictures of when they were much younger. In one of them, they were embracing in a wheat field beneath an orange sky. In another, Leo was carrying Marie in his arms on a beach toward the water, though Marie looked like she wasn't too keen on the idea. I couldn't fight the tiniest bit of envy. Deep down, I'd always thought Clem and I would end up happy sexagenarians like Leo and Marie with a house full of photos, and the kids—and grandkids—visiting on weekends and holidays.

I grabbed a book off a shelf. It was a collection of Mark Twain short stories, a very early edition. I flipped it open carefully to a random page.

Q. How could I think otherwise? Why, look here! who is this a picture of on the wall? Isn't that a brother of yours?

A. Oh! yes, yes, yes! Now you remind me of it, that *was* a brother of mine. That's William,—*Bill* we called him. Poor old Bill!

Q. Why? Is he dead, then?

A. Ah, well, I suppose so. We never could tell. There was a great mystery about it.

Q. That is sad, very sad. He disappeared, then?

I read a little more then put it back on the shelf then took a thick album filled with photographs of North American national parks, which was serving as a bookend. I pulled it out carefully so as not to knock over any books and opened it. I took my time looking at pictures of the Grand Canyon, Yosemite, Lake Powell, remembering a road trip Clem and I had taken as newlyweds down Route 66 from Chicago to Los Angeles. As I reached to put the photo album back, I noticed something at the back of the bookshelf. It was a paper scroll that was partly unrolled and yellowed with age. I realized it was a rolled-up canvas. A painting Marie hadn't framed yet, I figured.

Which, for some reason, is hidden in the back of this bookcase, I thought to myself. I was surprised to feel my curiosity piqued. It was a like a whisper inside my head: *Do it, Pete.*

Don't even think about it, I told myself. *What's with this sudden urge to snoop?*

I tried to make room so I could squeeze the photo album back on the shelf. But the books were so perilously piled in place that the whole stack tumbled onto the floor.

Good job, klutz.

Downstairs, there was still talking and laughter. Good, no one heard a thing. Someone might think I was rifling through their things.

Though . . . wasn't I?

I picked up the fallen books and started to stack them again. That's when I realized they'd been positioned just so to leave a space of a few inches width behind them. A space for a rolled-up canvas.

Go on, take a look, the little voice inside my head said.

You are *not* doing this, I told myself. You're going to turn around and walk back up the hall, and knock on the door to see if Jip's ready. What you're not going to do is snoop around this canvas, which was so purposefully hidden. . . . But Marie had paintings hung all over the house. Why not this one? There was probably a good reason.

And whatever the reason was, something inside my head told me I had to know it.

C'mon, what are you waiting for? You know you want to do it.

I peeked back at the stairs. The sound of conversations continued to rise from the dining room. Besides, Marie and Leo's stairs creaked like they were going to split in two. If anyone started up them, I'd have more than enough time to stash the evidence.

The subtle scent of paint wafted up toward my nose as I unrolled the small canvas, which was about fifteen by twenty inches. It was the portrait of a child, a months-old baby. The baby looked like he was lying upon fluffy cotton, though it could have been clouds. The boy looked happy and peaceful. He radiated tranquility. His face was the most detailed part of the portrait, with bright eyes that followed and transfixed you. I stood almost hypnotized. I couldn't stop looking at it, but at the same time, it started to dawn on me that I'd overstepped my bounds. I wanted to put the painting back quickly.

At the bottom of the painting there was a signature. I was expecting to see the signature "M. Kogan," with the left side of the "K" connecting to the "M," which is how Marie signed her artwork (including the one I had hanging over my fireplace). Instead, it was signed, "Jean Blanchard."

Jean Blanchard, I whispered to myself. *Wonder who that is? Obviously another painter. Someone from town?* But why would Leo and Marie have a painting of a baby, signed by another person?

"Everything all right up there?"

Leo's voice from the bottom of the stairs almost made me jump. I quickly rolled the canvas back up and was about to toss it through one of the bedroom doors. But he was still downstairs.

"Yeah, just a little 'backup,'" I said as I slipped the painting back in its place. I walked over and poked my head out at the top of the stairs. "But nothing to worry about."

"Okay, no worries," Leo said. "Tell Jip dessert is on the table."

"Sure, I'll let him know. A little motivation can't hurt."

I walked back up the hall with the intention of rapping on the door again when I noticed something on the floor by the bookcase. A newspaper clipping.

I picked it up. I figured it had fallen out of one of the books I'd been perusing . . . or maybe from inside the canvas. It was half a newspaper page, carefully clipped. On one side was an ad with Asian characters. On the other, the side that was meant to be saved, was the following newspaper article:

THE STANDARD. Hong Kong, December 14, 2004

SAILBOAT FOUND ABANDONED, ADRIFT NEAR MAGONG

Crew, an American couple residing in Hong Kong, feared kidnapped

By Jim Rainsford

HONG KONG—Tuesday afternoon rescuers discovered a missing sailboat adrift 50 miles north of Table Island, in the Magong archipelago. Authorities had been searching for the *Fury* since Sunday when a helicopter rescue team spotted the vessel and confirmed the boat was empty at the time it was discovered. Rescuers continue to search for the boat's only crew, an American husband and wife who reside in Hong Kong.

The 39-foot sailboat was presumed missing Sunday afternoon around 2 p.m., after Kowloon marina managers reported it had left the previous day "without more than a day's worth" of provisions onboard.

A local fisherman alerted Table Island authorities about a vessel, apparently adrift and abandoned, several miles off shore. Authorities used the vessel's registration to confirm the port of origin and that it was, indeed, the *Fury*.

Although it's too early to know the circumstances surrounding the couple's disappearance, Magong Police sources say clear weather in the region rules out a storm-related accident on the high seas. Police are working under the theory that the couple, whose identities have not been released, may have been boarded and kidnapped by pirates. However, police say they "still have to analyze the evidence on the sailboat. And if it is a case of piracy, we'll have to await some kind of ransom demand from their captors. . . ."

THE TOILET FLUSHED, and I jumped. I quickly folded up the article and stashed it behind the books, in the space where the painting was hidden, hoping that's where it had come from. I folded my hands behind my back and waited for Jip to come out of the bathroom.

"All set, Dad," he said, looking relieved if not satisfied.

I hastily patted on him on the back, still shaken by a discovery that could mean nothing and so many things all at once.

I tried to act normal the rest of the night, but I guess it must have shown on my face. Judie tweaked my thigh under the table and asked, "Is something wrong?" I smiled and shook my head. About an hour later, the three of us started yawning and thought it was time to call it a night.

Back at the beach house, Jip and Beatrice complained that the beds were cold. And they were right. The sheets and comforter I'd set out the week before were cold from the moist sea air. So I went downstairs to warm up a pair of hot water bottles. But the kids were so exhausted that they fell asleep before I returned with them. I put them under their feet and I sat in the room awhile, watching them sleep.

I looked at the clock: It was after midnight. I should have been exhausted. I'd driven from Dublin that morning after a restless night, and after such a big and delicious meal, my body should be screaming for rest. But I wasn't even sleepy.

I walked downstairs, sat on the couch and flipped open my Mac-Book. I opened a browser window, went to Google and punched in the first words that came to mind: "Blanchard" +"Kogan" + "Hong Kong."

What was I looking for, exactly? Some kind of connection? Confirmation of some half-baked theory?

. . . an American couple residing in Hong Kong . . .

What if there was a simple answer? Maybe that was another *American couple, friends of theirs, perhaps. Did Leo ever mention Hong Kong in one of his stories . . . ?*

I spent the next two hours searching the Web with every pertinent word combination I could imagine: "Blanchard" +"Kogan"; "Hong Kong" + "Fury" + "Kogan"; "sailboat" + "Kogan"; "missing sailboat" + "Hong Kong" + "Leo Kogan" + "Marie Kogan" . . . But the Internet just spit out unrelated results. There was a Richard Kogan in Newport Beach, California, who ran a sailing website. There was a couple (Celine and Dario Blanchard) living in Martinique—an overweight man and a younger woman sailing throughout the Caribbean's crystal blue seas on their boat. But they didn't look anything like Leo and Marie. The search engine returned several entries about people named Leo Kogan, but none of them was my neighbor. There was a Leo Kogan who was a painter in Lyon. A Leo Kogan who was an attorney in New York. I searched for profile pictures on Facebook and LinkedIn. I clicked through image galleries for any references to a Leo Kogan. But none of them (at least not the two hundred or so I searched through) looked anything like the

Leo Kogan I knew. Same thing with Marie. At first, I didn't think it was strange. There are plenty of people who have managed to keep their personal information out of the black hole that is the Internet.

I finished up that boring and most unproductive investigation by searching my name in Google: "Peter Harper accepts BAFTA for best musical score" two years ago . . . "Peter Harper on the cover of *MOJO*," two years ago . . . "Peter Harper in a documentary of contemporary composers" two goddamn years ago. And finally, I stumbled upon Clem, who, to my surprise, had opened a Facebook account and posted pictures of a brilliant new life with Niels, something she'd never done with me. What, had she been embarrassed of me?

I clicked on a photo of the two of them kissing while sharing fruity drinks with little umbrellas in them on some idyllic tropical beach. I luxuriated in letting the rancor, hate, envy, and my bruised ego roil in my stomach for a while. Then I turned off the computer and went upstairs. I peeked into the kids' room. I brushed my teeth and lay on the bed, staring at the ceiling. I considered talking with Leo about everything. The painting, the newspaper clipping. I could say I found it by accident. (It was true, wasn't it?) But then I gave it up as a stupid idea. They'd been so well-hidden it might as well have had a "do not disturb" sign attached. And I'd looked anyway. No, I might as well admit I'd rifled through his wife's panty drawer. There was no way to bring it up without ruining our friendship. It was best to keep quiet. Maybe there was another way to broach the topic. Maybe it wasn't even important, at all.

I fell asleep eventually and had a dream.

In the dream, I had the window open on a clear, starry night, and I played the piano in the living room as the sound of the ocean added an accompaniment to the music.

It was a happy little tune. I'm not sure where it might have come from, but it was my best idea in long time. My hands floated over the piano keys, confidently, as if I'd been playing this unknown piece for years. The music poured out of my heart the way some of my best work had, and I thought, *I've got it back!* I thought about rushing off to write it all down before I forgot it, but I was so sure of myself and the piece felt so much a part of me that I was not afraid of losing it to the ether.

I'd call Pat that very night, even if I woke him. He wouldn't care, he'd be so happy for me. I'd tell him that I finally had it. That Peter Harper was back. My hands had reunited with my head, old friends. The hits would start rolling out. No more depressing afternoons, hopelessly struggling with chords. The fountain of ideas was bubbling again.

But then, as I played deeper into the melody, one of the piano keys stopped working. I pressed down, and there was a muted thud, like a hammer striking an errant finger. It was the F-sharp of the fourth octave.

And then I lost middle C. Then an E.

THUMPTHUMPTHUMP

I looked down at the keyboard and was horrified to discover it was covered in blood.

The keys were covered in my sticky fingerprints. Bloody fingerprints. I turned my hands over and saw my palms were covered in blood. But there was no wound. . . . Where was all this blood coming from? I pressed one of the keys and watched it produce a small red bubble. The red liquid oozed, dripped over the smooth, white ivory and viscously onto the floor.

I jumped back, frightened. The stool fell over, hitting the floor like a sledgehammer.

The piano lid was closed. I always left it open but apparently not on that night. I inched toward it, grabbed it with both hands and opened it carefully, like a mechanic opening a car hood. Instantly, I knew something was wrong. Where was the golden frame? Inside, there was only a deep, dark cavity. I reached in with one hand, trying to feel for the strings. Instead, I felt my hand dip into something wet and warm. The piano case was filled with . . .

My God . . .

Blood.

I lifted the lid farther to get a better look. Floating inside that bloodbath was a body. A naked body. Submerged in a deep, red pool.

Hands and feet tied. Judie.

"Help me, Pete," she moaned. "He'll be back any minute. He's going to kill me. Please, help me."

My entire body was shaking. "I'll get you out of there, Judie. Don't worry, I'll get you out." I couldn't find the bar to hold the lid up and I couldn't let go. . . .

"Please. *Please* . . . He's a monster. He's only going to toy with me awhile longer and then he'll kill me, Peter. He'll chop me up into a thousand pieces."

That's when I felt a presence behind me in the room. I closed the lid, drowning out Judie's pleas. I turned around. In the middle of room was a shadow.

"Time is running out, Peter," it said.

The figure was bald. There were horrible black spots on her skin that made her appear monstrous. Thin, like a skeleton. Just as she was in those final days, on her deathbed, when the chemotherapy had torched her from the inside out.

"Mom?"

She was dressed in her house gown. And despite her deathly appearance, her eyes revealed a sweetness and compassion that somehow transformed that nightmare into a good dream. I went to her but her figure became more ghostly, and she began to disappear.

As she faded, she parted her lips and said one last thing:

"Get out of this house, Peter."

THREE

SUMMER ARRIVED and so did the tourists. No longer could you blow through the only stop sign at the center of town. The streets were alive. In came a steady stream of cars, campers, and motorcycles riding up and down the coast. Our tiny Andy's supermarket/gasoline station stocked up on food, including a whole BBQ section. There was always a line that was three or four people deep at the register. All throughout town, there were fresh new faces and accents. Jip was obsessed with the water and waded in up to his neck until he couldn't take it anymore and ran out covered in goose bumps. After three days of it, I caved and drove into Dungloe to buy him a wet suit. No way did I want him to miss out on his summer because of the cold. Even though the weather was warm, this northern sea remained a frigid sixty-four degrees Fahrenheit. Beatrice, on the other hand, preferred to lay on a towel and read. On our first trip to Judie's store, Judie had given her the first Twilight book, and Beatrice was hooked.

Judie would drop by the house sometimes and we would all go

Title:
The last night at Tremore Beach :
Author:
Santiago, Mikel, 1975-
Item ID: 34200012963290

Due: **09/19/2017**

for an afternoon walk together. The paths between the dunes, naturally cut between the sand and the grass, were the perfect place to get lost on warm, summer afternoons. Judie and Beatrice would walk a little ahead of Jip and me and share girl talk. They seemed to be getting along so well. Jip and I were doing our own thing: searching for bugs, picking up sticks, and collecting weird or unique rocks—and taking them all home in a bag, of course. And ever since Leo had told him the Vikings story, he'd been certain we would stumble upon the buried treasure. He would race toward any shiny thing he saw in the sand, and a couple of times I even had to take a piece of broken glass out of his hands.

Mrs. Houllihan's store competed with Andy's for beach supply sales, so Judie was busy that week. On Tuesday, she asked to borrow my Volvo to pick up a big order in Dungloe: little plastic shovels, buckets and rakes; hammocks and beach umbrellas; swimsuits, sunglasses, T-shirts, and shorts. . . .

"Wow, you really think you'll sell all this stuff?" I asked.

"People go crazy for summer," she said. "And this looks like it's going to be a good one."

It's true that all the weather forecasts predicted beautiful weather for July and the first half of August. Maybe with a chance of a thunderstorm or two, but good weather overall.

A slight chance of thunderstorms (with ominous black clouds, thunder, and lightning strikes sweeping in unexpectedly at midnight, accompanied by a side order of hallucinations), but overall good weather.

After the trip to Dungloe and a long day unloading new inventory at the shop, Judie brought the car back, and I invited her to stay for dinner.

While the children played Frisbee in the backyard under a

darkening, starry lilac sky, Judie and I cooked together and chatted. It was a sweet moment, having her and the kids with me in that house by the sea, making a delicious dinner, and a DVD ready for movie night after. I was aware that my brain was trying to replace Clem with Judie, to put a patch over the fractured family I missed so much. But whatever it was, I knew I felt good. More than good: happy. It was a sensation I hadn't felt in a long time.

On the other hand, since the kids had been in town, Judie and I hadn't been intimate, much less spent the night together.

"Mmm, a big bear hug?" she said, as I wrapped her from behind while the kids' voices sounded in the distance. "Careful or they'll see us."

"I'm having a hard time controlling myself," I said. "Why don't you spend the night?"

She shook her head. "We already discussed that, Pete."

Yes, we had. It had sounded very reasonable then: She wouldn't feel comfortable spending the night with the kids in the house. It wouldn't be easy for me, either, but I guess I was more open to it. After all, Clem lived with Niels. And I'm sure my kids saw him in pajamas in the morning, brushing his teeth with his hair a mess and his face unshaven. Judie painted a much prettier picture.

"But, I mean, at some point we're going to have to . . ." I said, nibbling on her bare neck.

"Have they asked you anything?"

"No. Not yet. But I know they will. I know them. They're rolling it around in their little heads."

"What will you tell them?"

"What do I know? That we're friends with benefits . . . I don't know," I said. "What are we, exactly, Judie? Are you my girlfriend?"

She turned her head back to the tomatoes on the cutting board.

"Maybe it's too strong a word," I said.

"No," she said, "it's okay. You can say we're boyfriend and girl-friend."

I felt teenage butterflies at hearing her say it.

"Unless, that's a problem for you. . . ."

"No, not at all," I said quickly. "I mean, in the twenty-first cen-tury lexicon, 'boyfriend and girlfriend' doesn't mean we have to get married."

"In the twenty-first century lexicon, I like you and you like me, and we get along well, and we don't sleep with anyone else. We don't have to sign any document or wear a ring, we just have to be honest and open with one another. And we can call it whatever we like."

"Judie, that's the most romantic thing anyone has said to me in the last two years."

She turned to face me, rested her hands on my shoulders, and leaned in to kiss me tenderly.

"I'm not even trying to be romantic yet. Wait and see."

Just then, we heard Jip crying outside. Beatrice came running through the yard with the Frisbee in hand.

"Jip's hurt, Dad!"

We rushed outside. Jip was sitting on the grass, next to the sep-tic tank drain, holding his knee, and I immediately knew what had happened. He'd tripped over the goddamn drain I'd run over twice with the lawn mower.

"I've been meaning to get that thing fixed for months," I told Judie, "but I always seem to forget. It's hidden by the grass, and it's easy to trip over it."

I picked up Jip and carried him into the living room. Judie asked where the first-aid kit was, and I sent her to the hall closet. She re-turned with a metal box containing unopened packages of cotton, bandages, and iodine. Also in there was the headache medicine Dr. Ryan had prescribed, but which I'd not yet taken.

I soaked a piece of cotton in iodine and started disinfecting Jip's cut. He'd been chasing the Frisbee in midair and stepped into the open drain, tripping and banging his knee. It was an impressive battle scar, although not too deep, thank God.

"You think he needs a tetanus shot?"

Judie said it wasn't necessary since the cut had come from a rock.

"A little iodine should be more than enough," she said.

While I cleaned the wound, Judie asked about the beta blockers and the other pills in the first-aid kit.

"Is this what they gave you at the hospital?"

I said yes. "Thank goodness you decided not to take them," she added.

Beatrice sat down next to us and stroked her brother's hair while I finished rinsing out his wound with hydrogen peroxide.

Judie was standing next to us, but I noticed she'd fallen silent, studying a piece of paper she'd found inside the kit. I looked up and saw a surprised look on her face.

"Where did you get this?"

She reached down and showed it to me.

"Right, Kauffman," I said. It was the scrap of paper on which Dr. Ryan had written the name of the psychologist in Belfast. I must have tossed it in there along with the rest of the medicine and forgotten about it. "Dr. Ryan recommended him. He's supposed to be some kind of sleep-disorder specialist. Ever heard of him?"

"He was . . . my college professor, but I'm surprised Dr. Ryan would recommend him."

The look on Judie's face told me there was more to it. There was something like fear in her eyes.

"I told her about . . ." I glanced at Beatrice and Jip, wondering if

I should broach the subject now. ". . . about the dreams I had after the accident. She told me it might be a good idea to go see him. You think it'd be worth making an appointment?"

"Maybe. But I think it's a little early for such a drastic measure. Plus, it's been a couple of weeks and you haven't had any more of those nightm . . ." She stopped herself, looking at Jip and Beatrice. ". . . those 'lucid dreams.' Right?"

I thought back on the last one, which I hadn't told her about— where she was bound and held hostage in my piano in a pool of blood, moaning about a man who was coming for her. . . .

"Ouch!" Jip yelped, as I dabbed his cut with iodine again.

"Sorry, champ," I said, turning back to Judie. "Well, I'm still having strange dreams. But nothing like the other time."

"Is it because of the lightning, Dad?" Beatrice said. She always managed to find out everything.

Two days earlier, as we took a walk along the bluff, I'd told them the story in broad strokes, figuring they'd eventually hear it somewhere. I'd given them the stripped down version without all the morose bits (say, the part about me lying unconscious in a ditch for fifteen minutes). As far as the kids knew, Dad got out of the car to move a branch out of the road and a bolt of lightning struck "nearby" and "burned" him a little, the way someone might singe their fingers if they get too close to a candle.

"Yes, my love, because of the lightning," I responded, "but I'm feeling much better."

"Have you seen his tree-shaped burns, Judie? They're pretty wicked."

"Yes, Beatrice, they're pretty incredible. But they're almost gone, aren't they, Pete?"

They'd faded almost completely.

"And I'm sure the same thing will happen with the headaches. Still, if you want, I can put in a call to Kauffman and consult with him."

"No, forget about it for now," I said. "Let's give it a little while longer."

I took the bandage Judie had prepared and put it on Jip's cut. Soon, Beatrice and Jip were back in the yard playing with the Frisbee, though I warned them to stay away from the very back of the yard, where the drain was. I made a mental note: *Put something over that damn drain*, which I'd promptly forget the next day.

We finished cooking and the weather was so nice that we set the table on the terrace and ate by the late afternoon sun. Judie used the opportunity to catch me up on the outdoor movie night, which was just ten days away.

"Everyone's excited to hear you play. What do you think?"

I'd thought it over and decided I could play Ennio Morricone's *Cinema Paradiso*. It was a short piece I barely had to prepare for since I'd played it hundreds of times. Judie thought it was a good choice. She told me she'd secured a keyboard for the event. "That should work," I said.

"You might want to say a few words beforehand, too," she said.

"Like a speech?"

"No, nothing that grand. Just a little introduction. 'Hello, neighbors, it's an honor to be here tonight,' that kind of thing. You're the only person among these two hundred or so people who's ever been in a movie studio and talked to a famous director. They're all eager to know what it's like. Maybe just tell a couple of anecdotes, that's all. Nothing too heavy."

After dinner, we all settled in for a movie, and Judie went home around midnight. I watched the taillights of her Vauxhall Corsa disappear over Bill's Peak as I thought back on her strange reaction at seeing Kauffman's name.

He was my college professor.

A sleep-disorder expert. And a girl who has terrible nightmares she won't discuss.

Well, I guess she's not the only one.

THE NEXT MORNING, something sparked a connection. We'd set out on a walk along the beach, Jip hunting for treasures, Beatrice chattering away. We reached the end of the beach, where caves had formed among the black rocks, and Jip's bag was completely full of beach souvenirs, to the point where I'd started stuffing his finds in my pockets. Beatrice had started writing her name in the sand, B-E-A-T-R-C-E. . . .

"Duh! You're missing the 'I,'" Jip said.

"Okay, let's see you write yours, if you're so smart."

Beatrice chased Jip toward the rocks. He ran faster and faster—faster than I'd ever seen him run—as if real danger was nipping at his heels. I was laughing until I saw him headed for one of the rocky caves.

"Jip!" I called out. "Hey, Jip!"

But he was too far away, and the wind was blowing too hard for him to hear me. He'd accelerated and was six or seven feet ahead of his sister. He dove onto the sand and crawled into one of the tiny caves, which was too small for his sister to follow him into. She kicked sand at him, but he disappeared into the cave.

The mouth of the tiny grotto couldn't have been more than a foot and a half wide and the waves crashed near the opening. I got a sick feeling watching Jip disappear into that narrow blackness. I was almost sprinting by the time I got there. Beatrice was on her knees trying to see inside, but that damn cave swallowed every bit of light like a black hole.

"Jip!" I yelled, realizing I didn't care that I sounded mad and scared. "Get out of there, right now. It's dangerous."

My voice reverberated inside the cavern, a short, staccato echo. And then, silence. I felt my heartbeat quicken. Beatrice looked at me without saying a word. I think we both realized something was wrong.

"Jip, do what Dad says!" she yelled. "Get out of there!"

I was afraid that maybe he'd found another way out that led to the jagged rocks on the other side of the rock formation. The waves crashed there in violent white water. I climbed over the treacherous rocks, shredding my bare feet, trying to find another way into that den.

"Jip!" I sounded terrified now. "Can you hear me, son?"

The whole range of awful things that could happen flashed before my eyes.

I couldn't see another way in so I climbed back down onto the beach. Beatrice had crawled into the opening as far as she could, and I crouched down next to her.

"Can you see him?"

"Yeah," she said. "I think I see him."

"Jip!" I yelled again. "Listen to me, son. Please come out of there. There are big waves on the other side and . . . I don't want you to get hurt."

A few seconds later, Jip appeared out of the darkness, crawling back out the way he'd crawled in.

The second he was out, I swooped him up in my arms, checked him over for cuts, and blanketed him in kisses.

"What happened in there, son? Tell me . . ."

But Jip didn't say a word. He threw his arms around me and buried his face in my neck. He was shaking, and I felt the warmth of his tears coursing down my skin. I couldn't understand what had happened. I'd witnessed the whole thing, his skirmish with Beatrice, the splashing, the chase. Nothing out of the ordinary between two quarrelling siblings.

"He had one of his weird episodes," Beatrice said. "It'll pass. You just have to give him a minute."

"Weird episodes?" I asked. "What are you talking about?"

"He gets them sometimes. Mom told the psychologist about it. But it's nothing serious. He just gets quiet, as if he's in another world. Sometimes he gets all sweaty and nervous. You just have to let it pass."

We went back home and I got Jip into a hot bath—"How are you feeling? Warming up yet?"—using the opportunity to lavish some attention on my poor boy.

"Yeah . . ."

The tub filled up to his belly, and gradually I felt Jip's shivering subside. I continued soaping him up, taking his tiny ears between my fingers, slippery like a pair of minnows.

"What happened down there, son? Why were you crying?"

Jip remained silent at first. It took almost a minute for him to speak. He scrunched up his face.

"I was scared."

He nearly whispered it, like a secret he didn't want anyone else to hear. I lowered my voice to match his.

"Scared of what?"

"Someone was coming. A monster."

"A mon . . . ?" The words caught in my throat. *Don't sound sus- picious, Harper.*

"Who was it, son?" I said, finally. "Did you see its face?"

"No . . ." Jip said. "I just . . . *felt* it. All of the sudden."

"When your sister was chasing you? It was just her behind you."

"Yeah. But there was something else, too."

"Something else?"

I ran my fingers through his shampooed hair, taking the opportunity to kiss him on the head. And I remembered what my father had told me in Dublin: *It's passed down from parent to child.*

Why not? I said to myself. *What makes you think you'd be the last one?*

"Has this happened to you before?"

"Sometimes," he said.

"What is it you feel when it happens?"

I rinsed the shampoo from his hair and Jip opened his eyes. He looked up at the ceiling as if trying to remember.

"I'm afraid. Afraid that something's going to happen."

"That something's going to happen . . . to you?"

"To me," he said, playing with the soap suds, "or to somebody else."

"Like, who, for example?"

"Mr. Elfferich, the security guard at school."

"What happened to him?"

"His son died in a car accident."

"And you had a feeling something was going to happen to him."

Jip nodded.

"Before it happened?"

He nodded again.

"Did you tell your mom about any of this?"

He shook his head no.

"Have you told anyone? The therapist your mom took you to?"

I pictured poor Jip sitting in that therapist's office, squirming in his chair to keep an unspeakable secret, as the psychologist probed with textbook questions that would never arrive at the truth.

He shook his head again: no.

"Does it happen to you, too, Daddy?" he asked.

"I think so," I said. "I never know when it's going to happen, either."

"Is it bad?"

Jip had opened his eyes wide, searching. He was listening intently now. This was a BIG QUESTION, in capital letters. Like, *Is there a God?* or *Where do babies come from?* I could see it on his face.

"I don't think it's bad or good, Jip. It's like having ears. Sometimes you hear something nice, like music. Other times, you hear things you don't like, such as noise. I think that's all it is. Neither good nor bad. We only perceive things."

One day, I'll tell you about your grandmother and your great-grandmother. One day, when you're older, I'll explain a lot of things, son.

"Okay."

"Whenever it happens, you can always talk to me. You can tell me about it, okay?"

". . . I will. So, can we fill up the bathtub a little more?"

"Of course," I said, turning on the faucet. "But you can't stay in too much longer or your skin will get all wrinkly."

"Yeah, Dad."

We fell silent as I watched Jip shape the suds into sailboats. I was scared for him, as if a doctor had just diagnosed him with a rare and incurable disease. It was probably what my father had felt for my mother every day of her life.

ON A SPLENDID Tuesday morning, I got a call from Leo and Marie that the O'Rourkes had invited us out on their sailboat with their children.

The pier was five miles outside of town, in a lagoon where a dozen sailboats were docked. We drove out, and the O'Rourkes were already there with their twelve-year-old twins, Brian and Barry, who immediately turned their attention to Beatrice. She wore a wide-brimmed hat we'd bought at Judie's and movie-star sunglasses. The twins immediately fell under her spell and argued over who would help her across the gangway. But Beatrice, who was used to hopping on and off of boats in Amsterdam, bypassed the whole scene by leaping onto the boat unaided, to the boys' amazement.

I hadn't seen Frank O'Rourke since the night of my accident, so I took the opportunity to thank him for his help. He had been the one who found me and carried me to Leo's car. Of course, Laura went on and on about how she had been the one to tell Frank what to do. Good old Frank just nodded, a case of Budweiser in his arms.

We sailed along the coast, past a landscape of fabulous cliffs, vast salt marshes, and ancient watchtowers, lighthouses, and homes even more remote than my beach house. Marie, who'd spent her years in Northern Ireland bird-watching and reading about them in books, gave us a graduate-level review of all the local migratory birds. In the spring, she said, you could find birds that had traveled from as far as Africa and Canada.

Laura and Marie were in the back of the boat on either side of Jip, who sat, strapped into his life vest, scouring the ocean with his binoculars for a glimpse of a dolphin or whale. The twins sat similarly on either side of Beatrice at the bow of the ship, trying to win her attention with stories and boating trivia. They must not be as boring as their mother, I thought as I watched Beatrice laugh with her new friends.

Meanwhile, Leo, Frank, and I sipped our beers at the helm.

"I'm trying to convince Leo to make the investment of a lifetime," Frank was saying. "There's this sailboat for sale right at the port where we dock. What about you, Harper? You interested in sailing?"

I admitted it was something I'd always wanted to get into but had been too lazy to pursue. Frank encouraged me to take the plunge and even offered to give me lessons.

"The season begins in May and ends in October. You have almost half the year to sail and there's always wind in Donegal."

Frank left the wheel to ask his sons to give him a hand with the sails. He left Leo at the helm. I couldn't help but think of that newspaper article I'd found. The temptation to probe further was irresistible, and this seemed a good moment to try.

"Maybe it is a good idea to buy one of these," I said, hoping to steer the conversation. "Have you been sailing long?"

"A few years now. I learned in Thailand, but I've only ever sailed small boats. Twenty, twenty-two footers. Nothing as big as this. But dammit if O'Rourke isn't giving me a taste for it," Leo said. "What do you think, Pete? Should I blow the rest of my life savings on a boat?"

"I think you'd better ask your wife first," Marie chimed in, as she came over to find a soft drink.

"So what does my lovely wife think?" Leo asked, pouting his lips for a kiss.

Marie gave him a peck on the lips and caressed his shaved head.

"I don't think our retirement allows for that kind of luxury," she said. "If you wanted a sailboat, you should have run off with that rich German heiress you met. What was her name . . . ?"

"Okay, okay . . ."

"You know he had a rich girlfriend, don't you, Pete? She was a guest in one of the hotels in Dubai where he worked. She called him on the phone every day with some excuse to see him."

"Oh, she had big plans for me . . ." Leo joked. "I was a pretty good-looking guy. Maybe I should've given it a shot, huh? Run off with her? Maybe I'd have a big sailboat by now."

"And maybe I could've found myself a hunky aerobics instructor instead of a funny little old man."

"Who you callin' old?"

As they play-fought, I turned and let the ocean breeze blow through my hair and clear my mind.

The last few nights, I'd had some free time, and I'd started playing around with online searches again. In a way, I was ashamed of myself for continuing to snoop (and even taking the paranoid step of then erasing the search history on my MacBook for fear of someone finding me out). But the memory of that mysterious newspaper article hidden in a bookcase kept eating away at me. My second round of searches finally turned up something. I found a story about the *Fury*'s disappearance in an Australian newspaper's electronic archives. But this one was more of a summary and didn't include any pictures or a description of the missing couple. I couldn't find any other record of the incident. The crew of the *Fury* seemed to vanish without a trace—or at least, no other newspaper had bothered to write about them being found.

And then there was the painting of the baby by one J. Blanchard, hidden just as carefully. My mind spun some wild theories, but I tried to force myself not to go down that path. I've always hated gossip, and I didn't like being the one spinning conspiracy theories about my friends. Whatever the explanation might be, it didn't matter: Leo and Marie were two of the closest people in the world to me, like family, and I must refuse to pick apart their lives. I decided I wouldn't Google them again. "Bad karma is like a termite," Judie had told me once. "It burrows deep inside your mind and eats you from the inside out."

A few hours later, we came upon a pod of dolphins to the north, and we decided to follow them into the deeper water. It's one of those moments that remains etched on my memory. I remember the feel-

THE LAST NIGHT AT TREMORE BEACH

ing of standing on the bow of the ship with Jip, the wind and sea spray in our faces, as we yelled every time one of those magnificent creatures came to the surface alongside the boat. "Look, Daddy, look! There's another one!" he cried, and I held him close to me, partly out of love for my son and partly out of fear of the endless blue sea.

That night, as I cooked dinner, Beatrice showed up next to me in the kitchen with a look on her face that said, *Ask me what I'm thinking*.

"Is Judie your girlfriend?"

"My girlfriend?" I said as I moved the skillet over the gas burner. "She's a friend. A very good friend."

"But you kiss, don't you?"

"Well . . . yes. I guess that makes us boyfriend and girlfriend. Are you all right with that?"

"Yeah," she said, stuffing her hands in her pockets with an expression that now read: I knew it.

"So," I said, trying to change the subject, "let's talk about something else. Like, say, boyfriends."

"Boy*friends*? I only have one, Dad."

"Wait a minute, what?"

"Mom knows. She lets me."

Touché. Game, set, match.

"Go on and set the table, would you?"

"And now I'm going to set the table," she said, turning on her heel and leaving the room.

That night, after dinner, we finally broached the topic of the argument at school. It had all started with a humiliating situation. The kids came in from recess to find the chalkboard reading, "I may be annoying, but you're flat-chested, Bea Harper!"

"I hate it, Dad. I hate everyone at school. They're all so stuck up. I want to leave. I want to go back to my old school!"

I promised I would talk to her mother about it. And I suggested that while we "tried to fix all this," she should try to find the silver lining. It didn't sound like the kind of place where I'd want to be, either, I thought. I'd talk with Clem about it, though I predicted what her response would be: "I'm not willing to risk Beatrice's future because of one bad year. She has a chance to have a great life, and it's my job to keep her from ruining those chances."

IT'S ONE OF THE aspects of our relationship where Clem and I never agreed. To her, my way of seeing the world was "juvenile." I thought you should do what you want, follow your instincts and see what happens. "You can't leave anything to chance!" she'd say. That was the mistake 90 percent of families made, she said. She thought securing a quality education was the most important thing a parent could do for a child. I'm sure it had to do with her own upbringing. Her dad was a drunk, a bridge worker in Haarlem, and her mother spent most of her time playing cards in a café. Clem had had to work for everything she'd gotten, paying her way through school, fighting for every inch, until she finally reached her dream job as an attorney at a big law firm.

"You ever wonder why they call me the dictator—the bad guy? Because I'm the one who's there every day, pushing them," she'd said.

"First, I had to deal with your failures. Then, I had to deal with your successes. You've become such an egomaniac. You spend twenty-four hours a day staring at your navel. And that may be good for a musician. But as a father and a husband, you're not worth a shit."

She had hurled that monologue at me about a year ago, while we stood by a police car and Niels got his lip butterfly-stitched by a paramedic—after I'd punched him in the mouth. I'd never seen her so pissed. I thought she was going to punch me herself. And I wish she would have. I deserved it.

Niels Verdonk, the man whose lip I'd just busted open, was a well-known architect in town. His design studio was in the same Prinsengracht building where Clem's law office was, and they'd met at a garden party there one night.

We broke the news in a textbook way to the kids, a long discussion that any family therapist would have met with approval. Despite that, watching Jip and Beatrice absorb the news was maybe the hardest thing I'd ever had to witness in my life. Beatrice was in denial for weeks. She figured we were just angry at each other, and that we'd be over it in a couple of weeks. Jip started wetting the bed. That's when I understood why couples stayed together for the children and even rationalized infidelity. "Look, Clem. Have your fling with Niels, do whatever you want. Just don't break up our family, okay?"

At that moment, I'd have preferred to not have had kids. It would have been better to be a twenty-four-year-old guy and suffer the pain in solitude. Maybe I would have taken a long trip, gone traveling. Maybe I would have gotten drunk every night. Gone to every party in town looking for hookups. Slowly regained my self-esteem. Instead, I set out to destroy myself.

I became addicted to pain. I was bent on torturing myself. That was around the time I stopped playing music altogether. I couldn't manage to play a single note, thinking about where Clem might be, what she might be doing, whether she was with Niels. . . . The hardest part was saying goodbye to my kids at the door where I used to wipe my feet. To have your children ask you why the hell you couldn't come in. To turn around and find yourself on a lonely road in a city you no longer recognize. In a world that seems hostile now, at every turn.

I started to follow her, first to work, then to bars and cafés where she hung out. Sometimes I watched as she and Niels met for lunch. They'd kiss and hold hands. And worse, sometimes I'd follow them to his apartment and wait outside in the rain while I imagined them inside making love. I kept up that sick game until they caught me. A neighbor had seen me standing outside Niels' apartment a couple of times and must have told him. One afternoon, he came out a side door and caught me by surprise before I could sneak away. He told me to leave, and that he never wanted to see me around there again. I started to get agitated. It was a lot to take in, never mind that I'd had one too many beers. I grabbed him by the throat and told him the real crime was seducing another man's wife. He was a foot taller than me and slammed me up against a wall. But I was the one fueled by rage, and I started swinging left and right. The rest played out like something out of a movie. The neighbors called the cops. Clem came down and was hysterical, screaming that I was crazy. Niels said he wouldn't press charges, but he didn't want to see me hanging around again or his lawyers would eat me for breakfast. Pat and a couple of other close friends tried to help me. The contract I had with FOX went to shit, and in a way I was glad. I couldn't string two notes together. I decided I needed to get away from everything. Even if it meant enduring the pain of separating from the kids. At that moment, I was no good to anyone, a detriment to everyone all around me. So I ran away. I found the house on Tremore Beach and realized it was exactly what I needed. To heal. To let the wound close. And maybe I had been a shitty husband and father, who only worried about his work, and who later only worried about his own fragile ego when he should have been there for his kids when they needed him most. How I would have wanted to be stronger, to endure my pain in a more dignified way. But things are the way they are, and I was trying to fix them the only way I knew how—not the way you see them played out in Hollywood movies, where the hero has an iron will and always knows the right thing to do.

》　》　》

THE WEATHER AT NIGHT had cooled, and I decided to light the fireplace. We didn't really need to, but Jip had wanted to use it since the day they'd gotten here. While the fire warmed us, Beatrice strummed the ukulele. Jip and I lay on the rug, coloring and drawing dinosaurs. "This is a Triceratops, Dad. This is a Stegosaurus. And this is a Brontosaurus . . . When it roared, it sounded like thunder."

For a moment, as I watched Jip draw and listened to Beatrice play, I allowed myself to imagine them twenty years down the road: Jip leaning over a professional drawing table; Beatrice holding a violin instead of ukulele, surrounded by other musicians, playing with orchestras around the world.

"Are you going to stay here forever, Dad?" Jip asked me as we drew an army of dinosaurs.

"You mean Ireland?"

Jip nodded without looking up from his work.

"Well, no, not forever," I said. "Just until I finish a few things."

"And then you'll move back to Amsterdam?"

"I suppose. Or maybe some other town."

It could be another city, after all. Someplace far enough from Niels and Clem, somewhere we didn't share the same circle of friends. Somewhere farther south, perhaps. Close to Maastricht or Breda. A house with plenty of land, maybe on the beach. I could mow my lawn, paint my fence, get to know my neighbors. Maybe they'd be cool, like Leo and Marie.

". . . either way, I'd make sure I was close to you."

"Will Judie come with you?" Jip asked, as if reading my own thoughts.

"Would you like her to?"

He nodded and smiled. Across the room, so did Beatrice.

"Please, dad, convince her!"

"Yeah," Jip added as he played with a toy dinosaur on my back. "Please!"

"Well, I don't know if she'll want to come. She's happy here with her store and her life. Maybe she wouldn't like the idea."

"She'll like it. You just have to ask her nicely. She's your girl-friend, isn't she? You do make a good couple. Everybody says so."

"Oh, yeah? Who's 'everybody'?"

"Leo and Marie. They were talking about it on the boat."

I laughed as Jip made a menagerie of plastic dinosaurs crawl over my shoulders.

"Besides, it's not right for you to live here all by yourself. It's not right," Beatrice said, as if reciting a well-rehearsed speech. "Mommy has Niels, and you have Judie. That's the way it ought to be. Not like Grandpa who's all alone."

The reference to my father shook me. I looked up. Beatrice had turned to focus her eyes to her ukulele but her cheeks were bright red, as if she knew she had touched a nerve.

But I didn't say a word. This thirteen-year-old girl had made me think. About myself. About my father. About the fact we weren't so different at this moment: hurt, in hiding, waiting for answers to fall from the sky, perhaps.

Beatrice's thoughtless strumming on the ukulele became famil-iar chords.

"*Somewhere beyond the sea . . .*" she sang,

"Hey, I learned to play that when I was about your age. . . ."

"*My lover stands on golden saaands . . .*" she sang louder, craning her neck.

I stood up and sat at the piano. My longtime companion who'd become my nemesis.

I leaned in without pomp or ceremony. Jip sat on my lap, and I gave him a metronome to play with. If all my old professors could have seen me, they'd have thrown up into their top hats. But what did I care?

We started to play together.

"What other songs are in that book?" I said, nodding to the songbook we'd bought along with the ukulele at Judie's store. "Anything from the Beatles?"

"'*In My Life*'?" Beatrice said, reading the index.

"*There are places I remember . . .*" I hummed.

"Who are the Beatles?" Jip asked.

"Your mother hasn't played you any of their songs yet? Christ Almighty . . . That's it, I'm officially taking over your musical education."

"How's it start?" Beatrice asked.

"Don't worry about the riff. I'll pick it up on the piano. You just play the chords."

"Okay, cool."

"What should I do, Daddy?" Jip asked.

"Hmm, let's see. Okay, Jip, you have to keep the rhythm going, tapping just like this: one, two, three, four. . . . It's easy. Just keep doing that."

Music wasn't Jip's talent, but he knew how to keep the beat.

After a couple of false starts, the Harper Orchestra began its overture. What a great moment . . . The fussy old piano put on her party dress and began to move with style. Beatrice played the ukulele fearlessly, with personality. The two of us sang the lyrics together.

And just like that, we were a team again.

Someone once said if you want to know whether you truly love or hate a person, you should go on a trip together. And to that I'd add: If you want to truly see into someone's soul, you should play music together. That afternoon, the three of us saw into one another's souls. It seemed only appropriate that it was a Beatles tune. I got goose bumps as I surreptitiously tried to wipe the tears that swelled in my eyes at witnessing these beautiful creatures, my children, here with me, after everything we'd gone through. They'd weathered the storm their parents had rained down on them, and greeted the sunshine with a smile.

That night, a strange wind blew outside. My headache, which I hadn't felt all day, suddenly returned. *Tick. Tock. Tick. Tock . . .* like an old-fashioned clock.

I closed my eyes and waited for it to pass.

FOUR

I MANAGED TO SLEEP for a few hours, but eventually, the pain returned and awoke me with a sudden stab that made me yell out, "Oh, God!" I lay in my bed, disoriented. There was a storm swirling outside. A storm that shook the house just as it had the last time. And that's when I knew it: I had returned to that unknown place.

The ache recoiled, like a venomous snake that has just struck its prey. It settled back into the depths of my head with a dull, moderate throb, the *ticktock* that had become my cellmate. I was covered in sweat, but I lay still, in the middle of my tussled bed. I didn't want to move, and I didn't want to be there. I closed my eyes and tried to fall back to sleep, but I couldn't. The storm, the night sweats, the headache, all of it conspired to keep me awake.

Not to mention the pounding. On the door downstairs.

This can't be happening. Not again. I'm not getting up, it's just another bad dream.

But I *had* heard it. It was hard to hear over the howling wind, but clearly the noises were coming from downstairs. With my heart already pumping hard, I listened close. In my mind, the tiniest sound—a creak of the stairs, the wind, the house settling—became the sign of a killer who had broken in. Suddenly, there was another thud downstairs, this time clear and strong. There was no denying it anymore: I was awake and this was happening. I immediately feared that the kids had heard it, too, and if I didn't get up to see what it was, they would. And that would definitely be worse.

I opened my eyes wide.

Is that you again, Marie?

I thought back on my last conversation with Judie. Was I having one of those lucid dreams she told me about? It seemed impossible. Everything around me felt tangibly real. I could feel the sheets beneath me, my pajamas drenched in sweat. I reached up and touched my head, feeling my disheveled hair on the soft pillow. Outside, the wind raged and shook the house. But wasn't that normal in Donegal?

Forget it. Just go back to sleep.

I tried taking three deep breaths and told myself these bad dreams would vanish as quickly as they'd appeared. I lay perfectly still in the silence for about a minute and heard nothing, only the storm outside. Wind, rain, the rumble of distant thunder. *Now sleep*, I told myself. *One sheep, two sheep, three shee . . .*

There it was again! A solid, forceful thud. The sound of a door slamming open.

I jumped out of bed this time. If this was all a dream, as Judie said, then it was the most vivid dream I'd had in all my life. That's when I remembered the notebook.

I felt the carpet beneath my feet, my toes wiggling through the blue wool fibers. Yes, this *seemed* real. I reached for the closet door handle and noted the cold metal in my hands, the texture of the worn brass between my fingers. You'd have to be high on mescaline to perceive this kind of imagined detail. It was as real as real could be.

I opened the closet door and was greeted by squeaking hinges and the wafting scent of mothballs someone had scattered before I moved here. I fumbled around in the dark for my black coat. The small notebook Judie had given me was in the pocket where I'd left it, along with a lighter and a scrunched up Kleenex.

Dreams don't feature rumpled tissues, do they?

I sat on the edge of the bed and turned on the lamp on my nightstand. I laid the red 3M notebook with the spiral binding on it to write. I even noted the price tag still affixed to the cover: seven and a half euros. A pencil was wedged inside the spiral ring. Yellow with black lines and a pink eraser on the end. I pulled it out, opened the notebook, and began to write:

A storm woke me again tonight. And there may have been some pounding on the door, too. I'm not sure. I'm going to go take a look. It all *feels* real. This pencil in my hand. The feel of the paper beneath my fingers . . . It all just *is*. NOTE TO SELF: confirm that the notebook cost 7,50 €.

Just when I started to doubt that I'd heard anything at all, when I had finally convinced myself this was all a dream, I heard another noise downstairs. It sounded like something being dragged. A door slammed at the same moment as a burst of thunder crackled, and I couldn't tell where the noise was coming from. I wrote down one last thing before getting up.

I'm afraid, and my fear is real. I'm going to take a look downstairs. I heard something moving.

Jip and Beatrice were asleep in their rooms. I didn't turn on their bedroom light but in the half-light I could see their delicate forms breathing under the covers. I carefully closed their door and headed downstairs barefoot. A draft of cold air blew up from the living room, and I could feel goose bumps spreading beneath my pajamas.

Everything downstairs was draped in shadows. The windows were black and blue squares in the dark. Stormy wind and raindrops jingled against the glass. A thud made me swing around toward the entryway, where the door was standing wide open.

The door was open a sliver, banging against the frame. So that's the noise I'd heard. And that's the source of the icy draft.

What if Marie's on the other side of that door? Alive? Or dead?

I took a deep breath and approached the door.

Let's get this over with. . . .

I was shaking by the time I reached the entrance hall, either from the cold or fear. My keys were dangling from the lock. I could have sworn I'd locked it before going to bed, like I always did.

I was tempted to close it and go back to bed. But I didn't. If this was real, I needed an explanation. If it was a dream, I needed to understand what it meant, once and for all.

I whipped the door open as if trying to surprise the person or phantom that might be hiding on the other side. A gust of icy wind and rain blasted my face. If I'd had the notebook in my hands, I'd have written: *The rain's cold. The wind is real. I can hear the ocean crashing in the night. The air is redolent of salt.*

In the hallway closet, there was an old pair of rubber galoshes. I stuffed my bare feet into them and put on my thick, yellow anorak. I grabbed my keys from the sinister-looking hook and stuffed them in my jacket pocket. I flipped the switch for the outside lights.

It had stopped raining, but the wind was still howling. The ocean, dark in the distance, roared as waves broke onto the shore. The dunes shone icy white in the night, as far as the eye could see.

As my eyes searched the horizon, I suddenly noticed the fence. *Broken again! The wind was shaking it like a baby's rattle.*

I walked over and crouched down next to it. I had just finished painting it, and it was still newly white. But something had mowed it down, knocked it over just like the other night. Two of the slats were snapped in half, and a section of about six feet had been flattened.

It was crazy to try to convince myself this was "just a dream." I could feel the jagged stump of the splintered fence. I could sink my hand into the hole it had left behind in the thick, cold mud. I was crouched down, trying to figure out what the hell was going on, when suddenly there was a bright flash of light behind me, briefly illuminating the front of the house. At first, I thought it had been a bolt of lightning. But when I turned around, I noticed a light beyond the top of Bill's Peak.

It flashed again and lit up the blackness like a lighthouse beam. But this was no lighthouse. The light was moving. And it was coming from the direction of Leo and Marie's house.

I stiffened against the bitter wind that rustled my hair and raincoat.

Is that where I'm supposed to go? Is that where I'll find the answers?

The light swept across the sky, illuminating the clouds, and the rainfall picked up again. I had a feeling in my gut, but I had to see for myself. I started up the path along the top of the hill toward their house.

The crunching gravel under my feet, the noise of the wind in my ears, the cold rain soaking my hair. Again, this couldn't be more real. And still, I doubted it. That was why I didn't take the car. I didn't dare drive and end up in an accident. It was safer to walk. The worst that could happen if I woke up was to look like an idiot in his pajamas, out wandering around in the middle of the night.

I'd gone about halfway when I realized the light seemed to be coming toward me. The beam flashed and spun and then disappeared behind the hilltop. At the same time, I heard what sounded like the rumble of a car engine approaching.

I slowed down. The lights reappeared, and this time they clearly were pointed in my direction. The sound of the engine grew louder, coming right at me. Just then, as I stood in the middle of the road, a huge vehicle swerved around the bend. And it was coming fast. Too fast.

I thought it must be Leo. My mind saw the four lights (a pair of headlights and lower fog lights) and assumed it was Leo's Land Rover. I even stood in the middle of the road and waved my arms so he would stop and explain what the hell he was doing driving around like a maniac in the middle of the night.

That two- or three-ton giant leaped over the rise like a raging bull, kicking up sand that its taillights illuminated like a trail of blood. I assumed it would veer left and take the road toward Clenhburran. Perhaps there had been some kind of emergency at his house. . . . But to my shock, the mechanical bull kept barreling right toward me, down the path toward my house.

"Wha . . . ?"

I stood paralyzed on the road, a sand dune to one side, a ravine to the other. And only then did I realize he wouldn't have enough time to stop.

"Stop!" I yelled.

The truck roared over the narrow highway at full speed. Leo must have been blind or drunk because he didn't even try to stop. I shot a glance at the dune and the ravine. *It's one or the other!* I leaped over the edge of the gorge just as the SUV sped by, missing me by inches.

I landed hard and let out a muffled groan. The SUV roared by, spraying a blinding cloud of sand in my face and mouth. I tumbled down the side of the hill, scraping against twisted roots and thistles, and banging against the occasional boulder until I came to rest in a bed of thorny bushes.

Well that ought to do it, I thought. *Now, you'll open your eyes and you'll be back in your bed, under the covers. The bumps and bruises will stop hurting in a minute. . . .*

But when I tried to open my eyes, they were full of sand and so was my mouth. *Lucid dream, my ass.* This was as real as getting your balls caught in your zipper. It hurt. And dreams don't hurt.

I sat up and felt a pain in my side. It hurt to breathe, but I didn't think I'd broken a rib or anything. I spit out a mouthful of sand. I rubbed the sand out of my eyes with my pajama sleeve and opened them. I was at the bottom of Bill's Peak, and I'd narrowly missed several jagged boulders that easily could have busted my head open. None of this was funny anymore.

I'm going to kick your ass, whoever the hell you are, I thought as I stared toward the road.

My ears, apparently the only part of me that hadn't been injured, heard brakes bringing a car to a halt. It could only be coming from one place: the car had stopped in front of my house, where my children were asleep in their beds. My blood pumped as I shot up and ran back toward the house.

I ran parallel to the dunes until I could properly see the vehicle parked next to mine. But it wasn't Leo's Land Rover.

It was some other vehicle.

It was a van with a sliding door. When I was sixteen, I'd dreamed of buying one, tossing my surfboard inside and setting off to surf every beach on the south of France. From what I could see in the dim light, it was dark red, with chrome wheels and LED taillights that shone in the darkness.

There were people standing around the van. I counted three. Who were they? I couldn't tell from this distance.

I was close now, some fifty feet away. I stormed across the road toward these assholes who'd run me off the road and nearly killed me, my blood boiling. I was about to yell out, "Are you crazy?" and start pounding each and every one of them. I thought maybe they were tourists or surfers who'd gotten lost. Either way, they were going to get it, God help me.

But as I came closer, I got a better look at one of them. A big guy, wide as a tank, no neck. This was no surfer and he wasn't dressed like any tourist I'd ever seen. Dressed all in black, with a mid-length trench coat, he looked more like a mortician. He walked around to the front of the van, and stood in the headlights. I saw something glimmer in the hand he held behind his back. Something that made me stop in my tracks. Something that made my angry rant catch in my throat and left me momentarily breathless.

He was carrying a huge knife.

I felt my heart pound in my ears.

Once, on a flight from Amsterdam to Rome, the captain announced that we had to make an emergency landing. I remember that moment so clearly, hearing his voice over the loudspeaker, everyone looking around at one another thinking, "Did he just say what I think he said?" as our pulses raced. *This can't be happening to me*, we all thought. *This only happens on TV. In the movies. In books . . . but not to regular people in real life. Not to me.*

But in fact, it had happened. And now, it was happening to me again, on this beach. They were criminals. The crew of Eastern Europeans that Marie (or was it Laura O'Rourke?) had mentioned a few weeks ago. They'd come to rob my house, probably after looting Leo and Marie's. *What had they done to them? What were they about to do to us?*

I ducked down behind the cliff wall and tried to think fast. My throat had tightened. It felt like going out for a swim and suddenly discovering you were about to be attacked by a shark; there was no way to outswim it to shore. You had to ball your fists up and attack it first—punch it right between the eyes.

I peeked up over the ridge, feeling exposed, like my head was totally out in the open. But they didn't see me. The fat guy was walking toward the house when someone else got out of the van and stopped him to say a few words. From what I could tell, it was a woman, also dressed in dark clothes. But her back was turned, and I couldn't see her face. For a minute, I started to think maybe it wasn't that band of criminals, despite the gleaming knife. Maybe they were just lost, I hoped. Maybe they weren't here to hurt us at all. What criminal would let himself be seen so obviously? And then it dawned on me that this was the scariest part: They weren't afraid of being seen.

The fat guy and the woman were locked in discussion while the third person waited next to the dark red GMC van. I couldn't make out his face but he was smoking. He blew plumes of smoke into the air that caught the van's headlights.

I noticed the house remained dark. I prayed that Beatrice might look out the window, see the three strangers and go to my room to wake me. And, not seeing me, that she'd know something was off and call Judie, or the police or the damn firefighters or whoever.

She's a smart girl, Pete. C'mon, Beatrice, grab hold of that blasted iPad you love so much and start sending emails and tweets and Facebook messages to everyone you know! Call for help!

I skirted along behind the dune, keeping my head low so as not to be spotted. I was only a few yards away now and could hear them speaking, quietly, calmly.

Just give me one more minute. Just one more, I prayed.

If I could reach the wooden stairs from the beach, I could climb up along the side, without being seen and work my way toward the back of the house. But then what? Hell if I knew. Grab a knife from the kitchen? I thought I'd seen an ax in the shed once. Then barricade myself in the room with the kids and play defense, I guess.

The van was parked where the lights didn't shine on the front lawn or the front of the house and the living room window. So when I reached the top of the wooden steps, I lay flat and crawled along the grass toward the patio where we ate breakfast every morning. I hid beneath the outside table and chairs, rested, and took a moment to take in the situation.

The fat guy headed toward the house with his hand still behind his back, hiding the knife. The other guy, Smoking Man, walked up with him. He was tall and slender and moved like a snake, in comparison. He wore round-frame black glasses like an evil John Lennon. His hair was cut into a bowl shape and it hung like he'd been doused with a bucket of water. He wore a leather jacket and skinny black pants. And he was carrying a massive handgun.

I lost sight of the fat guy. He must have reached the front door. But now John Lennon was headed my way. I skittered under the table and hid between the chairs. I pulled my knees in, made myself into a little ball, and held my breath.

I watched his legs pass by. Polished black shoes with a thick silver buckle stopped suddenly in front of the table. I heard other footsteps stomp up the lawn. It was the woman. She spoke in a whisper, but I managed to overhear.

"Just grab the bitch. Leave the rest. Got it?"

Smoking man gave a little laugh. He carried on around to the back of the house. The woman stood for just a moment and then returned to the van.

Just then, it sounded like someone rang the doorbell. It must have been the fat guy. The sound of the ringing shattered the stillness. It echoed throughout the quiet house. Maybe the kids hadn't heard it.

Meanwhile, I was hiding under the table, hugging my knees, scared out of my mind. The skinny guy was at the back door, or maybe he'd already managed to get in. Or maybe he wanted to make sure no one ran out that way. What could I do? He'd see me the second I rounded the corner.

But then an idea popped into my head: the sliding glass doors to the living room. We usually never locked them because of a faulty latch. It was my only chance. If they were open, I could slip inside the living room unnoticed. But I was scared that any noise the door might make would amount to a death sentence.

The doorbell rang a second time, and my thoughts returned to the kids. *Please, God, don't let them wake up.* I spun around and faced the doors. I put both my hands on the glass and pulled. At first, it was stuck but on my second attempt it started to slide. It was a big, old door with a rusty track. But maybe with all the wind, no one would hear it. The doorbell rang again, followed by thumping on the door. I'd managed to slide the door open enough to slip in, but one of the chairs' legs was in my way, and I didn't want to make noise moving it. So I gave the door another couple pulls, and finally, I had room to sneak in.

I crawled into the room as the doorbell rang a third time.

"Hello?" someone on the other side of the door yelled. "Is anybody home? Hello, we're having trouble with our van. Is anyone there?"

I looked all around. I didn't see anyone inside but I wasn't sure. Lennon's doppelganger might have broken in through the kitchen and be stalking the halls with that big pistol. I crawled to the fireplace and grabbed a poker from the hearth. The perfect tool for splitting open somebody's skull. I skulked toward the kitchen, poker in hand. The back door was closed. It locked with the same key as the front door. I guessed the gunman was still outside, though he might have come in and locked the door behind him.

I turned up the hallway and looked in both directions. All clear. Not a creature was stirring. The creaky old wooden floors would have given them away.

I climbed the stairs slowly, one at a time, the poker cocked and ready to strike as my heart thumped in my chest. I had no idea who these people were or why they'd come to kill us, but that didn't matter. As far as I was concerned, this was like a rabid dog trying to attack my children and me. What do you do with a rabid dog? You put it down. If I had to kill them, fine. It was self-defense. I couldn't give a shit about the law right now.

The upstairs hallway was dark and silent. The door to the kids' room was open a crack. Their room was all shadows, and no one was moving inside. I found it odd, suddenly, since the man downstairs was ringing the doorbell and pounding on the door. Or maybe they'd woken up and were hiding somewhere.

I whispered their names urgently—"Jip . . . Beatrice"—but no one answered.

The knocking downstairs had stopped. The fat guy must be looking for a way in without making a lot of noise. Or maybe the skinny bastard out back had managed to pick the lock and would soon come sneaking up the squeaking stairs.

The old hinges to Jip and Beatrice's room creaked as I eased the door open. My reptilian brain had taken over and sparked my fight or flight responses. My muscles were tensed. My hearing was ten times as sensitive. My pupils were saucers in the dark.

But the room was still.

There were two lumps, one in each bed. I approached the nearest. Jip was asleep the way he always slept, the sheet pulled up to his chin and one little hand peeking out next to his face. I held my hand near his mouth and felt his hot breath, relieved.

I gently shook him awake.

"Wake up, son," I whispered.

He opened his eyes, puzzled, and was about to say something when I gestured for him to stay quiet. I crept over to Beatrice and woke her, as well.

"There are people in the house. Don't make a sound," I said. "Beatrice, do you have your cell phone with you?"

"People?" Beatrice said, her eyes betraying fear. "Thieves?"

"Yes," I said. "They broke in to rob the place. Do you have your phone?"

"My cell? It's in the living room. In my backpack," she said.

"Dammit. Okay, get under the bed and don't make a sound. I'm going to go grab mine from my room."

"Don't go, Daddy!" Beatrice whimpered.

"I'll be back in a minute. Hide under the bed."

Beatrice grabbed her brother and they slid under Jip's bed, the one farthest from the door. I headed for the door. I hugged the wall and peeked out, but didn't see anyone in the hallway. In two giant steps, I was in my room.

My room faced east and was right over the front door. I tossed the fireplace poker on the bed and crawled on the floor so no one outside could see me through the window. I tried to remember where the hell I'd left my cell phone. Maybe it was in the other pocket of my jacket? I reached the closet and opened it carefully. (*Wait, had I closed it earlier?*) Again, the hinges creaked. I rifled through the dark for my coat, and it fell to the ground. I reached in the pocket and felt familiar cold, metal rings. It was the notebook Judie had given me.

I turned to the nightstand where I could have sworn I'd left the notebook just a little while ago.

But the pencil was still in the metal rings. I opened it. The pages were blank.

I crawled over to the window, feeling a rush of contradicting emotions. On one hand, relief; on the other, concern. I poked the curtains open and looked outside. Stars illuminated a clear sky. There was not a single cloud, not a trace of storm. The ocean curled softly onto the beach. No van was parked in front of my house, and the white picket fence was perfect, intact.

I felt my knees go weak.

It happened again. Jesus Christ, it happened again.

There was no van. No killers at my door.

FIVE

I WOKE JUDIE in the middle of the night with a desperate phone call. "I don't want to hear anything about lucid dreams. This was no dream."

It took her twenty minutes to pull on a pair of jeans and race down the winding roads in her Vauxhall to my house. She came through the door like an ER doctor, ready to act. Jip was still shaking and Beatrice sat on her bed, fighting back tears.

I was sure this hadn't been some dream.

Sure, everything else had disappeared. Even the note I'd written in the notebook she'd given me. *I'm afraid and my fear is real*, I remembered writing.

"But . . . are you sure, Pete?"

"As sure as I am that you're standing here, Judie. Down to the fact the notebook cost seven and a half euros. I remember reading it in my dream."

Outside, everything had vanished, as well. There wasn't so much as a tire track that didn't belong to Judie's or my car. I grabbed a flashlight out of the shed, flipped on the outside lights, and walked around the house with Jip and Beatrice at my side. They didn't want to be alone even for a second. They were terrified, and I couldn't blame them.

To start with, the fence was perfectly intact. White and straight and not a scratch on it. I told them that in my "nightmare" the fence had been broken and knocked over. I remembered sticking my fingers into the rain-soaked hole where the slats had once stood. But now, the fence was as solid as a hundred-year-old oak.

And then there was the matter of the storm. Judie told me there hadn't been a drop of rainfall in the night. All you had to do was feel the dry ground to know she was right.

"But I . . ." I stammered as I ran my fingers through my dry hair, "I remember walking in the rain. I'm sure of it! I put on these boots and I was out walking for more than five minutes before I came across that van . . ."

I showed her the sand on my raincoat, boots, and pajamas. I showed her the scratches from my fall down the side of the ravine. I showed her where I'd banged my chest when I dove off the road. I was sure if we grabbed the flashlight and went up the road, we'd find my footprints in the sand.

"I believe you, Pete, but . . ." she said, gesturing toward the kids, "what good would it do?"

IT WAS ALMOST daybreak by the time the kids managed to fall back asleep. Judie had told them three back-to-back bedtime stories, and they were still wide awake at the end of the last one. Then, she sang an old Irish ballad, and her voice filled our home with warmth and peace. She shooed our ghosts and fears away. The memory of their father running around the house with a fireplace poker, like a madman, slipped away. I heard their breathing slow, each breath deeper and longer, their little mouths open slightly, as they watched and listened to Judie from under the covers, until their eyelids gave in and they drifted off completely.

"Daddy just had a bad dream. He's very sorry to have frightened you. Now, sleep. Sleep. And tomorrow will be a beautiful day."

She came to my room when the children were down. My head and my heart were in pain. I took pills for one and whiskey for the other. Then I collapsed into bed. Judie sat on the edge, next to me. She resisted lying down, regardless of how tired she must have been. Outside, the sun began to rise.

"If Clem were in Amsterdam, I'd send them home right away," I said. "Their father may be an idiot, but he's not crazy."

"Pete . . . you're not crazy," Judie said, gently taking my glass of whiskey and setting it on the nightstand. She turned and ran her fingers through my hair. "Something's going on, but you're not crazy."

"So what's the matter with me? What if I have another hallucination and mistake them for the thieves and bash their heads in with a goddamn poker?"

It sounded frighteningly plausible. I noticed Judie react, but she tried to reassure me.

"You don't know that there'll be a next time."

"That's what we *want* to think, Judie. That's the best-case scenario we're hoping for. But tonight, I frightened the hell out of my children. I pulled them out of bed in the middle of the night and told them they had to hide. That was this time. What happens next time? I won't put my kids—or you—in harm's way. I want you to be completely honest with me. Do you think I might be schizophrenic?"

She couldn't help chuckling.

"Where did you get *that* idea?"

"From the Internet. Dr. Google. I read that schizophrenics sometimes hallucinate."

Judie asked for a cigarette. The pack was on the nightstand, and I handed it to her. She lit one and launched two streams of smoke out of her nose.

"Yes, there are some mental illnesses, like schizophrenia, where the patient 'sees' or 'hears' things that aren't really there. But there are a host of other symptoms associated with that disease that you don't display. Your 'visions' are very organized, for instance. You always know when they start and finish."

"And that makes it different?"

"It does. That sets you apart from the vast majority of cases of schizophrenia or delusional disorders. Although I can't swear there aren't other cases like yours. In my opinion, there's something else going on with you. Something medical science can't so easily label. Like, where did those three distinct characters come from? And that recurring image of the broken fence? If I had to bet money, I'd say the answers lie with Jung or Freud and not a lobotomy."

"You mean, you think there's a hidden message in all this?"

"It's just a hunch," Judie said, "but why not? It seems like you 'exist' inside these dreams. You move, walk around, hell, even jump off the side of a cliff when you think something's trying to attack you. It's as if you're living out your dream. As if you're wearing a pair of virtual reality goggles. But none of that changes the basic question: Why are you having these dreams?"

"*Why am I having these dreams?*" I repeated to myself. "Why? It feels like a warning. Like something's coming. It's like the whole picture is coming together a piece at a time. The first time, it was Marie. She was frightened. Something had happened to her. Then, in Dublin, there was that image of the dead bodies . . ."

"What happened in Dublin?" Judie asked.

I remembered then that I hadn't told her or anyone else about my vision with the newspaper article.

"The night I stayed at my father's house, I had another . . . 'nightmare.' I believed I saw a newspaper on the dining room table. There was a story about a massacre in Clenhburran. A family had been killed. Then, I flipped the light on and everything vanished. Just like tonight. Just like every night. I'd forgotten about it . . ."

"Is there anything else you think is important?"

"I don't know. I don't remember anything else. The fence is always broken. And I guess that makes sense because the dream always takes place on the same night. And tonight, it seemed like these assassins were looking for someone. A woman."

Judie finished her cigarette and snuffed it out in the ashtray. She sat quietly, thinking for a long minute.

"Do you think I'm crazy, Judie? Because right now, you're one of the only people in the world I can trust. Recently, everything's been so . . . strange. I see things that aren't there. I've even started doubting Leo, Marie . . . even you."

"Why me?"

"It's nothing. It's stupid, forget I said anything."

"No, tell me," Judie said. "I want to know."

"You . . . were in one of my nightmares. Something horrible happened, horrible like all the others. And later, you gave me this strange look when you found the name of that doctor, Kauffman, scribbled on that scrap of paper in the first-aid kit. Tell me I'm imagining things, please. Tell me I'm just being paranoid."

Her deep brown eyes, almost black in the dark room, locked in on mine.

"What happened in your nightmare, Pete?"

I took a long drag off my cigarette.

"I don't know if you want to know. It's terrible."

"I want to know."

I tipped back the rest of the whiskey until the ice cubes tumbled against my lips.

"You were tied up. Tied up and scared. Someone was coming to get you, to hurt you, and you were begging me for help. You said he was 'going to kill you.' But maybe that dream was a remnant of real life. There are a lot of nights where you . . . well, you have those horrible nightmares. I guess I internalized that, and it came out in my dream."

"Tied up . . ." Judie said. Her lips had started to tremble. "Was there someone else in the dream?"

"Yes . . ." I said. Her face grew more tense.

"A man?" she asked, and now, I saw she was frightened.

"No. It was my mother," I said, "telling me I had to leave this house."

Judie covered her mouth with one hand. I couldn't tell whether she was crying, but I could tell she was breathing faster. I leaned back. Suddenly, our roles had reversed: She had become the patient and I the doctor.

"Judie? Are you okay?"

"Yeah, just, a little stunned, Pete."

"Did I say something to . . . ?"

"Let's just drop it for now. This isn't the time to discuss it."

I took her by the shoulders. The morning light that crept into the house fell softly on her face. I was looking at a different Judie, now. She was pale. Terrified.

I tried to hug her, but she pulled away.

"I think it's better if I lie downstairs, on the couch. You should try to get some rest, too. Tomorrow's another day."

"But Judie . . ."

"Not now, Pete. I need a minute, okay?"

She went out of the room and I heard her sigh in the hallway. I had definitely touched a nerve, something deep inside. I was about to get up and go after her, but I knew her enough to know there was no fixing this right now.

The sun had risen over the horizon by the time I managed to fall asleep. But before I drifted off, I decided two things. First, that I would go see that Dr. Kauffman and be cured of this by any and all means necessary. And I'd do it immediately. I wanted to be rid of it for good. I wanted my life back.

The second thing I decided had to do with Leo and Marie. If I was sure of anything at this point, it was that all of this was somehow connected. I didn't know how, exactly, but that's what I need to figure out.

SIX

A GARDA SERGEANT named Ciara Douglas met with me the next day in the small police station in Dungloe. The cop at the front desk, a chubby and ruddy officer, had given me a hard time when I asked to see someone in charge.

"What exactly do you need?" he'd asked. "To file a complaint?"

"No, I just want to talk to somebody in charge."

"Are you a journalist?"

"I already told you, no. I'm a resident of Clenhburran. I just want to meet with an officer."

Thinking back on it later, I should have said I was a writer or a criminology student.

Honestly, I probably shouldn't have even gone. Why, after all? To ask if some characters from my nightmares were actually real? But that morning, I felt like I had to do something, to try to take control of the situation somehow.

"Look, all appointments go through city hall. You should start there, and they'll assign the appropriate . . ."

"Honestly, buddy, it'll take ten minutes, tops. Isn't there someone here who could take ten minutes out of their day to speak with me?"

Ciara Douglas was a tall woman with a stern look, and black hair and green eyes. I waited for her for half an hour, and when she arrived, you could tell she thought this was a big waste of her time and wanted to get rid of me as quickly as possible.

"Tremore Beach? That's the little beach in northern Clenhburran, right? Didn't know there were many houses up there."

"Just two. My neighbors, the Kogans, and me. They live there full time. I'm just renting out there for a few months."

"All right, Mr. Harper, so how can I help you? What would you like to know?"

Faced with this serious-looking Sergeant Douglas, with all those stripes on her sleeve, I realized how stupid this was going to sound. I decided this was going to require a little imagination.

"Well, see . . . the other night over dinner, a couple of neighbors mentioned some . . . security issues. They said they heard about some criminal activity in the area. Something about a band of Eastern European thieves, or something like that. And, well, since I live alone . . . and actually, my two children are in town visiting . . . Well, I was just wondering if you thought it was worth getting a monitored alarm or something like that. . . ."

Sgt. Douglas stretched her long lips into a smile, something I figured took some work for her.

"Look, Mr. Harper. I can't tell you whether you should get an alarm or not. What I can tell you is that there have been a couple of break-ins, but mostly in empty summer homes, and certainly there hasn't been anything major. There was a big robbery of construction material from a site near Letterkenny two weeks ago, and we apprehended two suspects, both of them Irish. Nothing to do with any Eastern Europeans."

She sat quiet for a moment with the tips of her fingers together in a little pyramid and an expression that said, "Is that sufficient!" But I wasn't going anywhere just yet.

"Have you heard about anything like that happening out in rural areas? Something like, say, a group of international smash-and-grab thieves. Guys who ride around in a van robbing houses . . ."

Sure, it was something I'd seen once on *COPS*. And maybe Sgt. Douglas thought I was some kind of amateur detective or a bored tourist. *Maybe he's waiting for his wife to finish up at the beauty parlor,* she must have thought.

"No, sir. This is Donegal," she replied. "We don't have those kinds of problems here, thankfully. For those types of crimes, you'd have to be in southern Europe or someplace like that, where all the rich people vacation and the real crime is. Here, people break in to steal copper pipes or plasma TVs or maybe rip off a car to take it to a chop shop. Little more than that. You can rest easy, Mr. Harper. Now, do you have any other questions?"

She drummed her fingers on the desk. She looked at me impatiently.

"One last thing, actually. Have you ever had any calls over on Tremore Beach? Anything . . . out of the ordinary?"

"You mean from one of the two houses there?"

"Yes."

"I can look into it. But you know what? I think there's a reason you're asking me all these questions."

"Excuse me?"

"Is there something you want to tell me, Mr. Harper? I'm curious about all these questions regarding your house. Maybe you're having some kind of issue with your neighbors?"

I was tempted to tell her everything. But I resisted the impulse. *Oh, sure, I'll just tell this cop I've been having nightmares, and that's why I came down to see her.* I'd sound like a serious head case. And with my kids visiting (and my recent divorce), that wasn't the kind of attention I wanted or needed.

"Maybe it's just that the house is so lonely," I ended up saying. "The real estate agent warned me about it, but I didn't listen. Sometimes, I hear noises at night and it keeps me up, worried with all those rumors about foreign bandits invading homes. I guess I'm a city boy at heart."

Sgt. Douglas stared at me, not quite believing my story.

"It happens," she said, finally. "Especially if your kids are visiting. Maybe your antenna is up a little more because of it, Mr. Harper. Relax. It's probably just nearby sheep or the wind. In Donegal, we sleep with our doors unlocked."

SEVEN

I WAS GLAD Marie wasn't home when I knocked on the Kogans' door that afternoon. Leo said she was in Clenhburran finalizing the details for movie night the following Thursday.

"Where'd you leave the cubs?" Leo asked.

"They're in town with Judie. They went off to watch the seals over in the port."

"Want a beer?" he said, disappearing into the kitchen. "I know it's early, but I just got back from a long run, and I'm parched."

"Down by the cliffs?" I said loudly as Leo bent into the refrigerator.

"Yessir," he yelled back. "Ran from here to Monaghan. Hell of a trek. Noticed there's a lot of humidity in the air, though. Hope movie night doesn't get rained out."

Leo came back from the kitchen with a pair of Heinekens. I took one and thanked him.

"So I hear you're the big act. Got your speech ready?"

"No, not really. I'll probably talk about the benefits of living in a small town, the simple life . . . I don't know, something like that. Or maybe I'll quote something out of a book."

"Small town, big headaches, that's what I always say. Now we've got the town gossip Laura O'Rourke going around saying we're secretly rich because I called to ask about that sailboat. It must be true because everyone's whispering about it over at Durran's! Ah, well, at least Frank's a good guy. He's been trying to talk me into it. And who knows? Maybe I'll trade my house in for a boat. You know, I actually love the idea."

The kids couldn't stop talking about how much fun they'd had on the boat. And Leo said he thought we could do it again before the kids returned to Amsterdam. That was only a week and a half away.

We sat on the couches near the fireplace.

"It's got to be hard to let them go again, huh?"

"Really hard," I said. "They only just got here, and already it's almost time for them to go."

"No doubt. They're great kids, Pete. And you can tell they adore you. But you're planning on going back, too, isn't that right?"

"I guess so," I said. "After I record a couple things, I'm going to have to make a decision. Maybe I'll go back to Holland. Some city other than Amsterdam. I've got friends in Haarlem. I could put down roots there. I could see the kids every week. It could work . . ."

Leo took a long sip of his beer.

"We'll miss you, lad."

"I'll miss you guys, too. But don't worry, you'll have Peter Harper around for a while yet. What about you and Marie? Haven't had your fill of icy winds here yet? How long before you guys fulfill your dream of moving to Thailand?"

"Hmm. I don't know, Pete," he said, scrunching up his face. "Everyone has all kinds of dreams. But then you get older, and your dreams become porcelain figurines you keep on the shelf and only dust off every once in a while. Besides, Marie's in love with this place. And what's the saying? Happy wife, happy life."

I nodded in silence.

"So what happens with Judie, if you don't mind me asking. Does she figure into your plans?"

I smiled and took a long swig of beer. *And I thought I was the one who was here to ask questions.* I tried to answer Leo with a look and smile, but he was expecting actual words.

"I don't know. I think she's happy here, tending to her store and living in her cosmic world. Maybe she won't want to give that up."

"Or maybe it's just a matter of asking her," Leo said, chuckling. "If there's anything experience has brought me—aside from all these wrinkles on my face—it's knowing that sometimes all you have to do is say out loud what you want. She's a great girl."

"I think so, too," I answered, "and when I see the way she is with the kids . . . it makes me imagine other things. But I'd hate to make them live through the same thing again, if you know what I mean."

"I do . . ."

He was about to say something else when the phone rang. Leo got up and went to answer it in the kitchen. He came back a little while later.

"Damn gas company. I don't think they could be any worse if they tried. Now they're telling me it'll be a week before they can get out here, and we've been out for two days. Thank goodness it's summer. Either way, I think I'd better go by Andy's to get a couple of tanks of gas for the generators. You busy today?"

I crushed the beer can.

"Actually, I came over because I wanted to talk to you about something."

Leo furrowed his brow for a minute and then smiled.

"Am I imagining things or did you suddenly get serious on me? C'mon, whatever it is, you can tell me."

I offered him a cigarette as I pulled the pack of Marlboros out of my shirt pocket. "It might be a while . . ."

"This *does* sound serious . . ."

"I just got back from meeting with the police in Dungloe."

Leo matched my gaze. He drank the rest of his beer and took one of my Marlboros.

"Let's hear it."

The story just poured out of me. It all flashed before my eyes, every detail crystal clear in my memory. The nightmares that had continued. The newspaper at my father's house in Dublin. Everything that happened the night before. The door banging open, the lights on the other side of the cliffs. The van that nearly ran me over by Bill's Peak. My tumble down the ravine. The two men and that woman. The gleaming knife.

I kept waiting for Leo to interrupt me with an observation or a joke to lighten the mood. But quite the contrary. He listened in total silence. His face was all seriousness. Not worry, not fear, not disbelief. He listened as if he were memorizing every last word.

When I'd finished, only the squawk of the seagulls and the crashing waves broke the silence that had fallen between us. Leo leaned back on the couch with his arms crossed over his chest, completely still. I couldn't tell what he was thinking.

"Well . . . what do you reckon about all this?" I said, lighting another cigarette. In less than half an hour, there were already four butts snuffed out in the ashtray next to me.

Leo sat up. He uncrossed his arms, puffed out a long sigh, and hunched forward with his elbows on his knees. He glanced at the side table which held several pictures of him and Marie.

"Jesus, I don't know what to make of it. We thought all this was behind you. But I can see we were wrong. I don't know what to tell you, Peter."

He bummed another cigarette and lit it. I stayed quiet.

"I know you, Pete, and you're an honest guy. I don't think you're exaggerating or making things up. If you're telling me this happened, I believe it did—or at least that you truly believe it did. All I can tell you is that no one has driven by Bill's Peak in the night. There was no van, and no three people parked in front of your house, at least not in the dimension or reality where I live. And no one has hurt Marie. Not that any of that helps you . . ."

"What if it's . . . something else," I said.

"Like what?"

"Like some kind of . . ." I looked up at the ceiling, fully aware at how stupid and insane this was going to sound.

"Premonition?" Leo said, finishing my sentence. He downed his beer and turned to gaze in the direction of the ocean. "Is that what you think?"

"I know it sounds stupid, but yeah, that's what I mean. Like something bad is going to happen. Something that threatens all of us. You, Marie, Judie, me, the kids . . . There's something I haven't told you about my family, Leo. It sounds a little ridiculous, but my mother believed she had a gift, a sort of sensitivity . . . to things that were going to happen. I feel like the same thing is happening to me, and the lightning only amplified it."

Leo looked at me but didn't say a word.

God, it really does sound stupid when you say it out loud, I thought during that long silence.

He got up and paced around the room, rubbing his temples and shooting me a furtive glance every now and then. You could tell he was really nervous. And who could blame him. Ultimately, I was telling him that a gang of killers was going to murder him and his wife.

"Let's say you're right," he said, finally. "Why do you think I could help?"

"I'm not sure, exactly. But it feels like this has something to do with Marie. It all started with her . . . and those people who were chasing her. Or that's the best I can make of this whole thing. Look, the last thing I ever want is to stick my nose where it doesn't belong, but there's something I have to ask you: Do you think there might be something to this? Is there a reason someone would be after Marie?"

"None," he said sharply, and turned around quickly as if he were trying to hide his face. "No. There's no reason I can think of."

I didn't believe him. And then, it was as if my lips were forming words I never gave them permission to utter. Before I knew it, I asked out loud: "Leo, who is Jean Blanchard?"

I don't know what possessed me to say it. But there was no taking it back now. I felt Leo was about to explode. It was as if I'd just lit a fuse.

Leo stopped in his tracks, his back to me, and stood silently for a moment in the middle of the room. Then he slowly turned on his heels to face me and asked, "Where did you hear that name?"

His voice was like a distant growl of thunder. I'd never seen him lose control of his temper before.

I was suddenly overcome with shame. I couldn't even hold his gaze. And then I told him—I told him everything. How it had happened when I'd taken Jip upstairs during dinner that night and had stumbled upon that rolled-up canvas.

I didn't know what he'd do. He might throw me out of his house for snooping and never speak to me again. Instead, he sighed as deeply as a man ever has, as if he wanted to forget everything he'd just heard, and fell back onto the couch, facing me.

"Jean Blanchard is a name I haven't heard in a very long time, a pseudonym Marie used to use years ago to sign her paintings. The last time she used it was to sign the portrait you found by accident—a painting of our only child, Daniel."

The name resounded in the air between us. His words knocked the wind out of me.

"Your . . . son?"

Leo looked up at me. The pain in his eyes made me regret everything I had said. I sat in stunned silence. I couldn't even bring myself to open my mouth to say I was sorry. What an imbecile I'd been.

"If he'd lived," he started to say, "he'd be about your age, now. Maybe a little younger. But he died before his first birthday, and the agony was so thorough that it nearly drove us insane. We named him Daniel. He was born premature in Brazil in 1972. The doctors said his heart was not developed fully. He only lived for three months, like a butterfly, like an angel visiting us on earth. I only saw him smile once, from inside that incubator-prison, which is all he ever saw of the world. But it was enough to remain etched in our minds forever.

"Marie painted that portrait during the depths of her depression, but she's never been able to part with it or hang it. Sometimes at night, she'd unroll it and just sit there, looking at it. She'd smile at it, whisper sweetly to it. She said she felt like she could speak to him. I was really worried. I decided to get a job as far away as possible from there. That's how we ended up in the Middle East, and, eventually, in Southeast Asia—trying to get away from that terrible memory. We never tried again to have kids. It was something understood between us. Time passed, and we got used to being alone, just the two of us. I guess we never were able to overcome the fear that it might happen again."

"I'm so sorry, Leo," I said. "I'm so sorry to have stirred up such painful memories."

"It's okay, son. I don't know whether it's your brain or God talking to you, but I appreciate you coming to me if you thought there was something I needed to know. But honestly, it's knocked me flat."

He didn't ask me to go, but I understood he wanted to be alone.

I can't believe this is how I repay you for inviting me into your home, for being my friend, Leo. By digging through your belongings and dredging up such old and painful memories.

I left their house feeling queasy. I wanted to turn around, bang my head against the door, and beg his forgiveness.

EIGHT

"I THINK I'm losing my mind, Judie. I want to go see that doctor."

It was around 8 p.m., and we were hanging out in the kitchen of the Houllihan's hostel. We'd already had dinner, and the children were in their bunks, Beatrice reading *Twilight* and Jip playing Angry Birds on the iPad. Judie had invited us to spend the night far away from the house that still gave her goose bumps. And I was infinitely grateful. All afternoon, as we ran errands around town and attended a meeting to finalize the details for movie night, I'd tried to put on a good face for the sake of the kids. And I'd done it mostly without a problem, until I was alone with Judie, washing dinner plates, and I couldn't hold back anymore.

"What a shitty day this has been. I made a fool of myself down at the police station, and what's worse, I think I hurt one of my best friends."

Judie knew immediately who I was talking about.

"I went over to talk to Leo. In hindsight, I simply went there so he could tell me what I wanted to hear: that I'm not crazy and that there's a reason why all this is happening to me. And all I managed to do was open some very old wounds. I made him talk about something deeply painful, and I admitted to rifling through his things the night we went over with the kids."

Judie gave me a dumbfounded look.

"You didn't . . ."

"It was almost an accident, the way it came out. But yeah, I did. I stumbled upon a couple things that were hidden on a bookshelf. Something was drawing me toward it, to look in there. . . . Actually, I think there's something you should know about my family. About this weird 'ability' that runs in the Harper bloodline."

While we washed dishes, in just above a whisper I told her about my mother, the Aer Lingus accident, and about the voice I heard the night of the storm, before leaving the house. About Jip and his incident over by the rocks, and how he could "feel" when something bad was going to happen. And that's when I realized I had been acting exactly like my dad. Hoping that it would simply go away if I didn't talk about it.

"So now you know. And you have every right to think I'm out of my mind," I said.

"Maybe you're not as crazy as you think," she answered.

I asked what she meant, but she raised an index finger to her lips and told me to follow her. We walked by the room with the bunk beds and saw Jip fast asleep, the iPad fallen to the floor by the bed. In the bunk above him, Beatrice was propped up on a pillow, reading with a small flashlight, absorbed in her book.

We descended the stairs in silence. Downstairs, besides the front door, there was another door that connected to the store. Judie opened it, and we walked through the shadowy space, amid miniature lighthouses, model boats, and shelves filled with second-hand books until we reached the back.

"I wanted to make sure they can't hear us."

"Hear what?"

After you told me about your dream the other night, I decided there's something you need to know. But first, I need you to tell me the story again."

She sat down and opened the small box where she kept her stash of weed.

"Judie, I'm not sure that I should. I've screwed up enough with my friends today. I don't want to hurt anyone else."

"I'm asking you to, Pete."

Okay, I said, and I described the scene again: her, with her hands and feet bound, inside the resonant chamber of my piano, in a pool of blood, begging me for help. A man was coming to hurt her.

Judie had rolled a small joint and lit it as I retold her the story. When I was done, I noticed she looked at me with a strange mix of fear and fascination.

"It's incredible, Pete. It really is."

"What is?"

"But everything fits. Especially after you told me the thing about your family. I think it's about time I told *you* something," she said, pausing. "That man, Donald Kauffman? It's true, he was my professor. But he also was my doctor. He treated me in the past. I was his patient."

"His patient?"

"Yes. There was a time in my life when I needed help. Before I traveled to India, I had a . . ." She stopped again to take hit of the joint and spoke through a puff of smoke. ". . . an accident."

I reached out, took her hand, and squeezed it gently.

"The scars along your side. The nightmares . . ."

She nodded.

"It was no motorcycle accident, although I guess you've probably figured that out by now. As for the nightmares . . . it's been years since I've spent more than one night with someone. You're the first. I knew you'd eventually have questions. I figured I'd tell you some-day . . . I *wanted* to tell you. But I was scared. Scared to open up a door I know is going to let in pain."

She took a long hit—maybe too long—and offered me the joint. I took it as she let out another cloud of aromatic smoke.

"You're one of the few people I can talk to, Peter. It's been a long time since I've told this story, but I think you have a right to know." She took a deep breath. "There was a man who hurt me. Who really hurt me. He's the one who injured my side. But that's just a scratch compared to what he did to my mind.

"And I still see his face at night. . . ."

She held my hand tighter without knowing it.

"It was five years ago. I was working at Princess Grace Hospital as a psychology resident. That's all anyone in Clenhburran knows about my time in London. But there's more. The real reason why I left.

"Every day, I'd go to Regent's Park to eat my lunch. That's where I met a man named . . ." She stopped for a second, as if just the name brought back a rush of memories. But she continued. "A man named Pedro. He was Portuguese and he worked at one of the take-out places near the underground station. They served falafel, my favorite, so four days a week, I'd stop in, we'd talk for a while, and then I'd head to the park to sit outside and eat my lunch with a book.

"I'd been going there for about a month. I noticed Pedro looking at me, and he was smart—cleverer than your average person—and he remembered every detail I'd told him about myself. And I liked him, too. I was single. I'd just broken up with my boyfriend of three years, and I wasn't looking for anything serious. I wanted to meet people who were fun, and Pedro looked like fun. He had a beautiful smile, and he always talked about his quaint little town in Portugal, about the beaches there, the food, the wine. I liked him even though he wasn't really my type. And one night, I agreed to have a glass of wine with him. We went to a bar near the park after work, and he insisted on treating me. He didn't want me to lift a finger and went to the bar for drinks. 'In my country, the men take care of everything,' he said, smiling. I felt this rush of romance. It had been so long since I had let someone wine and dine me.

"We started to drink and talk. Everything was going perfectly, but then I started to feel dizzy and sleepy. I even joked about it when I started yawning. I told him not to think I was bored of his company, but I was probably tired from a long week. He smiled and joked that he wouldn't take it personally. It was Friday, after all. I had a right to be tired. He told me about another place that was a little more lively, a club just down the street, and thought that might help me get my second wind. We went there and had another drink. But by that point, my eyes were starting to close as Pedro talked about his life, about his plans to buy some property in Madrid . . . and in the end he was the one who suggested it might be time to go home. 'But you can't take the tube in this state,' he joked, 'or you'll wake up at the end of the line.'

"My mind got hazy. I was sleepy, the noise of the club was dizzying, and it seemed like I'd gotten drunk too quickly. And for a split second, I thought I was making a mistake getting into a car with this total stranger. But I told myself I was being ridiculous, and I was almost falling asleep when Pedro helped me out of the bar. Just before passing out, I remembered I hadn't even given him my address. How stupid of me, right?"

Judie sighed. A single tear ran down her cheek, and she gave a weak smile. I squeezed her hand.

"Judie, you really don't have to . . ."

But she continued speaking as if she hadn't heard me.

"He raped me," she said, pursing her lips. "While I slept. And again, after I woke up, in this horrible place. A windowless room. Later, I learned it was a basement in Brixton. He'd tied me to the bed. Tied my hands and feet, Peter, just like in your dream."

"Holy shit . . ."

I reached for the pack of cigarettes in my shirt pocket. I took the last one and lit it.

"I was locked in there for two days. And in some way, I'm locked in there still. A piece of me has stayed locked in there forever. I knew there had been others, too. I saw desperate scratch marks on the walls, discarded women's clothing, stains on the floor that could only have been blood. I knew what was going to happen to me. I knew it instantly. I'd seen his face. He was never going to let me out of there alive.

"Before he left in the mornings, he'd inject me with something in the arm. Turned out it was heroin. I spent most of the day asleep. When I'd come to, I'd scream as loud as I could—well, as loud as was possible through the gag. I struggled against the leather bindings. I'd pull so hard—I'd amputate my own hand if that's what it took—and finally one of the straps started to come loose. I used to complain about how thin my wrists were and now they were going to save my life. Ironic, isn't it?

"The binding slipped right to edge of my thumb but I realized that's as far as it would go because of the bone. So I didn't think twice. I started banging my hand as hard as I could until I dislocated my thumb. I got my hand free, and pulled off the gag. I started yelling myself hoarse, calling for help.

"If Pedro had restrained me with handcuffs, I'd be dead now. But that son of a bitch didn't count on me waking up before the drugs wore off. I found out later the evil bastard had killed his mother down there first, and then used the basement to kill three other women. Three poor women who weren't lucky enough to escape like me. These women—they were thirty-eight, forty-one, and nineteen. I didn't want to know more than that. How long they'd been in there. What finally happened to them. The only thing I ever asked the cops for was a picture of each. I try to imagine them smiling, in a better place. It helps me to think that somehow they helped me escape that day, as if they spoke to me: 'You can do it, Judie. Pull your hand out as hard as you can. I couldn't, but you can!'

"When Pedro came through the door that afternoon, I knew someone had heard my screaming. He looked scared, frantic. I started to scream again, and he jumped on the bed, knelt on my chest and punched me three times until I was knocked nearly unconscious. He told me it was time to get rid of me the way he'd gotten rid of the others, and then he told me exactly how he was going to do it, the way you rehearse a speech in front of a mirror: He was going to chop me up in his bathtub and burn the pieces, one at a time, in the house's furnace. But since I'd been such a bad girl, he was going to gag me again, and do it all while I was still alive.

"Thank God a neighbor had heard the noise and called police. The cops knew the neighborhood. They'd been there a few months earlier when a taxi driver swore he'd seen a man carrying a drunken woman who matched one of the missing women's descriptions, the last victim. Between my screams and the neighbor's phone call (a young Indian man named Asif Sahid who I still call every Christmas), the police raced down. They banged on the door, and Pedro swore I'd pay for what I did. He plunged a butcher knife deep into my side—once, twice—before police broke down the door and shot him dead, with a bullet right to the forehead."

"The scar . . ."

"Yeah. That was his final act. But of course, it wasn't the end of the story. I didn't sleep for six months afterward. I was terrified. The nightmares ruled my life. I'd wake up screaming, or rather, howling with fear. Completely by accident, I discovered a way round the problem: I slept at a youth hostel. Surrounded by thirty or so people snoring in their sleep—call it safety in numbers—was the only way I could manage to rest.

"But it wasn't a cure. One night, while I was working at the hospital, I was making rounds alone when I saw a man who looked like Pedro coming down the lonely hallway. I panicked. Forget that I'd seen his death certificate and even his body. My irrational mind thought he had survived somehow. I hid in a janitor's closet and spent the night in there, crying.

"I started self-medicating, first with prescription drugs, which were easy to get at work, and later with harder stuff. I couldn't stand to be alone, ever. I started going to bars and making friends—the bigger and tougher the better. I became sullen and needy . . . I guess one day I woke up in some strange house, with a man I didn't know and realized things had gotten way out of control. The hospital did the best thing they ever could have done: They fired me. My boss, a guy I used to think was an asshole but now I deeply respect, said they'd tried to look the other way, ignore my missing work or how disheveled I looked when I did show up. But he said I just was in no condition to be back at work. He's the one who told me about Dr. Kauffman and suggested I make an appointment with him in Belfast. More than suggested, actually. He stood by as I dialed the number. And so I went to see him.

"Kauffman listened to my story and told me I need to see him in Belfast. 'My method is intensive, but it works. I think in as little as a month, we can fix most of the damage.'

"It was my first time in Ireland, and I loved it immediately. On the weekends, when I wasn't meeting with Kauffman, I'd rent a car and travel around the north. That's when I decided I'd like to live here. One time, I ended up lost here, in Clenhburran, and that's how I met Mrs. Houllihan. It was raining cats and dogs, and hers was the only place open. She gave me tea and offered me a place to spend the night. (In those days, there were no hotels in Clenhburran.) She was a lovely woman. She loved to travel and had been all over the world. We spent the whole night talking, and although I never told her the whole truth about me, I think she intuited it, somehow—or most of it, anyway. She confided that she hoped to retire in a few years and didn't know who she might turn the business over to. I think she knew I'd want it, so she wasn't surprised when I accepted right away . . . 'But first I have some things I need to take care of. A brief trip,' I told her.

" 'Of course, child,' she said, 'but don't take too long.' That night, for the first night in more than a year, I slept without any medication or tricks of any kind. The next morning, when I came downstairs and went down to the harbor and saw the old men feeding the seals, I decided I loved this place.

"In about a month and a half, Kauffman and I had made real progress. I still had nightmares, though, and Kauffman was honest with me about it. 'You'll most likely continue to have them. Maybe forever. They're scars from a very deep wound. But at least we've stopped the bleeding.' And that was true. The hypnosis helped me put some distance between me and the monster. The voice in my head was a muffled sound I could finally manage. That's when I knew I was ready to grab my backpack and go. And that's what I did. I went to Vietnam, Thailand, India, Nepal. Spiritual retreats. Meditation. I learned to control my emotions, to accept them as something inevitable, but to keep them in their proper place. When

I was ready to return, Mrs. Houllihan was still waiting for me, ready to hang it up and retire to Tenerife."

"I'm glad you came back," I said, squeezing her hand and kissing it. "I'm glad I found your way back to Clenhburran."

"Me too, Peter. So now you know the truth. And maybe you're not so crazy."

"Agreed. But in either case, I want to see Kauffman. I don't trust myself, anymore. I have to try to take control over whatever this is. And right now he sounds like my best option. Can you help me get in to see him as soon as possible?"

"Consider it done," she said. "I'll take care of everything."

NINE

FIVE DAYS LATER, Donald Kauffman opened the door to me at his home on Archer Street, in Belfast. Judie had called him on a Tuesday, but his schedule was so full that only as a personal favor to her did he agree to see me, and then on a Sunday, his day off.

He was a short man of about sixty with an owl-like countenance and tufts of hair growing out of his ears, but he was vivacious and had a commanding voice; he wore a black turtleneck the first day I met with him. He oozed genius, and, according to Judie, it's exactly what he was: a preeminent scholar in the field of hypnotism, the author of books studied at universities around the world, an innovator of techniques that had changed the practice of psychiatry and psychology the world over. His practice was in the basement of his home, a warm and inviting space with high windows through which you could see the legs of people walking along the sidewalk outside. Shelves stuffed with books reached the ceiling. And on his small wooden desk still more books were piled beside a small typewriter with something half-written.

I started to thank him from the second he opened the door, but he just waved me off.

"Don't mention it," he said. "Come on in."

Dr. Kauffman offered me a cup of tea and a comfortable spot on his tan leather couch. He wasted no time getting right to it.

"Judie told me you were seeking help but maybe you should tell me about your situation in your own words," he said.

Seated cozily on the couch, I told him the story from the very beginning. The lightning, Marie's midnight run, the macabre apparition in the newspaper . . . all the way to the van with the three strangers . . . gangsters, assassins, whatever they were. I described each one of them making sure not to leave out a single detail.

Kauffman watched me with a penetrating stare, not saying a word or taking a single note. He leaned back in the other couch with his arms crossed over his chest and barely moved an inch in the time it took me to tell him the entire story of my nightmares. I felt better just sitting and telling him everything.

Then, he asked me a few questions about the dreams. Did I ever look at a clock? No, I told him. . . . Did I ever call anyone over the phone in the middle of the dream? My phone was always disconnected, I told him. Why hadn't I woken up my kids when I heard someone banging at the door? I told him I didn't want to worry them. "Tell me about that last night, Mr. Harper. When, exactly, do you think the intruders in your dream disappeared?"

"I'm not sure. I guess the moment I got back inside my house."

We took a short break, and he went out for a smoke while I used the restroom. I called Judie from the hall to see how everything was going. Jip and Beatrice had been a little worried when I told them I wouldn't be going with them to the Belfast zoo because I had to see a doctor.

"They're having a great time, don't worry," she said. "How are *you* doing? How's Donald?"

I told her he was smoking his pipe, and that made Judie chuckle.

"That's a little trick he uses to force a break in the conversation. He always does it."

She told me that she and the kids were on their way to Burger King and later they were thinking of catching a movie. Kauffman said we were in for an intensive session, and we might be at it until five or six.

"Tonight when I get out, we'll all go to dinner together," I told her.

I headed back to the basement. Kauffman was reviewing some notes he'd scrawled in his notebook. I sat back down, accepted another cup of tea, and asked him what he thought about all this.

"An unusual case, to be certain," he said without looking up. "I've heard of similar cases, but much more fragmented. Yours is like an opera in full. You have a truly interesting brain, Mr. Harper."

I smiled, although I wasn't sure whether to take that as a compliment.

"Forgive the joke, Mr. Harper. When you spend your life hearing peoples' stories, you can't help getting somewhat excited when you hear something out of the ordinary. Something like your case. Undoubtedly, the electrical shock caused by the lightning strike is at the root of your visions. It seems to have acted as an emotional amplifier. Perhaps, it is psychosomatic, which would explain why all your brain scans came back normal. I honestly don't think there is anything physically wrong with you."

"You mean to say I'm imagining the pain in my head?"

"Not so much that you're imagining it. Rather, we're looking in the wrong place for the source of your pain. The medication you're taking is having no effect, a classic sign of a psychosomatic disorder. On the other hand, before we go any further, I'm going to give you the name of one of the best neurologists in Dublin. If you want a second opinion, go and see him. Tell him I referred you."

As for the visions, Kauffman was sure they were a kind of parasomnia.

"I'm practically certain of it," he said.

I'd come across that term during my Internet searches and learned it was very similar to a sleepwalking disorder.

"How do you explain the fact I can remember everything?"

"Well, to begin with, that's what *you* believe to be true," he said. "There's no way of knowing whether you actually experienced what you think you did. No one saw you do the things you remembered doing. How can you be sure you actually threw yourself down the side of a ravine? Perhaps you simply bumped into a door inside your house and your mind interpreted it as something else. The sand you say you remember could have come from anywhere. All of these things could be constructs of your mind, Mr. Harper. Interpretations your somnambulant mind created to explain the sensory input. These things are often confused for 'lucid dreams' or 'astral voyages.'"

"But . . . the first time it happened, I actually drove my car to my neighbors' house and woke them up. That was no recreation. I was *there*."

"I don't doubt the events, per se. But there are many verified cases of sleepwalkers driving vehicles. There are even cases of people having sex while in a somnambulant state. Why, I had a patient who cooked while she was asleep and dreamed she won several cooking contests. Don't torture yourself, Mr. Harper. Your visions are simply a result of your mind creating terrible rationalizations to explain your nighttime adventures."

"But, how did I come up with this crazy explanation? The van, those three characters who felt so real. I could even hear their voices."

"Believe me, you could have taken it from anywhere. They could be people you met briefly in real life—in another city, on the train. . . . The brain can take information, like someone's face, store it away for decades and bring it back in a dream as if you had conjured it out of thin air. Have you heard of Freud's *The Interpretation of Dreams*? There's quite a famous story in it where a man dreams he can cure animals with a medicinal herb whose name he remembers upon waking up: *Asplenium ruta muralis*. The man, by the name of Delboeuf, is amazed to learn the next morning that that is the name of an actual medicinal plant. Moreover, it's more amazing because he doesn't know anything about plants or botany! Not until sixteen years later does the mystery solve itself. He's visiting a friend in Switzerland when he stumbles upon a book of medicinal plants and opens it to find writing in the margins—in his own handwriting! Sixteen years ago, he had come across this book, made a note, and his brain filed the name of that plant away until one night his mind dusted off the information from some forgotten corner of his mind and presented it in a new light, within a dream.

"That's how it often happens. And yet the first thing that comes to our mind is some kind of paranormal explanation: past lives, reincarnation, even visions like the ones you seem to be suffering from. But the answer is one hundred percent scientific. Memory and the human brain are vast mysteries that science is only beginning to understand, Mr. Harper. We can put a man on the moon, but we still don't know what's going on inside our own heads! In a creative mind such as your own, one that's used to expressing deep sentiments, an electrical shock like the one you suffered could easily be the cause of the radical episodes you're having. As to what these images mean, we could easily spend the next year in psychotherapy trying to figure it out."

"You think there's something I'm trying to tell myself through these visions?"

"Well, what do you think?" Kauffman said. "Do you have a perfectly happy and harmonious life?"

"No," I said, too quickly. "I . . . well, I'm recently divorced. It was a bitter pill. Two kids caught in the middle. And I think it affected my professional life, too. I'm a music composer, and I'm stuck in a terrible creative rut."

"Have you considered that all these visions might have something to do with the fallout from your divorce?"

"In what way?"

"In innumerable ways, Mr. Harper," he said. "Your family life was shattered, your life was unbalanced. It could be that these 'attacks' you're dreaming of are merely your mind's way of revisiting the trauma. You might have tried to 'make yourself forget' too soon."

Dr. Kauffman turned his head and got a faraway look, as if he were chasing an old memory himself.

"It could be your way of expressing an overprotective instinct for your children. You've found your role as father diminished after the divorce, and now that your children are with you again, your mind might be creating these threats so you can reaffirm your function as the family protector. Who knows . . . these are only theories, after all. We should begin therapy to get at the root of the issue, but it will take time. Right now, the priority is addressing your sleepwalking. You're worried about your children, and I understand the concern. But it's more likely you'll end up hurting yourself if these episodes continue to occur. Have you ever heard of clinical hypnosis?"

"You're going to hypnotize me?" I said, unable to hide a small smirk.

Kauffman smiled back.

"I understand your skepticism, Mr. Harper. The media and a handful of charlatans have helped create a myth around the field of hypnosis. But believe me when I tell you that this discipline has been recognized and proven effective by the medical community, particularly as it pertains to the treatment of somnambulism. You will not lose consciousness, or not necessarily, and you won't be 'in my power.' I'm not going to brainwash you and make you rob banks like in that Woody Allen movie. In any case, the entire procedure will be video recorded, and you will get a copy of the tape. Would you be willing to participate in this kind of treatment?"

"I'll do whatever's necessary to get better, doc."

BY NOW, it was two in the afternoon, and the Venetian blinds were completely closed to block out the afternoon sun. Kauffman left one window half open, though, to let in a breeze and a little bit of ambient noise from the world outside. He went upstairs and came back with a video camera, which he went about mounting on a tripod and pointing at me.

"I'm not a magician, Mr. Harper, only a guide. It's up to you to open up the doors for me. I want you to be in such a deep state of relaxation, that you forget you're even here with me. So start by relaxing your body one part at time, breathing deeply and at a steady pace. You're a musician, so I know you can even tell me what time you're keeping with each breath. . . . Ah, an *andante* tempo, yes . . . Now, I need you to slow it a little more. First, to *adagio*. Now, with your eyes closed, picture your toes, your ankles . . . can you feel them relaxing? We're giving them a little vacation, allowing them to go completely limp. Let's move a little higher. Your knees are still too tense, relax them. . . ."

I'm not sure how long it took for me to slip from *adagio* to *lento moderato*, but I began to feel lighter, and soon Kauffman started to describe something and asked me to imagine it.

You are walking alone in a desert. But the weather is fair. There's a light breeze. Now I want you to look off and focus on a fixed point in the distance, a mile or so away. There's a pyramid in the distance, can you see it? There's nothing else all around you. Keep walking toward it. . . .

For some reason, my mind painted the desert sand a rose color. It was a nice, calm place, just as the doctor had told me. The sky was filled with green-tinged clouds. I walked until I reached the pyramid, which, to me, was a dark, cobalt blue. Dr. Kauffman asked me to look for a door in one of the pyramid's four sides. He said I would instantly recognize it once I saw it, and he was right. It was just as he'd said. It was an elliptically shaped door lightly covered in sand. I used my fingers to trace the edges, and I cleared off the sand until I found a metal pull.

Open it, the voice (the doctor's) requested, and I did.

You will find a set of stairs near the wall, leading to a dark downstairs. Go inside and begin to slowly descend them, one at a time. Take a breath, then a step. A breath, then another step . . .

It was easy. I took one careful step after another. There was always another step waiting for me in the darkness, and it seemed like I was going down stairs for an eternity. But it didn't matter. *Pyramids are enormous*, I thought, *and these stairs go down a very long way. . . .*

It felt good to go down them. Great, actually. And the voice was always there to tell me what I should do next.

When you reach the bottom, grab a torch, and walk down the hallway. We're getting close, now. Very close, now, Peter . . .

The hallway was very narrow, and there were wide steps—they reminded me of some I'd seen in Venice years ago—that continued to take me downward. The small, rectangular bricks on the wall reminded me of my old high school gym in Dublin. *Ten laps for being late, Harper! Yes, sir!*

I kept going down the hallway in darkness, my mind filled with questions. What's the point of all this, anyway? In life, you get what you get, and that's it. Play the hand you're dealt, Peter. I'll be waiting for you, my son. *Who is there with you, Peter?*

"I feel it. I think it's my mother."

Don't worry. Everything is fine. Keep walking. Breathe . . .

We finally arrived at the end. I'm not sure when. The inner sanctum of the pyramid was an ancient and enormous space, a large vault illuminated by hundreds of votive candles spread along the ground. It reminded me of the exam hall in the Amsterdam conservatory. *It's audition day, but no one has arrived yet*, I thought.

Concentrate, Harper. Fear is your friend. Use it to your advantage.

The voice told me to turn my attention to a large screen in the middle of the hall. It was a huge movie-projection screen. *What do you want to see, Peter? What do you want to watch on the big screen?*

"Can I really choose?"

An image of Clem's face appeared on the screen.

It was just as I recalled her on that fateful day. The day where hot became cold and in which everything turned on its head. I'd wanted to think back on it, but my mind had always distorted the memory.

She sat in the kitchen in her gray sweater, stirring a cup of tea that had gone cold. She was waiting for me. "Where are the kids?" "They're with my mom, Peter. I didn't want them to be home . . . today . . . because I have something I need to tell you. . . ."

Then, as if by magic, that vault, that inner sanctum, it all disappeared and faded into sky.

Where are we headed now, Mr. Harper? the voice asked.

"Good question!" I yelled. "I'd like to know that myself."

Now, I found myself at Bill's Peak, and it was nighttime. The enormous thundercloud was floating overhead, spinning and roiling and about to unload on me once again.

What do you see?

Lightning. It was the actual bolt of lightning that struck me, its trail frozen in midair: a phosphorescent scar, a tear in the blackened sky. It was detailed just so, right where it had landed near the old tree.

I approached it cautiously. I knew what it had done to me, that it could easily spark and leave me charred on the ground. I was just two feet away now. Could I touch it? I reached out and touched what felt like a glass wall. A huge, fractured glass wall. And then, on the other side of it, I saw something moving, a person coming toward me through the rain and darkness.

Who was it, I wondered, as I shuffled backward, scared. Was it one of those three assassins?

It took me a minute to recognize him. He had a ratty beard, a white T-shirt soaked in blood, and a tired look in his eyes. "You're a piece of shit," I used to say when I saw myself in the mirror in the mornings—and that's exactly the image standing before me now. It was a version of Peter Harper on the other side of glass.

But the other Peter Harper was hurt and scared. He had seen me, too, and was headed toward me. He was limping and holding his side. His face was swollen and blood was trickling from his lip.

He came right up to the glass, standing equidistant from me. He raised his fist and pounded onto the glass. Everything shook.

That face . . . He never so much as opened his mouth, which looked as if it were full of something. Blood, maybe. His eyes seemed wild, and clearly there was something wrong with his mind.

Peter, are you okay?

He pounded against the glass again and again. The other Harper was pounding on a nonexistent door—and he wanted to come in.

I started to tremble. "What do you want from me?" I yelled.

Peter, it's time to come back. Okay?

"No! Wait. Not yet . . ."

Despite my fear and disgust, I came closer to that shattered glass and stared right into my monstrous self's eyes. He looked scared, and I could see tears of blood running down his cheeks.

"Tell me, Peter. Tell me what you want . . . !"

We're going to count to three, Mr. Harper. One . . ."

The light became brighter and brighter. I felt myself drifting away from this place.

"C'mon, you son of a bitch, say it! Tell me what you want!"

The other Peter Harper started to open his mouth to say something. A thick, viscous liquid dribbled out. He edged right up to the glass, and I put my ear up against it to hear.

Two . . .

In a hoarse and desperate voice, he whispered, "It's too late. They're all dead."

Three.

TEN

AT THE END of a very long day, I watched as Judie and the kids came down Archer Street toward where I was waiting outside of Kauffman's building.

Dr. Kauffman had chosen not to meet with Judie before my session, maybe because he wanted to maintain a professional stance. When we were saying goodbye in the hall, Kauffman said he thought it'd be a good idea for him to see me again. "We hit on a couple of interesting things during our session. It would be good to revisit them." We agreed to meet in August or early September when the children were back in Amsterdam. Until then, he encouraged me to relax, enjoy my time with the kids, and to take as little medication as possible. "If you have another vision, try to write down what you remember. Send me an email if it happens again."

THE NEXT DAY, we drove back in silence under a steady rain. My thoughts were still jumbled. After a long and intense session with

Dr. Kauffman, I barely shut my eyes that night. Judie was off, too. Returning to Belfast had unhinged her a bit. That night, when we slept in separate hotel rooms, she'd had really bad nightmares. Beatrice, who'd shared a room with her, told me about it over breakfast the next day.

"She moved around all night, as if she were scared of something. I woke her up, and we fell asleep later, holding each other the rest of the night."

We paid a visit to the Giant's Causeway on the way home. The weather didn't stop Beatrice and Jip from getting out of the car to explore that almost mythical labyrinth of basalt columns which faded in and out of a foggy mist.

The children explored the massive columns, and when they ducked behind one formation, Judie and I gave each other a deep, loving kiss. With the children around, we'd forgotten the taste of each other's lips. I sat back and admired her beautiful face that bore a wrinkle or two of experience and a few scattered freckles around her nose.

We listened to the children laughing and yelling in the distance. I held Judie's hands firmly in mine.

"I'd like to talk about something with you."

I felt her body tremble. My opening line had all the makings of a serious conversation.

"Hey, don't worry, I don't have an engagement ring stashed in my jacket pocket," I said, laughing.

She nodded, wordlessly.

"I've been thinking about returning to Holland, or Belgium, at the end of the year. I want to be closer to the kids. I realize I need them in my life, and there's no getting away from that. Seeing them every three months just isn't enough."

Her face changed. She pursed her lips, and there was an uneasiness in her eyes. Maybe she would have preferred the ring, after all. Maybe this was sounding like goodbye.

"You're right," she said. "I agree with you . . . it's what's best. They're two great kids. They deserve to have their father nearby."

I felt her wanting to pull away, but I clung to her gently.

"Wait. That's not all. I was wondering if you'd come with me," I said.

As the words left my mouth, I was a fourteen-year-old all over again, asking my high school crush for a date at the Tara train station in Dublin.

Judie's eyes widened, and she let out a nervous laugh.

"To Holland?"

"Yeah . . . well, anywhere on the continent, really. Germany, Holland, Belgium. We could have our pick as long as there was a train to Amsterdam. Look, Judie, I could help you open another store, something like Mrs. Houllihan's, and you could set it up just as you want. You're such a hard worker and you have so much talent, I know you'd make it work, no matter where in the world you set up shop."

She laughed.

"I . . . don't know what to say, Pete." She held my hand tight. "Thank you. Thank you for including me in your life. I really wasn't expecting this."

Her reaction wasn't what I was expecting either. (How about a nice, resounding, "Yes!" and her jumping into my arms, saying she'd follow me wherever I went?) The rain let up a bit.

"Well, it's all just kind of happened, hasn't it? It doesn't feel like we're rushing anything. I have really strong feelings for you. We're more than just a fling. And, well, I was wondering if you felt the same way."

"I do," she said, drying her eyes a bit. "This is all so . . . unexpected."

Unexpected. I felt a big "but" coming on. My heart sank.

"Can I think it over a bit? It's not a 'No.' You've caught me totally off guard. I hope you understand. I can't make a big decision like this on the spot. I'm sorry if that doesn't sound so romantic."

I squeezed her hand.

"Don't worry. I know we've never even discussed this. It's crazy, I'm sorry. I'm an idiot for putting you on the spot."

"No, Peter, it's okay. But just understand this is . . . big. It's a big change for me."

"No, of course, Judie," I said.

The children reappeared from behind a column, two little water nymphs in red and yellow ponchos.

"Dad! Judie!" they called. "Come check this out! We found a *huge* crab!"

I put on my best smile. Judie acted fine when we found the crab and later in the car as we drove back to Clenhburran in the rain, I put in one CD after another until we got back to town. I guess I didn't feel like talking.

PART THREE

ONE

A BLACK VAN with the name Blake Audiovisuals was parked in front of Chester's store, with its sliding doors open. Two workers dressed in black carried boxes, speakers, and rolls of cable into the store.

"Where are they going to set up the screen?" Donovan asked.

"Over there, at the end of the port, by the overhang," Chester replied.

"Well, I don't see any scaffolding. I'm not sure how they're going to do it."

Chester, Donovan, and Mr. Douglas had taken the day off to soak up the excitement around the port. With a can of Bavaria beer in hand and leaning up against the snuff-and-stuff store, they commented on the comings and goings of people and equipment.

It was the day of the outdoor movie night, and you could feel the anticipation around town. The idea they'd initially hated and criticized months ago over beers at the pub was a lot more interesting now. *So the women had come up with this whole deal?* "With what money? Ah, city hall funds. We didn't even know that money existed! Hey, we could set up a screen for the Six Nations Championship instead, next time! What do you think?" They all nodded, smiles on their faces, their Bavarias half-finished. But in their hearts, they understood their women had more tenacity than them, and that when the funds were available next year, they'd win that battle again.

"How's it going, Harper?" one said as I walked up. "So we hear you're going to play the piano tonight. Can't wait to hear it. Beer?"

I declined with a smile. I'd only come for some smokes and the morning paper. And to ask if they had seen Judie. She wasn't at the store, and some of the women had told me she'd be down by the port.

"I thought I saw her down by the fish market. They won't let us in while they're setting up. Ah, but they'll let you in. Get in there, and tell us what the women are up to."

The men erupted into a barroom guffaw. Chester bared his six teeth proudly. We stepped inside, and he charged me for our regular transaction: cigarettes, an *Irish Times*, and a copy of the most recent thriller that had made it to town. Back out on the street, Donovan was asking the tech where they planned to mount the screen and how. The tech, a big, sweaty kid with reddish hair and beard, told them there was nothing to mount because it was a big, inflatable screen that would be anchored to the ground to keep it from blowing away. That took the four old-timers by surprise. "Inflatable? Like one of those bouncy houses for the kids' parties?" "Yeah," the kid told them, "with one side painted a reflective white for the projector."

"Go figure . . ." Donovan said.

I used the opportunity to tell the tech that I was the one who'd be playing that night. I figured the piano would be arriving soon, too. "We'll set it up in front of the screen and slide it out of the way when you're done," he explained. "But make sure they get it here early so we can do a sound check."

I bid farewell to the amateur engineers and headed to the fish market, a huge warehouse of concrete and rusted metal, which had become the logistical nerve center for the event. A dozen women were dusting off chairs, and setting up food and drinks that would be served that night: Cadbury hot chocolate for the kids, gallons of hot water and Barry's tea bags, a barrel of beer. The owners of Andy's were going to set up a snack bar and a popcorn machine. I spotted Judie and Laura O'Rourke working at a table in the back, folding blankets the church had donated in case it got cold that night.

"Where are the kids?" Judie asked when she saw me.

"They made some new friends and ditched me."

When we got to town that morning, the O'Rourke twins were waiting for Beatrice by the entrance to Mrs. Houllihan's. "We planned it through WhatsApp," Beatrice said, explaining how she'd managed to make arrangements without a phone. They brought along a couple of English girls ("Oh, yes, Becky and Martha," Laura O'Rourke had said. "Such wonderful girls.") who spent the summers here, as well, on a beach about five miles from ours. And there was another boy who was a little older, who turned out to be Mr. Douglas' youngest son. The boy, Seamus, invited them to take a spin on his small motorboat, and Beatrice and Jip came to ask me for permission to go. One of the O'Rourke boys was with them, as if to help them convince me. "We'll stay in the lagoon, I promise. We've got life jackets for everyone, even Jip. And we'll be back before dark, in time for the movie."

It wouldn't hurt to give them a little freedom and, honestly, I could use the time that afternoon to get the piano set up and tested before my mini concert that night. And after a short trip with their dad and his girlfriend, the kids could use a day off to enjoy some time with their new friends. I gave Beatrice money so she could buy something to eat at Andy's, but I left her with specific instructions. "Beatrice, don't lose sight of Jip. And make sure he wears his life jacket every second, okay?" "Yes, Dad." "And you, Jip, pay attention to your sister and don't straggle away from her, okay? And don't take off your sweater. You still have a little bit of a cold. Got it?" "Yes, Dad." "And don't do anything crazy just because you might see another kid do something crazy, okay?" This time, a chorus of "yes, Dads."

I found Judie.

"So, how's everything going? Need a hand with anything?" I asked.

"Everything's under control down here," she said. "What about the piano?"

"They should be delivering it soon, no?"

Judie stopped what she was doing and looked up at me, surprised.

"You mean, you didn't get my message?"

"Message? What message?" I asked as I stuffed my hand in the coat pocket where I kept my phone. I pulled it out and saw the unread message icon.

I clicked and read it: "Mrs. Douglas couldn't bring down the piano herself. Could you go to her house to pick it up? It's 13 Elijah Road. It's just past Andy's on the right."

It had been sent nearly two hours ago.

"Ah, I didn't see it. I'm sorry."

"There's still time," she said. "Do you think you could take care of it?"

I was impressed at the way Judie could make a request on the order of, "Do this or I'll kill you!" and make it sound like sunshine. Of course, I wasn't about to explain to her that a concert pianist shouldn't be lugging around his instrument just hours before his performance, that he should be relaxing with his feet up. This wasn't Royal Albert Hall, after all; it was a fish market in Clenhburran, and I'd already agreed to help.

"I'm not sure if it'll fit in the Volvo," I said. "I'll have to try folding the seats up."

"Mrs. Douglas said her cousin Craig has a van we can use, but he lives in Dungloe. Think you could try it first, and then call me if it doesn't fit?" She sounded stressed.

"Of course," I said. "I'll handle it."

I said goodbye to her and the other ladies and hurried up the road.

On my way to my car, I passed the group of guys still leaning unproductively against Chester's convenience store. We waved to one another, but I had no time to waste. I hurried to Judie's store, where I had parked my car. Just as I got there, I saw Marie step out of the store, and I had the sudden desire to turn and run in the opposite direction.

It was the first time I'd seen her since my talk with Leo, and, actually, I hadn't seen him since, either. The day after that catastrophic conversation, I'd tried to call him, but he wasn't home. And then I left for Belfast with Judie and the kids, and I'd spent the next few days trying to forget about everything that had happened, thinking I should call him when I got back. The devastated look on his face gave me knots in my stomach.

Marie was carrying a cardboard box filled with the corrected programs. She said she was on her way to drop them off at the fish market and asked where I was headed. I told her about the misunderstanding with the piano and said I was on my way to Mrs. Douglas' to pick it up.

"Okay, perfect," she said, resting the box on the Volvo's roof. "So you can drop me and the box off at the port, and I can help you with the piano."

I nodded, a little surprised. I'd expected her to be somewhat cold with me—or perhaps Leo hadn't told her anything? I helped her put the box in the backseat. She sat in the passenger seat, and I turned around to head out of town.

I didn't know what, if anything, Leo had told Marie about our talk, so I avoided the subject altogether. She asked me about my trip to Belfast, and before I could tell her about sightseeing at the Giant's Causeway, she told me Leo had mentioned my appointment with a sleep specialist.

"How are you feeling? Do you think it helped?"

It had been three days since I'd come back from my appointment with Kauffman, and I did feel better. I was sleeping better, for hours at a time, and my headache had faded into the faintest discomfort, which I only felt late in the day. A little aspirin did the trick, now. I told her Dr. Kauffman was convinced my pain was psychosomatic, and I had started to believe him.

"Psychosomatic? So . . . it's all in your head?"

"Something like that."

"And is there anything new with your dreams? Those nightmares? Leo told me you had another one."

So he had talked to her.

"Yes," I said, trying to sound as normal as possible. "Kauffman theorizes that it's an invention of my mind. Like being asleep and awake at the same time. Apparently, he thinks I get out of bed, walk around my house and garden and my brain invents a story around it."

"And what do you think, Pete?"

"I just want to forget all this ever happened, Marie. I'm going to see Kauffman again to continue therapy after Jip and Beatrice go home. I'll do whatever it takes. I just want my life back."

We'd reached the end of Main Street, where it intersected the state highway. I stopped to let two tractor trailers with French plates whiz by and then turned right.

"Pete, Leo told me everything that happened," Marie said. "About your conversation, about what you found on our bookshelf. About Daniel."

I felt myself tense up.

"He also told me you thought this might be some kind of warning. A premonition."

I was supposed to turn right after Andy's, but I completely missed the turn. I forgot about everything.

"I'm so sorry for having snooped, Marie."

Marie touched my arm lightly, as though there was more she wanted to say. I looked for a place to make a U-turn.

"It's okay, Pete. I'm not going to lie, it hurt. But we understand. Leo was very sad the first day, but then he thought about calling you. I told him to wait until you got back. We know you're a good man. We knew it from the first day we met you. Remember that day? We dropped by unannounced and made ourselves at home, basically pushed our way in. And you looked at us like, 'Who are these crazy old people?'"

I laughed hard, and so did she.

"It's hard for us to make friends," she said. "It gets harder every time. Maybe it's old age, or maybe it's our nomadic lifestyle. We've become a lot more cautious with people, and it's hard for us to open up our hearts. I'd like to think you're one of those special few."

"I'd like to think so, too, Marie."

"Good. Well then, let's forget about all this. Leo may be a little harder to win back, but it's nothing cracking open a beer won't fix. And as for your nightmares . . . well, let's hope that doctor is right, and it's nothing more than some kind of hallucination. But if there's anything else you ever want to know about us, anything at all, just say so."

"Anything?" I asked, trying to joke around—although there was, actually, one other thing on my mind.

"Yes. Whatever it is, Pete."

I thought about bringing up the thing about the *Fury* and the missing couple, but it felt like a bad idea. I wanted to repair my friendship with Leo and Marie and leave that episode behind.

We arrived at the Douglases' cottage in silence. It was a resplendent white house whose yard was covered in gnomes, plastic dragonflies, and other weird knickknacks. Keith, their oldest son, was waiting for us. Collecting dust and cobwebs in the living room was the piano. It was an electronic Korg with eighty-eight keys, foot pedals, and a beautiful stand around it that was, thankfully, detachable. It would probably sound decent, I thought.

We folded the Volvo's seats back, and Keith helped me carry the keyboard, the stand, and a stool to the car. After three tries, we finally got it to fit, with the keyboard lying diagonally.

We drove back to town, and Marie and I didn't broach the sensitive topic again. We talked about the weather, the movie, anything but that. It was my turn to have them over for dinner, and I promised to do it before the kids returned to Amsterdam.

I parked the car as close to the port as possible, next to a barrier that closed off the street. ("CLENHBURRAN MOVIE NIGHT. Apologies for any inconvenience.") I got Donovan and another kid to help me carry the behemoth to the red carpet the Blake Audiovisual guys had set up in front of the screen.

One of the techs was testing the projector and the sound equipment, and music was playing over the speakers. He came over when he saw us walk up with the piano.

"Did you bring the cables? We need one for each stereo channel," he said.

"Cables?" I said. "I thought you'd have them."

The guy sighed and wiped the sweat off his forehead. We needed two cables, each at least six feet long, to connect the piano to the mixing board. We looked inside the stool, where there were only two songbooks, one of Clayderman scores and another of Beatles songs for beginners. Mrs. Douglas had never needed to plug her keyboard into an external speaker so she had never needed the cables.

"Let me see what I have in the truck," the kid said.

No luck. They had microphone cables, but those wouldn't work for the keyboard.

"Nobody told us to bring cables. You think you can find any?" he asked.

"I have a set at my house," I said, checking my watch. It was 6:15 p.m. "If I hurry, I can be back in less than half an hour. We'd still have some time for a sound check."

"Bring two, if you have them. Otherwise we'll have to broadcast in mono," he said.

I ran to the car. When I was inside with the windows up and out of earshot of any townies, I was free to shout out what was on my mind.

"How the hell did you let yourself get talked into this goddamn mess?"

I fired up the car and raced out of town.

I reached home in less than fifteen minutes. At that time of day, the ocean seemed aflame. The large, orange sun, only a couple clouds at its heels, radiated at full strength. The beach was empty, and out at sea you could see a couple of sailboats. I thought about

Jip and Beatrice and their voyage on the lagoon. I prayed they hadn't thought to do something crazy like go out into the open water.

I backed the car into the driveway so I could make a quick getaway. I went into the house and headed straight for my box of gear in the living room. I had cables, chargers, an external hard drive, and a host of other gear to connect my MIDI player to my computer so I could record my music. I found what I was looking for right away, a pair of thick cables that were exactly what I needed, and wished I'd thought to bring them that morning.

I tossed the cables on the passenger seat and started up the car. I was determined to make even better time back to town with the sun at my back. The sooner I got there, the more time there would be for a sound check. I was worried the Korg would take some tinkering to sound right. I had one hand on the hand brake, the other clicking in my seat belt as I floored it. But, to my surprise, the car had the opposite idea. I'd left it in reverse, and it shot back at full throttle. Before I could take my foot off the gas, I felt an impact.

CRACK!

The engine stalled, and the car came sputtering to a halt.

"Shit!" I swore, as I pulled on the hand brake. "Haste makes waste. . . ."

Only as I was unbuckling my seat belt to see what I'd hit did it wash over me what the only possible, sinister, answer could be. "C'mon, this has to be a bad joke," I murmured to myself.

My fears were realized the second I opened the door, stepped out of the car, and walked to the back. It could only be "that."

The bumper had rammed into the fence, about a yard and a half from the gate, snapping four wooden slats in half. The impact had ripped them right out of the ground and dragged them across the dirt.

The fence . . .

If anyone had seen me in that moment, I imagine they would have thought I'd lost my mind. I stood there, quietly in shock at this minor—yet major—domestic demolition. For some reason, I pictured Dr. Kauffman telling me all of this was just a product of my subconscious. "You saw this image somewhere before, you internalized it, and now your mind has brought it back to the forefront."

You sure about that, doc? I personally don't remember ever running over a fence in my life.

Except this one.

I squatted down next to the trampled section of fence and studied it. It was exactly as I'd seen it in my nightmares, the white, broken slats laid in a row, like piano keys. It felt like I was looking at the last piece of a jigsaw puzzle. The final message.

I started to try to fix it, as if by doing that I could easily undo everything. I kneeled on the grass and tried to straighten a couple of the slats. But that pile of wood and splinters wouldn't stand. It was hopelessly destroyed, broken.

I heard myself say, "C'mon, Peter, it's just another damn coincidence." But it didn't matter. Deep down, I knew I'd stopped listening to "rational" explanations. I jumped in my car and peeled out of there, with the vague notion that maybe this ought to be my last night in this town.

"CAN WE SLEEP at your place tonight?"

Judie looked surprised.

I had just finished the sound check and everything was ready to go. Every seat was full, and it was standing-room only in the makeshift auditorium. (A lucky few sat on an improvised terrace Chester had set up in front of his store.) It was a perfect summer night for a movie. There was barely a breeze, and a canopy of stars in a clear, dark sky surrounded the screen, where photos of actors from the 1950s and 1960s played in a slideshow from Judie's laptop.

"Yes, of course you can stay, Peter," she said. "Is something wrong?"

"No, nothing. It's just that we'll probably finish late here and . . ." (not that that ever stopped us from driving the fifteen minutes back to the beach on any other night) "well, I just think it'll be more comfortable for the kids."

"I understand," she said, "of course. I actually love the idea. Plus, the hostel's empty today. But . . . are you sure everything is okay with you?"

I was tempted, really tempted, to tell her the truth. *Remember the fence that always appears broken in my dreams, Judie? Remember how you said you thought it might mean something? Well, it's broken right now, exactly how I saw it in my dreams. I've seen it. It was a premonition. And if the fence is broken, then everything else is going to happen, too. Marie, the men in the van. Everything. Do you hear me, Judie?*

But I didn't say that. I kept it all to myself. Why? Judie had enough to worry about that night, and I didn't want to add to it with my own *Twilight Zone* fantasy. Maybe she would try to rationalize it: "Okay, so the fence is broken. It could be that you broke it subconsciously. It could be that, in the back of your mind, you're trying to make all the pieces fit." Dr. Kauffman would probably agree with her.

Or maybe the fence wasn't even broken at all. Maybe I'd imagined it. As the night went on, I started to convince myself of that.

At exactly 7:30 p.m., Mrs. Douglas grabbed the mic and gave it a nervous *tap, tap,* "Can everyone hear me?" The crowd buzzed then fell into a hush. I stood off to the side of the stage with my arms crossed, trying to focus on what I was about to play.

"Good evening, neighbors and guests," Mrs. Douglas began. "Welcome to the first annual Clenhburran Outdoor Movie Night."

There was clapping and cheers, and Mrs. Douglas smiled.

"A few months ago . . ." she said, having to raise her voice. "A few months ago, when our friend Judie Gallagher proposed this idea, the ladies of our cultural organization almost burst out laughing. It was crazy: Set up a theater outdoors? In Donegal, no less . . ." There were a few chuckles in the crowd. "But at the same time it rang of idealism and adventure, and we loved that. And it looks like Lord Almighty agrees, because He's given us a beautiful summer night to kick off the event. So let's take advantage of it before He changes His mind!"

More laughter and applause: Mrs. Douglas had them eating out of the palm of her hand. I looked out to the crowd, but the spotlight in my eyes only let me see into the first few rows. Night was falling, and I worried whether the children had returned. The O'Rourke kid had said they'd be back "before dark," but what time was that exactly? I told myself they were fine; they were probably sitting in the audience right now, waiting to watch their dad play.

"We've chosen two films to kick off the event. A short film and a feature-length film. Judie has prepared a short presentation on each," Mrs. Douglas said, handing the microphone over to Judie.

Judie had changed into a tight little black dress at the last minute. She'd put up her hair and decorated it with a red rose to match her lipstick. She took the mic and smiled at the crowd.

"Thank you, Martha. Good evening, friends . . ."

There's no way of knowing whether you actually experienced what you think you did. I thought back on Dr. Kauffman's words from just four days ago. *No one saw you do the things you remembered doing. All of these things could be constructs of your mind, Mr. Harper. . . . These things are often confused for "lucid dreams" or "astral voyages."*

What if this were just another vision? I wondered. *What if I hadn't really broken the fence, at all!*

But I'd felt it with my own hands. And I was sure there would be some kind of white paint on the Volvo's bumper. I decided right then that I would go back that night to make sure. Maybe I'd call up Leo so he could see it with his own eyes, as well. And Dr. Kauffman, too. Better yet, why not call up all my friends and family. And the whole damn police force. And the national guard . . .

"Peter?"

I snapped out of it and saw Judie and Mrs. Douglas staring at me, gesturing for me to hurry to the stage. I shook my arms out and stepped out onto the stage.

"And now, without further ado, our illustrious neighbor, Mr. Peter Harper!"

The port broke into a thunderous ovation. It was the first time anyone had clapped for me in a long time. It was like having your favorite dinner for the first time in years.

I walked to the microphone and said something like, "Good evening, friends." I've never been much of a public speaker, and I tend to be brief. I said something about how good an idea this outdoor movie night was and how happy I was to be invited to play. Then, Judie asked me a couple of questions about my career. I focused on her beautiful face and managed to say something funny. Finally, I sat down to play. The moment I rested my fingers on the keys, I was able to push away all the other thoughts in my head. And, actually, I played amazingly well. It wasn't a complicated piece, but that night, my fingers seemed to radiate energy. I took solace in the piano and felt like hiding between the keys and staying there forever. The audience must have felt it, too, as they exploded in a fantastic, standing ovation when I struck the final chord and drew my hands away from the keys.

I don't really remember what I said after when Judie handed me the microphone. But I do remember the crowd shouting "encore!" At that moment, smiling at Judie, I realized how important it was that I be there that night, reacquainting myself with the public. This moment, this audience, those hundred or so people applauding, this was why I played music. Not FOX, not Pat Dunbar, not the TV stars. That was all smoke and mirrors. My self-pity, my misery, my self-imposed house arrest had made me forget the real point of my chosen profession: to tell a story with music. And a story without an audience is a party without guests.

Jip and Beatrice came running up the seawall, and when the applause finally died down, we sat in the front row of chairs. Jip sat on my lap and Beatrice squeezed in next to Judie. And when the first movie started, I wanted to forget about all the bad stuff and just focus on that moment of pure joy. Maybe I should start playing in front of the public regularly again. Get a band together and go on tour. I felt better about this idea than any new melody that might occur to me. And maybe, just maybe, the muse would return to me.

Before all that, however, there were still issues to resolve.

TWO

THERE WAS one last thing to take care of. And that night was the perfect moment to do it. The kids would be staying with Judie at the hostel. So no one would be in danger, except, perhaps, me. The house on Tremore Beach was calling me. It had sent me a clear and concise message that I should go there alone to learn its final secret. I knew it in my bones, the way I simply knew I shouldn't have gone out the night of the storm a few months back. The same way I knew my mother wouldn't live longer than a year the last time I saw her dressed in a hospital gown, as the hospital doors closed on her.

After the movie, the party moved over to Fagan's, where everyone insisted on buying me a pint. I graciously accepted every offer, while the children drank sodas with their new friends, sitting on barrels in the back of the pub, joking and laughing. Beatrice was proud to have a famous dad and her two friends, the English girls, shyly came over to ask for my autograph. "Beatrice said you wouldn't mind."

Leo and Marie came by, too. I was surrounded by the social club ladies, Donovan and his clan, even the flirtatious mail carrier, Teresa Malone, pressed her ample bosom up against me. But I managed to wriggle free and step off to the side with Leo. He unleashed one of his trademark smiles, which made his whole face light up, and he clapped me on the back.

"You were superb, Peter. Your music touched all of us."

"Thanks, Leo, really. Look," I said, lowering my voice, "I owe you an apology."

The gracious Leo Kogan patted my cheek like a kid and smiled.

"Forget it, Peter. You're already forgiven."

"But . . ."

"No buts. I'm serious. You made a tiny mistake—maybe not even a mistake, at all. I know you're a good friend. And that means more to me than some small indiscretion. As far as I'm concerned, it's forgotten."

"Okay. But at least let me buy you a beer."

"You read my mind. It's been a few weeks since we've sat on your back porch in the afternoon, tossed back a couple Belgians, and fixed the world's problems. Besides, that fence is going to need a second coat of paint pretty soon. . . ."

My smile faded a bit at the mention of the fence, and I nearly told Leo about what had happened that afternoon. But I still hadn't allowed myself to believe it had happened. *Don't screw it up again. Just leave it alone,* I thought. Instead, I promised I'd go to Derry that week and bring back a few Tripel Karmeliets I'd seen on sale. And we'd drink them watching the sunset, fixing all the world's issues, as friends, the way it should be.

We chatted for a bit longer, and then Leo and Marie said goodnight. The kids were spent, too, and around eleven, I told Judie we should probably get going. She still had a couple of things to take care of, so she gave me the keys to the store and told me to make myself at home. "I'll sleep in the office so I don't wake you," she said.

I put the kids to bed. We lay down and talked a little bit about their trip on the boat and how a crab had climbed up on Jip's leg. Beatrice seemed taken with Seamus, who'd piloted the boat around the lagoon. She told me how he'd taught her to dive head-first off the bow of the boat. I seem to remember him being a little old for Beatrice, but I guess he was a more attractive option than the O'Rourke boys. Besides, the older kids always seem to get all the attention. I figured I was about to watch a "made in Donegal" summer romance unfold.

They both fell asleep, and I lay watching them for a while, wondering if I should let myself fall asleep and forget all this business about returning to the house.

Judie arrived around twelve-thirty. I heard the door to the hostel open and shut and listened to her footsteps across the floor. Just as she said, she headed off to sleep in her office. That would make slipping out easier.

My watch read two-thirty when I decided it was time to go. The hostel was quiet. The children were asleep. Their steady breathing and their small bodies lying gently under the covers filled me with tenderness. I kissed each of them goodnight.

I dressed in the bathroom and tiptoed down the stairs, trying not to make a sound. It would be hard for Judie to hear me leave from the back of the store.

The town was fast asleep after its big night. The street was plunged in darkness. Windows shuttered, cats asleep on rooftops, the distant sound of some night owl's television set.

The Volvo was parked down by the port. I started it the way you tear off a Band-Aid: quickly and without hesitation. Someone likely would have heard the car start up. Maybe some neighbor even peeked out his window out of curiosity. I drove slowly up the main drag until I'd passed the last of the houses on Main Street. One mile down the road, I turned up the narrow road that led toward the beach.

Nighttime seemed even blacker on that dark stretch of road through the countryside. The sky was clear. Stars shone like silver buttons against the void. The bog on either side of the road was a wrinkled shroud of darkness over the earth. My headlights illuminated dried, twisted tree trunks, the occasional nocturnal bird perched on their branches, and the suddenly twisting highway. It was a good thing I was driving slowly that night.

Eventually, my eyes adjusted to the darkness, and I could make out the horizon. A golden beam from a distant lighthouse sailed over the dark ocean toward the western sky.

It wasn't long before I reached Bill's Peak. My headlights swept over the old lightning-singed elm. I turned left and started down the slope. My house sat dark and still. As I approached, I saw the downed fence. I'm not sure what would have been worse: to find the fence intact and realize my mind was still playing tricks on me or to find it broken. The way it was. Demolished on the ground.

It hadn't been my imagination, after all.

I parked the car a few yards away from the house. The scene was exactly as I'd seen it in my visions. Except that there was no storm overhead that night.

I stepped out of the car and stood in front of the house, ready for whatever came next.

A gentle breeze blew in, rustling the tall grass, a cricket singing its song somewhere in the yard. But nothing else.

I stood there for nearly thirty minutes, smoking a couple of cigarettes outside the car. Maybe I was supposed to do something else?

Well, the visions had started when I was in the house. *Okay, then. Let's do it. Let's go inside the house.*

I opened the door like I was an intruder. Everything was as I'd left it that afternoon in a rush. The box with the electrical gear was on the living room floor with its contents of cables and other technical equipment strewn around it.

I sat on the couch. Outside, the crashing waves were the only sound. I flipped through the magazines on the coffee table, and I was even tempted to turn on the television. This was stupid. . . .

Maybe I was wrong, after all. I'd thought I had the power to make the visions come at will. Where did I get such an idiotic idea?

I got up and went into the kitchen to pour myself a glass of water. Then I climbed the stairs and checked every room. The beds were unmade, and clothes and books were strewn on the floor. I picked it all up. The drive out here shouldn't be a *complete* waste of time.

I headed to my room. My bed was unmade, too. I lay down, pillow folded behind my head, and kicked off my shoes. I sat the ashtray on my stomach and grabbed a cigarette. Only three left, now. I lit it, took a deep breath and blew a long puff of smoke into the darkened room.

Time to go and stop being such an idiot, Peter Harper. Nobody's coming. Not tonight. No Marie in her nightgown. No van full of murderers. Better to spend what's left of the night with Judie and your children, and forget about all this shit. Tomorrow is another day. And who knows? Maybe the visions are gone for good.

I closed my eyes and thought of Judie and that night a few months ago when we were alone in this very bed. Her on top of me, grinding her hips. No one could hear us way out here in this house on the beach, and she loved that. She liked being able to moan as loud as she wanted.

I took another drag.

God, I wish she were here right now. . . .

And that's when I noticed it. The throbbing. Growing stronger inside my head. It started like it usually did, a gentle beating in my temples, a sort of fluttering in my veins, until the pounding spread all over the inside of my skull, and what felt like a pair of headphones grew louder and tighter against my ears.

I opened my eyes and snuffed out the cigarette. It was about to happen.

In a few seconds, the throbbing became the blinding pain I'd felt too often before, that railroad spike that pierced one ear and all the gray matter in between until it came out the other side. I covered my ears and howled in pain, as if a dentist were drilling a rotten tooth without Novocaine. I writhed in bed and fell to the floor along with the ashtray filled with ash and burned out butts. Just as I opened my mouth to scream, the spike in my head suddenly disappeared. The pain dissolved into thin air. I lay panting on the bedroom floor.

Then, I heard a door slam out in the yard. A car door.

Outside, the wind had begun to howl. Rain pattered against the windows.

Abracadabra. Hocus-pocus. It worked. . . .

I lay in silence on the floor, my ears wide open.

I heard the sound of an engine. And voices. They're here. Again. Out in front of the house.

It was magic. And I was in charge of it. I nearly burst out laughing in my excitement. I had to contain myself and cover my mouth. Now, all that mattered was what happened next.

I dragged myself along the carpeted floor to the window. It was hung with pale yellow curtains I'd never really cared for, but that night I was glad I never threw them out. I pressed up against the wall and slithered up it like a reptile until I could peek out the window. *Voilà!* There were my old friends. Here we were, all of us reunited again.

Down by fallen fence, parked next to my Volvo, was the GMC van with the chrome rims, shining in the darkness like a UFO. Its two headlights and two fog lights lit up the front of the house like Christmas.

Well, here was a new scene. Something which I hadn't seen before in other visions, but which made perfect sense. The pudgy guy and the evil John Lennon dragged a body toward the van. The woman was either passed out or dead, her bare feet twisted inward as she was dragged along the ground. The men lugged her by her limp arms. Her head hung down, and she was wearing the same outfit as the first time I saw her. It was Marie. The men sat her on the ledge of the door and flipped on an inside light.

Now I could see she was still alive but completely out of it. She swayed as if she were drugged and kept mouthing something to the men. She was pleading, crying.

The other woman appeared from the side of the house. I couldn't make out her face, just her dark hair gathered up in a ponytail. All dressed in a black outfit, she headed right for the van and stood directly in front of Marie. She grabbed Marie by the hair and yanked it to lift her head. She slapped her twice across the face, hard. She yelled something at her that I couldn't make out and hit her twice again.

"Goddamn evil bitch . . ." I whispered.

It was time to stop being a coward and do what I'd come here to do. These were my visions, I had to remind myself of that. *I'm in control here. . . .*

But my body felt heavy. The ground felt like quicksand, and it was hard to breathe. I was scared. Truly afraid.

I turned away from the window. I crawled along the floor and out the bedroom door. I stood up in the hallway. The one good thing about having this crazy hallucination more than once was that I knew there were only three of them, and they were all outside. I hurried downstairs, determined to do something—but what that was, I wasn't quite sure yet.

Things were different in the living room, too. My box of tech gear wasn't spilled on the ground. The door to the terrace was wide open and the storm was blowing in. The curtains fluttered like the gown of some shapeless phantom, and the floor and television were covered in rainwater. The coffee table was knocked over, the magazines strewn across the floor, the couch cushions rumpled and scattered.

There was a familiar scent in the air. I recognized it immediately from the fireworks that filled the sky in Amsterdam on New Year's Eve: It was the smell of gunpowder.

Doors slammed shut outside. I wasn't about to let them get away. I rushed to the fireplace and grabbed the poker.

Maybe they'll shoot and kill me, but this is a dream, isn't it? You can't die in your dream, can you?

I ran up the hall with the poker in the air like Excalibur, screaming like a man possessed, "SONS OF BITCHES . . . !"

They were just getting into the van and shutting the doors. They must not have seen me or heard my war cry. I leaped down the front stairs and over the shrubbery, racing toward the van. But the sliding door shut with a thud, and the van's engine roared to life. It swerved and banged into the side of my Volvo, and then pulled away in a cloud of exhaust and sand.

"STOP!" I yelled as loud as I could, but the van was already racing up the hill without slowing.

No, it can't end like this. We're going to finish this, wherever it leads.

You know where they're taking her: to her house. And that's where Leo will be—dead or alive. Get in your goddamn car and follow them!

I tried to open the door to my car, but it was locked—even though I distinctly remembered leaving it unlocked. *Right, this didn't happen today.* The keys should be on the hook inside.

I ran back into the house. I looked in the key holder, but it was empty. Why? I rushed to the wrecked living room. The gunpowder smell was stronger here—stronger still as I reached the kitchen door. What the hell had happened here? The lights were off, but the reflected light off the stainless steel appliances was enough to reveal three people sitting around the table. Sitting still in the dark.

A man and two children, about the ages of thirteen and eight.

I stood frozen in the doorway. The sound of the fireplace poker falling to the ground seemed to reverberate for miles around.

I opened my mouth to say something, anything, to these three motionless figures who sat so still in the darkness. But I couldn't say a word. What would I have said, if I could?

Jip's eyes were open. He looked straight ahead, emotionless. His arms were resting on the table, his wrists duct taped together. He was shot diagonally through one side of his forehead. The hole looked enormous against his tiny head, a wound that barely bled. However, the back of his head was blown open like cruel jack-in-the-box, matter hanging out of the gaping wound and spattered against the back of the chair.

Beatrice was no longer Beatrice. She was slumped backward and didn't have a face. I couldn't tell her mouth from her eyes. She was a jumble of disfigured features. Her hands were also bound with duct tape, her legs beneath her twisted at impossible angles.

Finally, I looked at the man who could be none other than me. Somehow, I was standing face-to-face with my own corpse.

The body had slumped forward, leaning against the edge of the table. His mouth was half open, as if he'd wanted to say something the instant someone put a bullet through one of his eyes. As if he were cursing the slug that was about to burrow through his skull.

I approached the table and closed Jip's eyes. His cold eyelids fluttered closed like the wings of butterfly. My last shred of sanity drained out of me in a single tear.

I avoided looking at Beatrice again, her face a jagged void. It was too horrible to contemplate. I thought maybe I should put a plastic garbage bag over her. I didn't want anyone to see her this way.

Then I looked at my deceased self. At the eye that was still intact and looking straight ahead, as if still alive. I felt myself sinking, sinking, disappearing down a dark and endless rabbit hole. . . . Fade to black.

HE'S OVER HERE! Pete, Pete! Oh my God!
   Is he . . . ?
   No, he's breathing. Quick, help me get him into the car . . . !

SIRENS. SIRENS. SIRENS.
   I'm sorry, Clem. I'm so sorry. Our babies. Our babies!
   Easy, Pete.
   He's hallucinating. Poor lad.
   It's better if he just falls back asleep. Does it have to be so noisy in here?
   Sirens. Sirens. Sirens.

THERE WERE COPS HERE. The cops who were guarding the bodies in Dad's newspaper. I was suddenly surrounded by them. Strange faces who stared down at me impassively. They were taking me somewhere, and all I wanted was to see my kids. But they just kept saying, "Your kids are fine, Peter," as they groped for my arms. Why would they keep saying that, when I *knew* it wasn't true? I jerked my arms away. I wanted to go home, back to the house, back to my babies. But the arms clamped down on mine and wouldn't let me go. I fought back. I punched the air to get free and hit something that felt like bone. Someone screamed and then hands were all over me again. I fought even harder, swinging wildly. Then, there was a hive, a cloud of wasps all around me. "Goddamn wasps, leave me alone!" Then someone grabbed me by the throat and held me down. I could barely breathe. One of the wasps stung me on the arm, dug its stinger deep into me. And I sank back into my darkened hollow.

THREE

AROUND AND AROUND. My eyes danced around and around behind my eyelids. It was such a glorious sensation, a feeling of total well-being. I could picture my eyes spinning around their sockets like two tiny planets in separate orbits. I was having a beautiful dream—but then suddenly I wasn't.

Someone had pulled the stopper out of the bathtub filled with warm water in which I lay. The water drained out, and I started to feel cold. My naked body emerged, uncovered. It was so cold now, so cold that I couldn't even move my hands anymore. I tried to hug myself, but I couldn't.

Then a voice came out of nowhere and everywhere.

"You're in a hospital in Dungloe," it said. "Can you hear me?"

I tried to say something but my tongue lolled clumsily inside my mouth. I sounded like a drunk asking for one more drink at last call. I sighed, tired and frustrated from trying to communicate. I attempted opening my eyes, but everything was a celestial whiteness.

I could feel a presence at my side, and at almost the same instant, a pin prick of pain in my left arm.

"He'll rest now."

I DREAMED about Clem dressed as a fairy at a Halloween party. She was the most beautiful of all the moms. I watched her, spellbound, as she chatted with friends. I thought to myself, "You are the luckiest man on earth," as she went around tapping children with her magic wand, bewitching them. I was charmed, too.

I dreamed about my college apartment in Amsterdam. Everyone in the building was a musician. We were having a party, playing and laughing and drinking mulled wine. It was Christmas.

I dreamed about the day Beatrice was born.

I slowly opened my eyes. The light seemed too bright at first, but it softened a little at a time until the shadows in the room became objects.

I studied the ceiling, the fluorescent lights above me, the paint that was flaking away where it had been sloppily applied. There was a window in the room, and through it I could see a tree swaying in a gentle breeze. I could hear cars driving up a nearby street.

I still couldn't move my hands and realized they were tied to the bed. I struggled, but it was no use.

"Peter, we had to restrain you last night. Do you remember anything about that? Do you know why you're here?"

It took me a while to find exactly where the voice was coming from, but I finally saw the figure take shape before my eyes, a little blurry, yes, but I did recognize her. It was Dr. Anita Ryan. I lifted my head to try to get up but I was held down by the restraints. I let my head fall against the pillow. The room spun in a pleasant spiral, and I didn't have the strength to try to get up again. *What did I remem-*

ber? I remembered screaming and fighting against dozens of hands holding me down. I had wanted to see my children, but the hands wouldn't let me. I thought they were all against me. I could have sworn it was the assassins, but the voices all told me that everything was okay.

"My children," I said, and realized my voice was hoarse, and my throat hurt like I'd spent all night yelling at a death metal concert. "Where are my children?"

"They're in the waiting room, and they're perfectly fine. You'll be able to see them very soon."

"Very soon? Why not right now?"

"We want to make sure you're well enough first. You were in shock, Peter. Do you remember anything about what happened?"

"I . . ."

I closed my eyes, and could see the vision so clearly in my mind. Even nightmares had a way of fading with the morning, becoming a vague recollection that evanesced in the coming hours or days. But not this one. This image was fresh and clear in my mind. This was no simple nightmare.

"Your friends found you. You were passed out on the floor at your house. You'd driven there in the middle of the night for some reason. Do you remember why?"

"No . . . no, I don't remember anything."

The doctor's features came into sharper focus. Her intense green eyes studied me for a moment. Then she turned her gaze toward a plastic bag that hung by my bed. I traced a thin plastic tube from the bag to my left arm, where fluid was pumping into an IV.

"What is that?" I asked. "What are you giving me?"

"It's a sedative. We had to give it to you so you wouldn't hurt yourself last night. You were very agitated."

"I want to see my kids."

"Relax, Peter, you'll see them in a minute. Right now, you need to rest. To get better."

The doctor spoke to me as if I were a child, but then again, I must not have been acting like much of an adult at that moment. She made a note in some paperwork and said she'd be back in five minutes.

I looked back up at the ceiling. At the fluorescent light. At the tree outside the window. What had happened began to dawn on me.

Your friends found you. . . .

SOMEONE CAME into the room. It was the doctor again, followed by a nurse and an orderly pushing a gurney.

"We need to run a scan," Dr. Ryan said, "and for that, we need to wheel you to another part of the hospital. Now, I know you. And I know that you're going to remain calm when we undo the restraints. Can I count on you for that?"

The orderly, a beefy character who easily could moonlight as a WWE wrestler, stared me down. The nurse's expression wasn't much better. I must have been some piece of work last night.

"I'll be calm," I said. "I promise. I think I can walk."

The orderly smirked like I was up to something. He patted the gurney.

"That's okay. We'll take you. This is more comfortable," he said.

As we moved through the hospital, the ceiling was a different color. Orange. The light fixtures overhead were different, too. Square. I counted at least a dozen of them as we wheeled down a long corridor. There were other people here, too. Some of them in hospital gowns, others in street clothes. They looked at me pityingly, asking why this poor devil was being wheeled down the hall on a stretcher. "He looks really young. Cancer?" "Some kind of heart condition?" "No, no . . . look at his eyes. And that long hair. Must be drugs."

A new room now. People spoke with one another without paying much attention to me. Back into the giant donut, the MRI scanner.

I was in the air again, carried by people. They lay me on another table, this one narrow and cold, and fed me into the giant machine. I closed my eyes. I didn't want to see anything anymore. But the noise was maddening. A mechanical clamor all around and a voice that whispered, "Now relax, Mr. Harper."

THE EFFECTS of the Valium were wearing off and my stomach started grumbling for food; I must have missed a few meals. When they returned me to the room, someone appeared to have been there ahead of me. A nurse came in wheeling a cart redolent of food. She parked it next to the bed and took out a tray that she laid on a moveable bedside table.

Dr. Ryan approached the bed.

"Peter, I don't think it'll be necessary to use the restraints again, but you will be under strict surveillance. Yesterday, you struck two orderlies as they were trying to treat you in the emergency room. You understand our concern?"

"I do."

"The hospital administration has asked us to evaluate you for possible transfer to a psychiatric facility, but I'm aware of your personal situation. So we're going to do everything possible to treat you here until we can figure out what's going on with you. Okay?"

"Okay."

Dr. Ryan exchanged a few words with the nurse, and they left the room together. Five minutes later, the nurse returned with

Judie. She had dark circles under her eyes. She wasn't wearing any makeup, and her hair was pulled back in a ponytail. She had a dark, wool sweater over her jeans. She looked the way you might expect someone to if they had suddenly had to jump out of bed in the middle of the night.

"I can stay here with you, if you like," the nurse told her.

"I'll be fine, thanks," she said.

The nurse eyed me with suspicion and looked back at Judie. *Christ, I must have made a real name for myself last night.*

"If you need anything, just press the emergency call button. The nurse's station is down the hall."

Judie nodded with a smile, and the nurse left the room, leaving the two of us.

"I'm so sorry, Judie."

I didn't know what else to say to her. She leaned in close and placed a delicate hand on my forehead.

"You didn't do anything wrong, Peter."

"I'm sorry I worried you. I'm sorry about all of this."

"It's okay, Pete. Everything's fine."

It sounded like the kind of *everything's fine* you tell crazy people.

"How are the kids?"

"Fine . . ." She didn't sound convinced. "They're worried. We all are, Peter."

She turned the moveable table until my dinner tray was in front of me.

"I think you should eat something."

"Judie, will you bring me a phone? I need to call Clem," I said. "This has gotten out of hand. She needs to come and get the kids."

She needs to take them away from here, far, far away. Before . . .

"Try to calm down, Peter. This isn't the best time to be making big decisions."

"Judie, they put me in restraints. They pumped me full of Valium. How much worse can things possibly get? I don't want them to fly back to Amsterdam alone. Wait, you! You could go with them!"

Judie fell silent, pursed her lips.

"They won't be going home alone, Peter."

"What do you mean?"

"The hospital's social worker has already been in contact with the Dutch embassy. They're trying to reach Clem now."

"Oh, God . . ."

I knew what this meant. Social workers. Embassies. They'd already come up with a diagnosis.

"The doctor said you don't remember anything," Judie said. "Is that right?"

"No," I said. "I lied to them."

"Why?"

"Because I don't think they can help me."

"Keeping things to yourself isn't going to help you, either. The other night you kept something from me, too, didn't you? The fence was broken—just like it was in your visions. You had hit it with your car, right? Is that why you returned to the house in the middle of the night?"

"Yes. But how did you . . . ?"

"I was there this morning, Peter," she said. "I went to pick up a couple things and that's when I saw it. Why didn't you say anything?"

"I wasn't sure it had actually happened. Plus, dammit, I didn't want to ruin anybody's night. When did they find me?"

"In the early morning. Jip woke up to use the bathroom and realized you were gone. They came downstairs to wake me. I figured you couldn't sleep and had taken a walk. But when I saw that your car was missing, I started to get really worried. I called you at home first. I thought maybe you'd forgotten something and had gone back for it. But you didn't answer. Then I called Leo. He's the one who found you."

"In the kitchen?"

"Yeah. You were on the floor. He thought you'd had a heart attack, so he called the ambulance. Then he realized you were hallucinating. You were saying things. About dead people. You said . . ."

"I know what I said, Judie. And I know what I saw. It was no nightmare. And it was no hallucination. It was . . . it was . . ."

"The future?"

The word fit perfectly in the context of that strange conversation. I'd thought it a thousand times before, inside my own head. But I never imagined how it would sound out loud.

I nodded.

"Yeah. That's what I think," I said.

"The fence breaks and ends up exactly the way you saw it in your visions; your visions are confirmed; and you worry the rest will come true, as well. That's your theory, right?"

I nodded again. Judie smiled. It was the most sane response to my insanity.

"Don't worry," I said. "I don't expect anyone to believe me. Besides, it's impossible. No one can see the future. That's why I decided not to say anything to the doctor. It's like Occam's razor: the simplest explanation is usually the right one. And the simplest explanation in my case is that I'm crazy, that I've had some kind of schizophrenic episode and I'm hallucinating. That's the diagnosis, isn't it?"

"There's no diagnosis, Peter. But yesterday you did react very violently when they brought you to the hospital. You busted one of the orderly's lips, and you smacked a nurse when she tried to give you a shot. Add to that a guy with two kids who's just gone through a divorce, and it doesn't paint such a rosy picture. The bad news is they're going to place the kids with a guardian until Clem arrives."

"What?"

"Leo's trying to talk to the director of social services right now. He's trying to convince them he and Marie can take care of them until Clem gets here, but you know how things get when children are involved."

"No! This . . . is a mistake."

"I'm sorry, Peter. I'm really sorry."

"Can I see them? Just for a minute, please?"

"In a little while. We have to wait for a decision from the head of social services. But they're fine, and they want to see you."

"How much do they know?"

"We told them you went to go pick up something at the house and fell down the stairs. I'm not sure they completely believe it, but I think they'll make an effort if you don't say anything."

"Of course."

Judie stood up and walked toward the door.

"Judie," I said before she reached the door. "All this stuff about my visions. Keep it between us, okay? I don't want to make things worse. I don't think it'll help matters if I tell them I can see the future."

She nodded.

"Oh, and one other thing. I'd rather the kids spend the night with you. If it's possible."

"Count on it, Peter," she said as she opened the door. "Now try to eat something. Your lunch is getting cold."

DR. RYAN returned an hour later, accompanied by another doctor, a tall, young guy with curly hair and round glasses who turned out to be the hospital's head of psychiatry. He hadn't been on call when I came in, but he was the one who called in an order for the IV medication (which hadn't been Valium, at all, but antipsychotics). He'd analyzed the case, taken statements from Leo and Judie, and had even had a long conversation with Dr. Kauffman in Belfast. He said he wasn't sure I'd be able to go home just yet.

"Mr. Harper, trust us, everything we're doing is for your own sake and for the sake of your children," he said.

Just hearing him say that made me nauseated.

He was at least ten years younger than me, and had the look of someone with a good family name. The kind of guy who plays golf with his father-in-law and has a beautiful wife. "Am I schizophrenic?" I asked at one point.

The doctor was quiet.

"Schizophrenia is an evolutionary diagnosis. There are many criteria you'd have to match, over a long period, before we could arrive at that kind of diagnosis. What we do know is you've had an acute psychotic episode. Though, we can't rule anything out just yet."

"There've been others," I said. "I've . . . seen other things, too. By the way, call me Peter, please."

"Okay, Peter. Dr. Ryan filled me in on the accident you had a few weeks back. For now, given your history, let's try to stay optimistic and assume all this has something to do with your accident. Dr. Kauffman agrees with this theory. Besides, the visual hallucinations suggest something other than schizophrenia. Either way, I've recommended you be admitted for the next few days until we can run some tests. I was hoping we could count on your consent."

"What does that mean? Is this voluntary?"

The doctors exchanged a furtive glance. I knew I was about to hear bad news.

"Mr. Harper, let's just say it's better if you stay voluntarily."

"What if I don't want to?"

"Then things get a lot more complicated, believe me. Right now, the priority is making sure your children are safe. And I can't recommend your being discharged at this point. We'd have to contact the legal department, and they would assign someone to investigate the case. In the meantime, we'd have to call social services and . . ."

"Come on, Peter," Dr. Ryan said. "It would only be a day or two at the most. We know you don't have any history of violence. It's purely a formality."

"But my children . . ."

The younger doctor cleared his throat.

"The hospital's social worker has agreed to let your friends take care of them, for the moment, at least until they locate their mother. It seems she's on vacation."

"Yeah, they're on a trip to Turkey. She's with a man named Niels Verdonk, her new boyfriend. He's a pretty famous architect. Maybe try locating him."

Dr. Ryan wrote his name down.

"As of now, there's no reason why your children can't stay with your friends. Besides, Judie is a licensed psychologist and everyone who knows her vouches for her that she's not out of her mind."

I laughed and the mood lightened a bit.

"Look, I promise I'll do everything in my power to make these tests go as quickly as possible."

I leaned my head back and closed my eyes as tight as I could, wishing for all this to be just a terrible nightmare. Wishing that I'd never been hit by that bolt of lightning. That I'd never had those stupid visions. But when I opened them, I was met only with the reality that these two doctors were waiting for my answer.

"Fine," I said, at last.

》   》   》

JIP AND BEATRICE came into the room the way you'd expect two children to visit someone's deathbed. Timid, scared, their eyes wide as saucers. But the second I smiled at them and told them to give their old man a hug, they leaped on the bed like a pair of tiger cubs.

Jip asked if I was still in pain, and I said, "a little," but that the doctor said it'd go away soon. Beatrice, on the other hand, was quiet. I could see doubt in her eyes: *If Dad fell down the stairs, then where's the cast on his broken leg? The neck brace? Even a single bruise?* But just as Judie had said, I soon managed to get her joking about something else.

Judie, Leo, and Marie came in a few minutes after the kids. Marie carried a bouquet of flowers and box of chocolates wrapped in ribbon that read, "Get Well Soon." Leo came ready with jokes. He joked he was going to buy me a helmet and make me wear it around the house. Sure, it was a dry joke, but it was effective. Though deep in his eyes, I could see the dark cloud of worry every time he looked at me.

I spent the rest of my visit with the kids trying to look animated, for their sake. But my smile was a fragile mask, ready to crack. Their smiling faces took me back to that horrific scene last night. I looked at Beatrice and saw that brutal crater and exploded skull where her beautiful face now was. And my little Jip with that hole in his forehead and that trail of "stuff" hanging out the back of his head. But I closed my eyes and hugged them close, covered them in kisses and wiped my tears with the back of my hand before they could see. I had the same flashbacks looking at Marie, who spent most of our visit on the other side of the room, talking with Leo and Judie. I still got goose bumps at the hallucination of those men dragging her and the woman slapping her, humiliating her, maybe just moments before executing her, too.

But I kept it all inside and played my part perfectly. The children would spend the night with Judie and make homemade pizzas in funny shapes for dinner. They'd play Monopoly and watch a Pixar flick. And after a few days, Dad would come home because the doctor said that he had to spend a couple of nights in the hospital. Daddy was fine, there was no reason to worry. I wish I could believe it myself.

At around eight, they said goodbye. Judie, the kids, Leo, Marie, all of them. Leo was the last one to leave the room. I don't know if he hung back on purpose or not.

"Leo," I said, as he reached for the door. "Can you hang on a minute?"

He stopped as if he'd been waiting for this moment. He walked over to the hospital bed with a heavy smile.

"What's up, Pete?"

"Two things. First, thank you. Thank you for bringing me here."

"Not at all, lad. Although you did hit me with a pretty solid right cross," he laughed.

"I'm sorry, Leo. . . . I was out of my mind. The second thing has to do with . . . what I saw that night."

His face darkened.

"Pete, I don't think I want to hear this."

"I know you don't. I wouldn't, either, Leo, but I can't live with not telling you this. Listen to me. Maybe I'm crazy, and all this is just a hallucination. We'll know eventually. If in two months I'm in a loony bin with my arms in a straitjacket, you can forget we ever had this conversation, okay? Just promise you'll send flowers and hide a flask full of whiskey in the vase."

Leo allowed a smile.

"C'mon, Pete . . ."

"No, really, listen to me. Until that moment, until the doctors decide I'm crazy, I want you to do me one favor, okay?"

"Okay."

"Do you own a gun?" I asked.

Surprise, if not shock, washed over his face.

"What?"

"A revolver, a hunting rifle, anything."

"Why do you ask?"

"Whatever you have, get it ready. Load it, keep it close to your bed, okay? In every single one of my visions . . . they're armed. You'll need some kind of firearm . . . if it turns out I'm right."

"Okay, okay, lad," Leo said, glancing at the door. "I'll think about it."

"And if you see a van pull up to your house—a dark red van with chrome rims and two men and a woman inside—don't let them anywhere near you. Okay? Shoot first, ask questions later, Leo. Will you do that? Promise me you'll do it, for Christ's sake."

"Okay, Pete, I promise."

I took a deep breath and sighed.

"I hope this is all just craziness, Leo. . . ."

Marie came in looking for her husband. Leo shook my hand and held it, and he gave me a look I couldn't quite place.

"Take care of yourself, Peter."

I nodded.

Marie came close again, and the two of us stared at one another for a long moment.

"Take care of yourselves, Marie."

"We will, Pete."

For a second, I thought I saw a flash of terror in her eyes.

FOUR

THE YOUNG PSYCHIATRIST with the curly hair and the little round glasses was named John Levey, and we spent the entire next morning talking in his office. He asked his questions, and I took my time answering, neither one of us in a terrible rush. I talked to him about my divorce, why I'd left Amsterdam, about my job and my kids. I talked to him about everything he wanted to know. I held nothing back, and tried to act normal, civilized, and inoffensive. . . . After all, he held the keys to my freedom: return home . . . or to the psychiatric ward.

We talked about my visions. He had spoken with Kauffman the day before, so he was aware of my episodes. But he wanted to hear my version of events. I told him everything while trying not to be too "emotional." I told it as if I were simply recalling a dream. The young doctor—dressed in a green Lacoste cardigan over a yellow collared shirt, corduroy pants, and Burton Derby shoes—took occasional notes and studied his pad. College boy, through and through. A young man raised among important men who tolerate zero mistakes. But he had his hands full with this case. It was clear he had no idea where to start with me.

He tried out several diagnoses, from a persecution complex to paraphrenia to paranoia. He mentioned great emotional stress (say, from a recent divorce, problems at work . . . sound familiar?) or low self-esteem. People in these situations, especially highly intelligent ones, construct a subconscious illusion. Something that helps them make sense of their new circumstance. A coping mechanism for their pain. But sometimes those fantasies estrange us from reality.

"Do you think that's what happening to you, Peter?"

"Oh, certainly, John, it's a possibility!"

Thirty-three-year-old John Levey wanted to nail this diagnosis. He needed all the books he'd studied at his very prestigious university to make sense, so I let him believe it. I even took the three pills they forced on me so I could return to my room. Maybe this is how it starts for crazy people.

Crazy Pete . . .

That night, with my head floating because of the medication, I considered the real possibility that I was losing my mind.

Nuts. You're going to end up absolutely nuts. Hell of a way to play out your days. At some "facility" somewhere. One of those lost souls who staggers around aimlessly in a hospital gown down a maze of hallways that smell like disinfectant. Ten pills a day. Mind numb. Chemically castrated. Shattered. Wandering the lovely gardens. Sitting on a bench all day watching the birds, talking to the flowers. An early retirement. Maybe it wouldn't be all bad. You wouldn't have to compose music anymore. There'd be no more successes, or failures.

These doctors, they were talking about visions, dreams, sleepwalking, and I was ready to believe them—to believe anything. But deep down, I was sure, I mean absolutely certain, about what I had seen, heard, and felt. What I had experienced had left bruises on my body and scars on my psyche: the fear, the sheer terror I felt as those people broke into my house, and the horrific result. It was all real. These weren't nightmares or lucid dreams or astral voyages. I had *seen* it. And suddenly, just like that, it all disappeared. It was like some sick joke. Like that loony cartoon toad, Michigan J. Frog, who sang (vaudeville-style) and danced only when he was alone with his owner.

Crazy.

Maybe there was no going back now. The lightning strike had broken something irreparably, and no one could see the damage. But think about all the things science can't explain! There was a word for that unknown gray area.

Crazy.

Society had a place for these kinds of people. And unless I managed to unravel this enigma, it was the only word that would ever describe me.

Crazy.

Between the pills, lunch, and a restless night, I fell asleep in the early afternoon. I took an impossibly long nap, and by the time I woke up, it was nearly nighttime. I looked out the window, and the tree outside was shaking in a stiff wind, its branches tossed into the air. The wind whipped and the sky had darkened.

I called the nurse, and it took a few minutes for the young blonde with the bored blue eyes to come into the room.

"We're understaffed today," she said, excusing herself. "I'll bring your dinner in a minute."

I told her not to worry about dinner and asked her instead what time it was. She said it was six-thirty at night. Thunder crashed in the distance.

"Is there a storm coming?"

"Oh, yeah," she said, "One of those big summer thunderstorms. The weatherman had originally said it'd be a clear night. But, there you go."

"A storm . . ." I repeated to myself.

"I'm sorry?"

"Uh, nothing, sorry . . . Is Dr. Levey in, by any chance? I'd like to talk to him."

"No, Mr. Harper," she said. "I think he went home at about five-thirty. But he's on call from home. Do you need something?"

"No, no, never mind. It's not important. I'd like to call my kids. Would you hand me my cell phone? It should be in my jacket pocket."

The nurse opened the closet and rifled around my coat until she found the phone. She brought it over and asked whether I wanted beef or fish for dinner. I said beef.

When she'd left, I called Judie at her store. It rang ten times, but no one picked up. It was almost seven and she'd probably already closed up shop. But she was supposed to be at the hostel with the kids. Or was she? I tried calling her cell, but she didn't pick up there, either. Where the heck could she be?

I started to worry. And now I was just thinking about Dr. Levey and his stupid little prep-boy smile, leaving me stranded in this goddamn place as if it were some kind of Club Med.

And now, this damn thunderstorm.

It's just a thunderstorm. It's totally normal for this time of year.

I started to wonder what would happen if I got out of bed, got dressed, and tried to walk out of the hospital. Would they sound the alarm? Sic the cops on me? Dr. Ryan had said that they were keeping me under "strict surveillance." And that my kids were with Judie only because it was "more humane" than sending them to live with protective services. No, it was better not to do anything stupid. I tried Judie's cell phone again, and this time it didn't even ring. The error message said the user wasn't available or had traveled outside the coverage area.

"Where the hell are you, Judie?"

We went for a drive, that's all. Maybe to Monaghan, since we never ended up going. Or maybe they're eating popcorn down by the port. Relax, Peter. . . .

I spent the next half hour in bed worrying, listening to the wind and rain pound the windows, thunder rumble in the distance, the storm still a few miles off shore. *I could swing by Clenhburran real quick, just to look things over,* I thought. *Take a drive, get some air, make sure everyone's okay, then come back tonight. Judie could drive me back. They probably wouldn't even notice I was gone. After all, the nurse was complaining that they were short staffed.*

Then I felt the phone begin to vibrate in my hands. *Good, it's Judie. Thank God.*

"Hello?"

"Peter?" The voice wasn't Judie's. It wasn't Leo or Marie, either. It took me a second to recognize her.

"Imogen?"

"The very same, dear. How are things going?"

Caught off guard by the phone call—from Imogen, of all people— I only managed a "good, fine."

"Sorry it's taken me so long to get back to you. I was scouting some property in Scotland, and I just got back from London. You don't want to live in a castle by any chance, do you? I found the most amazing renovated tower only twenty miles from Edinburgh. . . . Anyway, that's not why I'm calling. I've finally got what you asked me for."

"What I asked you for . . ." I said almost to myself.

"Yeah, about your house. You wanted to know if anything strange had ever happened there. The ghost your friend said she saw?"

"Oh, God, right. I'd forgotten all about that."

Thunder rumbled.

"Well, I didn't find anything about a ghost. But I talked to the realtor who used to represent the property before me, and she told me a pretty interesting story. Remember when I told you about the German guy who had rented the house before you? The guy who studied migratory birds? One of those scholarly, university types who wouldn't know how to fry an egg? Well, he had a weird story about your neighbors, the ones on the others side of the hill. He said somebody had broken into his house, and he was sure it had been them. Laurie, the other agent, asked him if he wanted to file a report with the police, but he said no. Said he looked, and he wasn't actually missing anything, it was just more of a feeling, like someone had been rifling around in his house. One time, from one of his hides, he had seen them meeting with some quote-unquote 'strange' people. No idea what he was talking about. He'd paid for six months but left after five. He didn't even ask for his deposit back. Have you seen anything like that?"

It took me a minute to say anything. My heart started pounding in my chest, and my mouth suddenly went dry as I started to struggle for breath.

"No . . . I . . . I don't know," I said, finally.

"Are you all right, Peter? Listen, if the house is a problem, we can switch you somewhere else. It won't cost you anything. There are other houses in the area. Well, not a ton, because it's the high season, but I'm sure we can find you something."

"No, it's okay, Imogen. Thanks. Thanks for everything. I . . . I have to go now."

I hung up the phone and realized how stupid I'd been.

Everything fit. All the pieces started falling into place. I knew it was time. . . . This would be my last night on Tremore Beach.

FIVE

I WAITED for dinner to arrive. The nurse's name was Eva, and even though she was in a rush to push the dinner cart to every room along the long hallway, I managed to engage her in conversation a minute. It turned out another nurse, Winny, was on her honeymoon, and Geraldine was sick; and although Luva was supposed to be on call, she had rung to say one of her daughters had caught a stomach bug and was throwing up all night. So she was all alone to cover the floor. "This place is an organizational nightmare. Everyone disappears at once, and one person is left to cover the whole damn place."

I told her not to worry about me. What was the medication I had to take again?

"One tablet of olanzapine and one of these blue ones before bed. I guess I could leave them for you here. After all, it's already past eight. . . ."

"Sure, don't worry. I'll take them right after dinner so I won't forget."

The second Eva closed the door, I jumped out of bed and started getting dressed. Thank God no one thought to take my clothes or shoes home, or that would have nixed my plan. But everything was in a plastic bag in the closet, along with a coat and some extra clothes Judie had brought from my house. When I was ready, I threw the hospital robe on over my clothes and left the room.

I paced up the hallway in no rush whatsoever, looking bored. I peeked in the open doors to see other patients watching television in their rooms, visiting with guests who spoke animatedly as they stared off into the void. With my three-day-old stubble and my dirty, long hair, I looked like just another patient as I paced along in my robe. People looked pityingly at me as I walked by, and I returned their sorrowful gazes.

When I reached the lobby, I found the admissions desk empty.

Outside on the steps to the entrance, a man was smoking. He was a lanky guy with sunken cheeks and hollow eyes. I asked him for a cigarette, and he grumbled as he handed it to me.

"Tobacco ain't cheap, buddy."

I smoked in silence, waiting for my ill-humored friend to buzz off. Meanwhile, I looked out at the street and saw it was nearly devoid of traffic. How the hell was I going to get to Clenhburran?

The wind picked up and started to howl. I recognized this sound. This furious whistling. Soon, the funnel clouds would arrive with their army of lightning bolts. But there was still time.

"Looks like a nasty storm," I said, trying to strike up a conversation, but the guy pretended not to hear me. He just kept smoking his cigarette.

A few minutes later, like a gift from the heavens themselves, a taxi appeared over the rise, heading toward the hospital, and stopped right outside the entrance. I still had the robe on, and Mr. Grumpy was still nursing his cigarette. What to do? If I tried to hail the cab in my hospital robe, I was sure to arouse suspicion.

The passengers got out, and the driver looked at us through the window.

"Need a taxi?" he called out.

I was about to say something when my smoking buddy waved him off before I could open my mouth.

The taxi disappeared back to wherever it came from. And just a few minutes later, so did my curmudgeonly companion. I sat alone on the steps, finishing my cigarette. I glanced back inside and noticed the admissions desk was still empty. I decided it was time to act. I whipped off the robe and stashed it under a nearby bench. Finally looking like a normal citizen again, I headed for the road.

There was a bus stop out front. The number 143 bus went from Dungloe to Clenhburran. But there was no telling when it would next be by. Waiting for a bus in Ireland on a Sunday is like waiting for a miracle.

I decided to hitchhike. It was common for people in that part of the country to catch a ride for a few miles. The hospital was close to Dungloe, and almost all the traffic came from that direction. But I figured eventually I'd stumble on someone going in the other direction toward Clenhburran.

Three or four cars sped by as a light drizzle began to fall. I tried smiling, putting on a needy face, even waving my arms as if there were an emergency. But that only made one driver step on the pedal.

A short while later, I saw a car pulling out of the hospital parking lot. I hurried toward it and approached the driver's window as the car came to a stop at the intersection.

"You headed east by any chance?" I asked pointing my thumb in that direction. "I've been waiting for the bus for an hour."

The driver was a young kid, and an older woman was in the passenger seat.

"Yeah, I'm headed that way. Where are you going?"

"Clenhburran."

"Oh, I know the place. I can take you as far as the gas station." I figured he meant Andy's. "It's just a few miles on foot from there."

"That would be great, thanks."

I sat in the back of the old but comfortable Toyota, whose footwells were full of empty soda bottles and old newspapers. The driver was named Kevin and his passenger was his grandma. They had been visiting Kevin's mother, who was in the hospital with an ovarian tumor.

"And why were you here?"

"Me? Oh, I, uh, was visiting an old friend. He broke his back in an accident. Poor guy's in a body cast, but other than that he's okay."

Kevin's grandmother asked what I'd said, and he told her again in a loud voice. That's pretty much how the rest of the drive went: Kevin would ask a question, I'd respond, and he'd repeat it to his grandmother, who seemed happy to be part of the conversation. The Frames' "Revelate" played on the radio.

Andy's appeared around a curve. In the distance, the storm was taking shape, like the silhouette of a phantom. The clouds extended like a heavy cloak over the horizon. I figured there was still an hour until it made landfall.

Kevin turned in to the gas station.

"We'd take you all the way home, but we're in a rush," he said.

I told him not to worry, that I'd be home before the storm hit. It was only ten minutes into town, and I figured I'd find Judie and the kids there. I thanked Kevin and then his grandmother, in a loud enough voice so she could hear me. The Toyota turned back onto the highway and disappeared around another curve.

Andy's had one of those little roadside cafés inside, the kind of place where your insides immediately regret having eaten. I'd skipped dinner, and my stomach had started to growl, so I considered going inside to grab a candy bar, but I decided it was better to find Judie and the kids first.

That's when I noticed a couple of vehicles parked out in front. Vans.

C'mon, Pete, just cross the goddamn street, and let's find Judie and the kids. . . .

They were probably tourists. There were a lot of visitors to the northern part of the country at this time of year. Probably camping. It was a long way from one town to the next. Maybe they were resting for the night.

One was a plain, white van. But the one next to it . . . I noticed something that made my blood run cold.

An unmistakable GMC badge on the front.

Dark red. Chrome rims.

It couldn't be. But it was. The van from my nightmares.

SIX

THERE WASN'T a single car pumping gas at Andy's. The wind scattered the pages of an old newspaper along the ground. From the speakers inside the café, I could hear the commentary on a hurling match between Leinster and Munster.

One of the newspaper pages took flight and wedged itself beneath the GMC van, which, in the fading light, appeared to be empty.

This can't be.

I walked up to the building as if I were looking at the items for sale outside. Firewood, bags of ice, dog food, newspapers.

I reached the corner. The white van was parked closest to the building. And right next to it was the GMC.

My knees started to shake.

It was a sparkling new GMC Savana, dark red, with Belfast license plates. Yes, there were a lot of vans like this one in the world. But how many red vans had chrome rims like this one? At least a few, I guessed.

I was so overwhelmed, I actually closed my eyes and told myself. *Wake up. Wake up in the hospital, right now, and eat your dinner.* But when I opened my eyes, the van was still there.

The windshield was covered in splattered bugs, so I figured it must have been on the road for a few hours. The air freshener hanging from the rearview mirror had a Hertz logo on it. *A rental . . .*

I pretended to shop for quarts of oil while I tried to memorize the license plate. I thought I remembered it, but immediately it went out of my head again. My mind was racing at a hundred miles an hour.

I walked around to the front of the store, and the automatic doors whooshed open. To the left, behind the counter, a teenage girl with acne smiled hello. I nodded back. With my mouth as dry as it was, I couldn't have managed a simple hello. To the left was the café and the convenience store section. I walked between two racks filled with magazines, potato chips, and chocolate chip cookies until I reached a column that obscured me from the café. I grabbed a magazine and pretended to read it.

Two tables were occupied. In one, a family was having dinner—probably the owners of the white van. Two kids Jip's age ran around the table, fighting over a toy, while their parents ate in sheepish silence, embarrassed by the scene their kids were making.

The other group sat by the window. There were four of them. Three—a brunette, a heavy-set man, and a skinny guy with sunglasses—I recognized immediately. The fourth was a tall, burly guy I'd never seen before, sitting next to the woman with a road map spread in front of him. The others drank coffee and ate sandwiches in silence, scrolling through their cell phones. It seemed like they were looking for something or some place. Tremore Beach, perhaps?

It's hard to describe exactly what was going on inside my head at that moment. It was all I could do to hold on to the magazine and stay quiet. What I wanted to do was stop them dead in their tracks, right then and there. To kill them. I watched them. From the outside, they could be anyone: people here on business or actors on vacation. And I was the only one who knew the truth about what they were here to do. I stuffed the magazine back on the rack. I went to the counter and bought a pack of gum. The teen offered me a two-for-one deal, and I said I was in a hurry. I left her a ten euro bill on the counter.

"Just one thing," I asked on my way out. "You see those four sitting in the back?"

"Yeah."

"Not the family, but the three men and the woman. You can see them, right?"

"Sure, of course."

"They drove up in that van, right?" I said, pointing out the window. "The red one? You can see that, too, right?"

"Um, yeah. Why?" she asked.

"Never mind. I thought I saw them earlier today in Dungloe. I think they're film people or something. Maybe they're scouting a movie location."

"Seriously?" the girl said, her mouth agape, her eyes wide. "My sister Sarah's an actress!"

"Well, maybe you should talk to them before they leave."

I left the store and walked slowly toward the road, my stomach sick and my head starting to pound with nerves. I crossed carefully. I was so out of it, I could easily have been hit by a truck. Plus, I didn't want those four to notice someone sprinting across the road toward town.

Once I'd crossed, I grabbed my cell phone and called Judie again. This time, the recorded voice said the mobile number I was calling wasn't available. Then I tried Leo and Marie. Neither their home phone nor cell phones rang, I glanced at the storm front thundering in the distance. Maybe the electrical storm was causing interference. It was hard to think straight. Only the feeling of panic was clear in my mind. I might have flagged down another car, or I could have taken a detour toward High Street, stopped by Fagan's and warned whoever was there about what was going on. Instead, I just ran. I wanted to reach Judie at the store, make sure my kids were safe, and then worry about the thousand phone calls I had to make—starting with Leo and Marie, the cops, the national guard, whoever.

First, I started toward Clenhburran, at a fast walk so as not to draw any attention, then a gentle jog, and, as soon as I was far enough away from the gas station, at an all-out sprint, churning my legs as fast as they could carry me.

For ten minutes, I managed to run at that pace, running faster than I'd run in the last ten years. I had to stop to catch my breath to keep from puking. The pills I'd taken at the hospital probably didn't help. Neither had the years of smoking a pack a day. I felt loathing for my soft and wimpy body as I tried to suck in as much oxygen as I could.

I looked back at the road. I could imagine the van flying down it any minute now. I started walking again, as fast as I could, a sort of desperate and exhausted march as my lungs tried to fill with air.

By the time I reached the first houses on the outskirts of Clenhburran, it started to rain. The neighborhood was deserted. I figured everyone was taking shelter over at Fagan's, with a pint and plenty of stories to last the night.

I hurried down the High Street but didn't run into anyone except a couple of kids who laughed at the way I panted and stumbled down the road. Judie's store was close, now, but none of the windows were lit up. I dashed around to the door that led to the hostel and pounded on it with my last bit of strength.

After a couple moments in which I caught my breath, I heard footsteps coming down the stairs.

Judie, I thought. *Thank God . . .*

But it wasn't Judie who opened the door but a big burly guy with an unkempt beard I thought I remembered seeing before.

"How can I help you, bud?"

I swallowed before I tried to speak.

"Where . . . is Judie?" My voice sounded stifled and hoarse, and it took the guy aback. He put his hands on his hips as if blocking the door.

"Judie?" the guy said, looking me up and down. "Who's asking?"

I wanted to yell at him, but I didn't have the strength.

"She's with my kids . . . please, tell her it's Peter."

Now, he seemed to get it.

"Oh, of course! You're the dad. They let you out of the hospital already? Judie thought you'd be there another couple of nights."

"They . . . they discharged me early," I replied.

"Oh, good, congrats. Well, Judie's not here. She went to go visit some friends of yours at the beach."

Hearing these words, I wanted the earth to open up and swallow me.

"What do you mean?"

"I think it's our fault," he continued, now a lot friendlier. "We showed up unannounced this afternoon. Since the hostel's usually empty, we didn't even call first, and Judie didn't want to leave us out in the cold."

I remembered where I knew the guy from. He was one of the musicians who used to play at Fagan's. It was this jerk's fault my kids were now in danger. Judie had taken them into the lion's den, on the night when everything was supposed to happen!

"Do you have a car? I need to borrow a car."

"We never drive when we come here," he said, winking and tipping back his hand as if drinking a beer. "But I can lend you a bike, if you want. Judie has a couple in the backyard."

I looked up and down the street. If I went over to Fagan's, somebody might be able to give me a ride . . . but how long would that take? The van hadn't come down the road yet, and I pictured the guys still sitting at the booth at Andy's calmly drinking coffee. Maybe they were killing time until it was darker. But I couldn't be sure.

"Yeah," I said, finally. "I'll take one of the bikes."

THE DARK PHANTOM continued to grow huge on the horizon. It loomed ever more black and fearsome. It was starting to come to a head, the storm taking shape and ready to unload on us.

As I pedaled the rusty bike, my legs felt old and tired. The storm winds had picked up even more and foiled my efforts to make quick headway. The rain grew stronger and stung my eyes, and the dim light made it harder to see the tortuous turns along the road.

I'd never traveled the stretch between Clenhburran and Bill's Peak on bike or foot, not even in good weather. I'd always driven, and since I never ran into anyone (with the exception of Leo and Marie), I'd always sped through this section in less than fifteen minutes. But tonight, this stretch of road seemed infinite. I'd been pedaling for fifteen or twenty minutes, and I still couldn't see the ocean.

I came to the first rise and passed a gnarled dead tree with branches like twisted claws. I stopped there for a moment to catch my breath. It felt like I was about a third of the way there. I looked back and saw the lights from Clenhburran diffused in the rain like watercolors. There were no cars coming up the road.

I tried the phone again. This time I didn't even get a recording. The screen showed zero bars.

C'mon, get back on the bike. There's no time to waste.

I went down a long slope and never let off the pedals. I remembered there was a curve at the bottom of the hill, and I got ready to turn. But the turn arrived before I could react. I guess I was going faster than I thought, or maybe I took it wrong. Either way, it was too late to brake when I felt the shoulder of the road sliding beneath my tires. I felt myself lose control as the bike skidded over rocks and finally jammed against some unseen obstacle. I went flying and landed hard against the spongy, wet earth, slamming my shoulder into the ground.

I heard a *crack* but didn't have enough breath even to yell in pain.

"Shit. Shit. Shit!" I yelled at the soggy and treacherous ground, while the rain soaked the parts of me that weren't already smeared in mud.

There was a terrible pain in my left shoulder. It wasn't broken, I didn't think, but I'm sure I'd dislocated it or something. I got up. The bike was lying on its side at the edge of the road. I picked it up with my right hand and guided it back onto the paved road. I got on, careful not to put any weight on my left hand, but when I tried to pedal, it was stuck.

I cursed every goddamn leprechaun in Ireland. I flipped the bike over and tried to see whether the chain had slipped off the gear, but something else must have been broken. It looked like something was wedged between the chain and the sprocket. A plate that was screwed in place was covering the rest.

I tried to rip off the cover but it was screwed tight, and I only managed to cut my fingers on the edge of the plastic. I kicked the shit out of the bike, left it lying in the road, and started down the path on foot.

Run, you bastard, even if it kills you.

But I couldn't run. I knew it. So I hobbled as fast as I could down the road. There was one more hill ahead and after that, a small decline that led down toward Bill's Peak. It'd take me another twenty minutes, but I'd get there.

The lightning, which had been flashing within the clouds in the distance, began to crash at last, still somewhere out at sea. Their brilliance illuminated the world below with each flash, casting long shadows on the ground. I dragged myself along in the rain like some desperate broken-winged insect.

It had been years since I last prayed. Years since I'd thought about God, at all. But in that moment, it was the only thing I could think to do. To ask the Almighty for forgiveness for having forgotten about Him and to ask Him one favor: that He might give me enough time to get to my kids.

Maybe God misunderstood my request. Or maybe He just has a sick sense of humor. It's all I can imagine after watching my own shadow form and stretch out in front of me. At first, I thought it was lightning overhead, but the shadow grew longer, and soon there was light all around. That's when I realized.

I turned around and saw the headlights of a vehicle fast approaching. It was too late to jump out of the way or to try to hide, so I just stood there, stock-still in the middle of the road, my hand shading my eyes from the oncoming car. It was all I could think to do: stand there and block the way.

As it reached me, I raised my hand and smiled. The van braked, and I could see it clearly now. As expected—as long-awaited—it was the red GMC.

SEVEN

I WALKED SLOWLY toward the van. I thought I'd stutter out of sheer panic if I found myself having to say anything. The driver's window rolled down. Behind it was the new guy, the character with the strong jaw I'd seen at the gas station. He was good-looking, like some kind of '60s movie star. Next to him was the woman, and for the first time, I got a good look at her face. Her black hair was picked up in a ponytail, and the dark eyes on her round, moonlike face were bright and cold.

"Thank God you came along," I said, my voice sounding worried. "I crashed my bike a ways back and . . ."

"Yeah, we saw it," the driver said, speaking with an American accent. "You left it right in the middle of the road. I almost ran the damn thing over."

"Oh, I'm really sorry," I said. "I was . . ."

Just then, without looking over, the woman said something in French. The driver nodded. Then he smiled, showing two rows of pearlescent teeth, and leaned on the windowsill.

"You live over on the beach?"

"Yeah. Why, you headed there?"

Stupid question. The road led in only one direction.

"We're on the way to visit some friends," he said. "Maybe you know them. Leo and Marie Kogan."

Yeah, I know them you evil son of a bitch. . . .

"Of course. They're my neighbors."

"Your neighbors! Wow, what a coincidence," the guy said. He glanced into his rearview mirror at the passengers in the back. "Randy, Tom, make room back there. Leo and Marie's neighbor is coming with us."

I heard the sliding door glide open.

"Hop on in. We'll save you a walk in this rain."

IN THE BACK was Randy, the John Lennon clone with the round sunglasses and the greasy, matted, long hair. He was sitting with his back to the driver. I sat across from him next to the stocky guy, Tom.

Nice to finally meet you, assholes.

Tom muttered something I couldn't make out as he made room for me, but I think it had to do with my appearance. Randy allowed a smile. "What happened to your bike, partner?" he asked.

His voice was low and raspy, like someone had snipped a couple of his vocal cords and replaced them with sandpaper. Like the driver, his accent was unmistakably American. His breath smelled like cigarettes.

"It skidded, and I fell," I said, my shoulder throbbing in pain. "Goddamn thing almost killed me. I'll come back for it later."

I noticed my voice was shaky from nerves, and my mouth had gone dry. I cleared my throat and tried to calm down. Tom and Randy smiled at each other.

"Sure. Later . . ." Tom said.

The joke lingered between them silently. I already knew what they were capable of.

I tried to focus. The van tore along the road and soon we were at Bill's Peak. What should I do? Jump at the driver? Gouge out his eyes and make him crash? I doubted it would work. Before I could pull it off, the fat guy would probably slit my throat with that knife (which I figured he was carrying under his Windbreaker). I scanned the inside of the van. It was too dark to see much. But I could see Tom and Randy's hands. Tom sat calmly with his hands in his lap. Randy cracked his knuckles in a nervous tick. No weapons in sight, but they couldn't be far away. Maybe if I got my hands on one of their guns. But how? I couldn't let them get to Leo and Marie's house. Judie and the kids were there. I had to think of something—and fast.

That's when I noticed Randy was staring at me. He had a small mouth full of small, pointy teeth.

"Got a smoke?"

"No, sorry," I said, reaching for my shirt pocket where I had the packet of gum I'd bought at Andy's. "Want some gum?"

"Just wait until we get there, Randy," the driver grumbled.

"Shut up, Frank," he said, and that's how I learned the driver's name.

"You live here year-round?" he asked me.

"Just for a couple months. I rent a house over the summer."

"Ha. Summer. You hear that, Tom? They call this summer in Europe."

Tom smirked and nodded that great big melon on his nearly nonexistent neck. The scumbags probably had already worked out what they were going to do. Maybe they'd even already decided to kill me.

"You guys American?" I asked. I wondered if I should make small talk, but it seemed like the most natural thing to do.

"Everyone except Manon," Randy said, nodding at the woman. "She's French. *Le France . . .*" he said, feigning a French accent. "We all used to work with Leo. At the hotel. He told you all about it, I'm sure."

"Oh, yeah. The hotel," I said.

"We were on vacation and thought we'd surprise him."

"Isn't that nice?"

"You here with your family on vacation?" Tom asked.

I smiled and coughed to give me a moment to think.

"Yeah. I've been coming here for years and know just about everyone in town. Actually, I'm having a big party at my place tonight. You all should come over. Tell Leo and Marie to come over, too."

"Oh, a party! Hear that, Manon?" he said, turning to the woman, who remained quietly looking ahead. "Maybe we can talk Leo and Marie into all of us going together. Do they live far from you?"

I watched the woman's face in the rearview mirror. She smiled coldly.

"No . . . not too far. And there are *loads* of people coming," I said. "You should come."

I thought it had been brilliant making up the story about the party and all the people I'd be expecting shortly. Maybe they'd call off their plan if they thought there would be too many people around. The lie emboldened me to keep lying. The fact Randy asked if I lived far from Leo and Marie made me realize they'd never been there. They didn't know the lay of the land, and that played in my favor. Not to mention there wasn't a single sign on the entire road.

We were reaching Bill's Peak when I cleared my throat and said, "When we get to the intersection, you can drop me off. I can walk from there."

"Oh, we couldn't do that," Frank said. "We'll drive you right to your door."

"Right," Randy added. "We wouldn't feel right sending you out in this weather. Any friend of Leo and Marie's is a friend of ours."

The three men laughed all at once. Manon, however, stayed silent in the front passenger seat. What was she thinking about?

They didn't look to be at all agitated. They were about to swoop on Leo and Marie like an eagle on its prey, and I guess they wanted to be sure about their surroundings. I thought maybe they'd already decided to come back for me after they'd taken care of Leo and Marie, to cover their tracks. Or perhaps they were going to kill me first.

Just then, I had an idea. It was risky, but it seemed like my only shot: I'd direct them straight to Leo and Marie's house instead. *With any luck, Leo will remember what I told him about the van and come out shooting. I'll be ready to duck on the floor of the van. Worst-case scenario, by the time they realize what's going on, the element of surprise will be gone. Leo has a radio. We'll just hole up in their house and wait for help to arrive.*

It was my only hope.

The van's headlights fell on the old tree at the foot of Bill's Peak, and I gulped. It was now or never. This night was going to end up in only one of two ways: with or without a bullet to the head. Right then, I could only think about giving Jip, Beatrice, Judie, and my friends a fighting chance to escape these monsters. I'd die content knowing I saved their lives.

"Take a right up here," I said as the van reached the crossroads. My voice was dead steady. The lie was out.

I noticed a silent tension among them.

"We'll drop you off at home, buddy," Frank said again. "Sure it's this way?"

"Yes," I said, trying to sound confident. "The Kogans' house is to the left, down that road. I live in the bigger house down to the right."

After a few seconds that felt like an eternity, Manon nodded at the driver, and he yanked the steering wheel to the right toward Leo and Marie's house.

Looked like they'd bought it. Now it was time to hold this poker face as long as I could.

THE STORM had reached the coast. Even at their fastest setting, the van's windshield wipers couldn't keep up with the pounding rain, as if we were inside a carwash. The scene was familiar to me by now. I'd been soaked by this rainstorm three times in my visions.

The van slowly descended the hill toward the house; there were lights on inside. I prayed that Leo wouldn't see the van pull up and come out to greet us. (Unless, of course, he came out firing.) Just then, I remembered the mailbox out in the yard and the name—albeit in small letters—that was printed on it: Kogan, not Harper.

"You can turn around right here," I said while we were still a few dozen yards from the house. "There's too much sand up by the house, and you're liable to get stuck with all this rain."

"You sure, man? You're going to get soaked."

"Yeah, I'm sure. It's a quick sprint to the house. It's just water, I won't melt."

Frank did as I said. He slowed down and swung the van around so that the sliding door faced the path toward the house. When he stopped, I reached for the handle, slid the door open and hopped out onto the sand.

"Thanks for everything!" I yelled over the blustering wind and rain. "You really saved my life!"

Frank rolled down his window, and his eyes lit up as he looked at the house. Next to him, Manon had lit a cigarette and the flame illuminated her soulless doll eyes.

"Nice house," Randy said, leaning up between the front seats and leering.

I didn't like the look of that smile.

"Thanks," I said, trying to hold his gaze. "Say hi to Leo and Marie for me. And tell them to bring you to the party later. It'll be fun."

Frank raised the window and turned the van back toward Bill's Peak.

I hurried to the house feeling like I couldn't breathe. As I reached the door, I glanced back and saw the van's taillights disappear around the bend. With my heart in my throat, I started pounding on the door with all my might.

"Leo! Marie! Open the door!"

The story was playing out yet again. A stormy night. Pounding on the front door. An unexpected visit in the night.

EIGHT

IT WAS LEO who finally came to the door. I didn't even wait for his reaction. I pushed my way into the house, tracking mud and rain-water onto their rug.

"Close it! Quick!" I said, wiping the water off my face.

Leo stood there in his jeans and checkered shirt looking stunned.

I scanned the room quickly, looking for the kids, Judie, and Marie. I'd expected to see them all sitting around the fireplace, playing Scrabble and drinking hot chocolate. But there was no one here.

"Where are my kids, Leo?"

My voice trembled. My whole body did. The panic I'd stifled in that van full of murderers finally came out. I wanted to cry, to scream, but first I needed to see my kids. To hug them and know they were all right.

"Pete!" Leo yelled. "What's going on? What are you doing here?"

Marie rushed in through the kitchen door, dressed in purple pajamas. I turned back to Leo. I spoke as fast as I could, my words running into one another.

"The kids, Leo. Where are they? There's no time. Are they here? We have to protect them."

"Relax, Pete. They're with Judie, and they're safe. What's happened? Did you check yourself out of the hospital?"

"Yeah. Yes . . . I . . . I saw the storm, and I thought this would be the night. And I was right. And then I stumbled across them at Andy's. . . . Leo, the people from my dream, they're here. The woman . . . the men . . . the van. They're here! I tried to get here first to warn you but I crashed the bike . . . and I ran into them on the way here. I managed to fool them. I told them this was my house, and they brought me here instead. I thought you'd all be together. Where are Judie and the kids? They weren't at the hostel. They told me over there that they were here with you."

Leo looked at Marie with an expression that could mean only one thing: *Run back in the kitchen and call the hospital.*

"Pete, listen," he said, trying to look calm. "You said someone drove you here in a van? I didn't see any headlights outside."

"No, Leo, this isn't a hallucination," I said, all of a sudden unsure myself. Is it possible Leo hadn't seen the headlights? But the girl at the gas station. She'd seen them. They were real. . . . "There are four killers outside, and when they realize I lied to them, they're going to come back here and kill us all. Tell me, where are the kids, Leo!"

Leo walked over to the window and looked outside. I joined him. Not a single light was visible outside, which was strange given how pitch black it was. We should at least be able to see the headlights of the van moving toward my house.

"Pete, why don't you have a seat," Leo said. "Let's talk a minute."

I backed away from him.

"Goddammit, Leo, I'm telling you the truth!" I yelled. "Where are the kids?"

Leo took on a blank expression.

"They're at your house, Pete," Marie said from the kitchen door. "They're with Judie. They went over to get some clothes to spend the night. They said they'd be right back."

It felt like someone had hit me in the chest with a sledgehammer. I put my hands on my head and replayed her words in my mind. I stood there stunned.

Home. They were at home. And I had sent the killers right to them. The van must be getting there right about now. The knife. That huge goddamn knife. Just as I had seen it in my visions. Right now, they were circling the house. About to go inside. Judie would have seen the headlights. Maybe she even went out to see who it was . . .

I ran for the phone in the kitchen, but tripped on the rug and fell hard before reaching the door, banging my injured shoulder. I moaned like a wounded animal.

"The phone," I told Marie, looking up from the floor. "We have to warn them."

From where I lay, I could only see her comfortable pearl-gray house slippers, but I knew she and Leo were giving one another a look. *Let's calm him down first, then we'll call the ambulance,* he'd surely mouthed to her.

"Marie. You have to believe me, please. They're here. Everything's going to happen tonight. Call my house, for God's sake. Please believe me!"

I leaned up on one elbow and saw her beautiful face filled with terror. And it wasn't just the shock of seeing me lying there, soaked in rain and sand, begging for my children's lives. It was something more. She was terrified at the possibility that I might be right.

"Please, Marie . . ."

She nodded, turned around and disappeared into the kitchen. I turned to Leo to ask him for his car keys, but he was already by the door, grabbing his brown leather bomber jacket.

THE LAST NIGHT AT TREMORE BEACH

"I'm going to take a look, God help me."

That's when it happened. The front door crashed open, the jackets and raincoats hanging by the entrance went flying. A cold wind gusted into the house like an angry dervish. For a second, we thought the hurricane force winds were to blame—that is, until Randy came through the door with a pistol.

Until that very moment, even I had doubts about my story. But there he was, crossing the threshold, gun pointed at Leo's head, while my friend backed up with his hands in the air. This was no hallucination.

Everything was happening too fast. I thought he was going to kill him right there. *That's it. It's over.* I cringed and waited for the gun to fire. Then it'd be my turn. And then Marie. End of story. But just as Randy had Leo backed up to the couch, he pistol-whipped him across the face, and Leo fell back onto the couch in a heap.

I was close to the kitchen door and started dragging myself backward toward it, until my back came to rest on the doorframe. Randy turned and pointed the gun at me.

"Hold it, you smart-ass son of a bitch," he said, in a gravelly whisper. His hair was wet and matted, and the superfluous sunglasses rested on the bridge of his nose.

I was frozen by the kitchen door when I heard the faintest sound, a door closing quietly in the other room. The kitchen was connected to the garage, whose side door led out toward the beach.

Of course, said a voice in my head which was surprisingly too calm. *This is when Marie runs down the beach toward your house. This is when she pounds at your door in the middle of the night. But you're not there to open it, Peter. The sequence is different now. It's changed.*

We were living a new version of the story. Would the outcome be different, too?

Tom appeared in the doorway behind Randy, his hair and clothes also soaked. From where I was, he looked like a human tank, made of flesh and bone. He strode across the room toward me and without saying a word, kicked me right in the stomach. I doubled over in the fetal position; it felt like my intestines had exploded.

"I hate the fucking rain," he said, putting his foot on top of my head. "These are expensive goddamn shoes, and now they're fucking ruined because of your sorry ass."

He pressed his foot against my head like a vise. I started throwing up as his weight came down on my skull with increasing force. I thought this was the end. My head was going to explode like a watermelon. But all of a sudden, the weight was gone.

He'd lifted his foot.

"Not just yet," he said.

I lay on the ground. Leo was passed out on the couch, blood dripping from his head. He might even be dead. Randy was talking on a cell phone.

"All clear here, Manon," he said. "Under control."

It wasn't long before the van's lights shone through the front window. It parked out front by the fence. There goes my plan, I thought. I didn't manage to keep the van at bay for long. *At least . . . Judie and the kids are safe.* There was still hope.

The woman came through the door. She stood in the doorway surveying the scene. I was on the floor, rocking with my hands on my stomach, trying desperately to breathe. The fat guy had nearly killed me with a single kick. Leo moaned and started to move on the couch. He was alive, after all. Randy had taken off his raincoat and sat by the front door. He could handle us both easily. He'd even put his pistol on the couch while he sifted through his pockets.

"Goddammit. I must have left them at the gas station. You got a cigarette on you, Tom?"

But Tom couldn't hear him. He was upstairs ransacking the house. You could hear furniture being tossed, glass breaking. He must have been looking for Marie.

Manon looked at Randy.

"Where's the woman?" she asked.

"I don't know," Randy said. "Tom's looking for her. Maybe this little punk here tipped her off. Tell you one thing, though. The old guy never saw it coming."

Manon turned and came toward me. I cowered and waited for another kick, or worse. She squatted next to me, grabbed me by the hair, and pulled it back so I was looking her right in the face. Our eyes locked.

"Nice try. Bet you thought you were pretty slick, huh, neighbor?"

She held something in front of my face. It was a GPS. I was staring at a detailed map of Tremore Beach. A red dot was pinned to Leo and Marie's house, to the right of Bill's Peak.

"You made all along," I said. "What were you waiting for?"

"You knew us in less than ten seconds. How?"

I opened my mouth to respond and noticed vomit dripping down my chin. I smiled.

"You wouldn't believe me if I told you."

She let go of my hair and let my head thud onto the floor. She stood up and called up to Tom.

The fat guy came thundering down the stairs a few seconds later.

"I looked everywhere. Nothing. I'll check the garage."

"Fuck," Manon hissed. She grabbed a device clipped to her belt and spoke into it. It wasn't a cell phone, but some kind of walkie-talkie.

"Frank . . . The woman's not here. Search the perimeter of the house. And watch your back."

She crouched back down over me. This time I watched her pull out a stiletto, the blade glinting between her fingers, and bring the point within inches of my eye.

"Tell me where the woman is—or I'll carve out your eyes, one by one."

"I don't know," I managed to say, even though the blade floated over my right eye.

"I'm going to gouge out your right eye, first. How's that sound? And then I'll make you eat it."

"I swear, I don't know! Leo was alone when I got here."

I felt the tip of the knife press beneath my right eye, and I closed them both. I felt the pressure increase. For a split second, I thought losing an eye wasn't so bad as long as she didn't touch my fingers. *They make glass eyes. I can still play the piano blind.*

"How did you know who we were?" she asked. I'd managed to stump them. I was glad. I smiled again. I felt another blow to my face, and my head rebounded off the floor.

Tom came back in from the garage saying he hadn't found anyone though someone might have been able to slip from the kitchen to the garage and out to the beach if they'd wanted to.

"Door's unlocked."

Manon stood up and walked to the couch.

"Wake up grandpa, here," she said, and then spoke into the walkie-talkie again. "Frank! The woman might be on the beach. Go take a look."

Looked like my eye surgery had been postponed. Tom grabbed me under my arms, picked up all two hundred pounds of me like he was lifting a carton of milk, and tossed me onto the couch.

Randy smacked Leo across the cheek. He was bleeding profusely out of a gash on one side of his face, but still he managed to open his eyes. With Leo awake, Randy sat back down, pulled his pistol out, and aimed it at us.

"Okay, Mr. Blanchard," Manon said, standing behind the couch. "Can you hear me?"

It took a moment for Leo's eyes to focus on her.

"My name is Leonard Kogan," he said. "You've got the wrong man."

"We know who you are, Leonard Blanchard. And you know why we're here. So let's stop playing games and wasting time, shall we? Where's your wife?"

"I'm telling you, you've got the wrong guy," Leo insisted. "My name is Kogan not Blanchard. You've made a terrible mistake. I'm just an American tourist. . . ."

Manon simply put her hand on Randy's shoulder.

"Right knee."

Before any of us could move, Randy aimed the gun and squeezed the trigger. A deafening *bang* rang out, and Leo lurched forward. He grabbed his right knee and fell forward on top of the coffee table. I rushed to grab him and laid him back on the couch. Leo was clenching his teeth so hard I thought he'd crack a molar.

"Let's see if we understand one another now, Mr. Blanchard," Manon said. "We can end this quickly."

A torrent of blood spurted from between Leo's fingers and soaked his pant leg.

"Goddamn bitch," Leo said through gritted teeth. "Marie is visiting a friend in London and won't be back for a week. You've wasted a trip."

"He's lying," Randy said. "Other knee?"

"Wait," Manon said. "We don't want him to bleed out. What do you say, Tom?"

"The woman was here. I'm sure of it. Maybe this other guy warned her. Or maybe she ran when she heard us come in."

Manon grabbed her walkie-talkie. You could hear the roar of the wind on the other end.

"Frank?"

"Nothing yet," he said, the storm howling behind him. "I'll keep heading down the beach."

I watched Manon's eyes scan the room and land on me.

"All right, friend. We really don't have to kill you. But we will if you don't tell us what we need to know. Where's the woman?"

"I don't know," I said. "I haven't seen her. I swear. Leo must be telling the truth."

Randy pointed the gun at my head. He was leisurely leaning back on the couch with his legs crossed like a gentleman and the pistol held casually, like a glass of wine. He was itching to kill me.

"Waste him?" he asked Manon.

Manon didn't seem in such a rush to see more blood run. Instead, she spoke into the walkie-talkie again. Frank had walked around the entire house and found nothing.

Randy brought the pistol sights up and aimed at my head.

"What do you say, Manon?"

"No, not yet," she said. "Let's see who's hiding in the other house. Maybe he really does have a family, and he is throwing a party." She fixed her cold, malevolent eyes on mine. I couldn't stop my eyes, my face, from flinching. Manon read me immediately. "Yes, I think there is some truth to this story. And maybe he won't be quite as brave after he sees what we do to his loved ones. We'll drag them over here and play with them awhile, until he tells us where Marie is."

"No!" Leo yelled.

I was so terrified, so desperate, I couldn't keep my mouth shut.

"You're screwed. We already called the cops over the radio. They'll be here any minute," I said.

"Not a chance. You didn't have time," Randy said.

But Manon just stood quietly, mulling over that scenario. She still seemed worried about how quickly I'd figured them out. If one of us had gotten to a cell phone, the cops would be on their way as we spoke.

"Tom, find the radio."

"It's upstairs, but it's off," he said. "There's no way they had time to . . ."

"I'll decide that!" she yelled. "Go upstairs and search the place again. See if someone might have slipped out an open window. And trash the fucking radio while you're at it."

Tom ran up the stairs. Meanwhile, Manon started talking over the plan with Randy right in front of us—I figured we were dead men right then and there. They had to move fast, she said. Randy would stay behind and watch us while Frank acted as the lookout with his walkie-talkie on. She and Tom would drive over to the house to have a look. She doubted there was any party planned, but they had to be careful. Maybe Marie had made it over there by now.

In a way, I was thinking the same thing they were: Could a sixty-five-year-old woman have run two miles across the beach in this driving wind and rain in less than fifteen minutes? I doubted it. But if she had managed to (and I prayed she had), Judie and the kids still had a chance.

Tom and Manon went out, leaving Randy and Frank standing guard. We heard the van start up and watched the lights pull away. The engine soon faded into the distance. I pictured the van headed toward Bill's Peak and racing at full throttle toward my house. The sequence hadn't changed so much after all.

RANDY SAT across from us, the pistol in his hand resting on his lap. Leo, lying next to me, writhed in pain. The blood wasn't gushing anymore, but now he was shaking. His teeth chattered.

"I have to tie a tourniquet or I'll bleed to death."

"Shut up!" Randy screamed.

"He's right," I said.

"Both of you, shut the fuck up," he said pointing the gun at us.

"What the hell's going on in there?" I heard Frank say from the other side of the door.

"The old man's bleeding out," Randy yelled back.

"Well do something, for Chrissake."

Randy rolled his eyes at me and gestured with the gun.

"Go ahead, do what you have to do. But don't fucking move from that couch."

"But how am I supposed to . . . ?" I started to ask.

"Use your shirt, Pete," Leo said, his voice sounding rushed. "Take it off and use one of the sleeves to tie off my leg. It should work."

Randy got up and walked toward the door, the gun still trained on us. He said something to Frank, who was on the porch, smoking a cigarette.

"Shit, man. Can't you wait until we're done here?" I heard Frank tell him.

I tore off my shirt and was about start tying off Leo's thigh. But he waved me off with his hands.

"I'll do it," he said. "You hold the pillows."

It didn't make sense to me, at first, but then I saw the look in Leo's eyes and knew he had something else in mind. I wrapped one of the throw pillows around his leg and held it in place while he started to tie the tourniquet. Our faces were nearly next to other's, and Randy was out of earshot, while Frank fished for a cigarette and matches from his jacket pocket.

"I've got a revolver," Leo whispered while he tied the tourniquet. "It's strapped to my right ankle, in a holster. Grab it. He can't see you from where he is. It's our only chance."

I looked at him in shock. *You didn't write me off, after all, you stubborn old goat.*

Randy was still by the door. It was hard to hear anything over the wind and the crash of the ocean. Plus, he probably figured he had nothing to worry about from some sixty-something-year-old man with a gunshot wound in one leg and a skinny, pale forty-year-old.

I was leaning slightly toward Leo, holding the pillow, and Randy was standing at such an angle where he couldn't see my hands. I reached one hand slowly down Leo's right leg, feeling for something beneath the hem of his pants. I finally felt a lump by his ankle.

"Hurry up!" he whispered.

In one quick motion, I lifted the cuff of his pant leg and felt the revolver, felt the texture of the gun's grip between my fingers. I grabbed it the very moment Randy walked back over to us. I looked up at Leo, and he looked back down at me without being able to say a word. *What should I do? Turn and shoot right now?*

But I didn't. I could feel the barrel of Randy's gun trained on us. He'd be a hundred times faster on the trigger than I would be. So instead, I tucked the gun under one of the couch cushions between Leo's legs. Leo just stared at me. One slip of my finger, and I might have accidentally shot his balls off.

As Randy sat back down, Leo quickly and slyly shook his pant leg to cover the holster strapped to his ankle.

"How's it look?" Randy asked as he blew out a puff a smoke, suddenly a picture of easygoing relaxation.

"Good," I said. "It should hold."

Randy jammed the cigarette into one corner of his mouth, threw his feet up onto a side table, and grabbed one of the picture frames that sat on it.

He whistled.

"So this is Mrs. Blanchard, huh? She looks pretty damn good in this picture," he said, flicking his ashes onto the carpet. "Although she's probably got another forty years on her by now, right? Either way, that's a beautiful woman. Maybe I can get a little alone time with her."

"You piece of shit," Leo spat.

"Hey, don't get all bent out of shape. We'll let her decide. Maybe when I put this gun in her ear, she'll feel better about going down and giving me a little satisfaction. What about you, neighbor friend? Got any hot little daughters?"

"You're a dead man, Randy," I spat. "I swear to God, you're going to die tonight."

I glanced at Leo and realized that with Randy sitting directly across from us, there was no way he was going to be able to get to his gun—unless we distracted him somehow. There had to be a way. . . .

"That's a nice fairy tale ending," he said. "Good conclusion to a novel. But the only ones who are going to die here tonight—slowly and painfully—are you two. And I guarantee you before it's all said and done, I'm gonna have a nice time with your wives and daughters. Frank, too. Isn't that right, Frank?" he called out, taking the cigarette out of his mouth and giving a dirty cackle.

Frank didn't answer.

"You and your wife shouldn't have done what you did. Now you're going to pay, Blanchard. And so is your neighbor's family."

"What the hell is he talking about, Leo?" I said, giving him an icy stare. "What did you do?"

Leo glanced at me, eyebrows raised.

"Oh, you didn't tell your neighbor, did you?" Randy said. "Your friends here probably spun you a nice little tale. Made themselves out to be a sweet little old couple. But they're just thieves. I'm going to love putting a hole in their heads."

"Shut up, you fucking snake. . . ." Leo hissed.

"No, I want to hear this!" I yelled. "About time I knew what the hell is going on. You put my whole family in danger. Right now, they're probably about to . . ."

"Better you don't stick your nose where it doesn't belong," Leo bit back. "This is none of your business, Peter."

Leo had figured out my plan. Or maybe he didn't; maybe he was totally serious. Either way, it was just the distraction we needed.

"None of my business, you old fuck?" I shouted. "You gave me this whole story about how you were a retired hotel security officer, and now we're all dead because of you!" I yelled.

Randy delighted in watching us argue.

"Shut your filthy mouth, or I'll shut it for you," Leo said.

"Oh, yeah?" I yelled back.

I lunged at him. I knew it might hurt his injured knee, but I tried not to land on it as I grabbed him by the shirt, standing right between him and Randy. He hollered in real pain. I could hear Randy laughing behind me but soon he half-heartedly said to get off of Leo. We heard Frank yell from outside, too. I watched as Leo slipped his hand between the cushions, grabbed the gun, and aimed it where my stomach was. This was the moment. I dropped to the floor and heard a terrible explosion over my head followed by a muffled cry of pain.

For the next few seconds, I lay pinned to the floor. There were two more shots. I heard glass shatter. Only later would I learn it was the window that overlooked the front yard.

I saw Randy's feet under the coffee table, saw them crumple underneath him as he rolled off the couch and then landed on the floor next to me, his round glasses slipping off to reveal his now-lifeless eyes, the burning cigarette falling from his lips.

"Peter . . ." I heard behind me.

It was Leo. He was lying on the floor, too.

"Did you get the other guy?"

"I think so, but I'm not sure. I saw him go down, but he got a shot off. He might be alive. Look, I can't move. You're going to have to check," he whispered, handing me the revolver.

With the cold metal in my hands, I felt an immediate rush of power. If I'd had my way, I'd much rather stay cowering between those two couches. But right about now, Judie and my kids would be getting an unwelcome visit from Manon and the fat guy. It might even be too late. But if God saw fit to give us this one chance, I had to make the most of it—and fast.

I eased my head up with the gun pointed out in front of me. Frank wasn't out there. At least, I couldn't see him from where I was. The front door was open, and you could see only part of the porch, and beyond that, sheets of falling rain. Where was he?

He might be hiding against the outside wall. There was no way to get to him, unless these bullets could fire through the wall. I lay there for another couple seconds, thinking: There was no time to waste; my kids' lives were in danger. Maybe in a rush of adrenaline—or a suicidal lack of self-awareness—I hopped up and ran toward the door in one motion. I blindly poked the barrel of the gun around the edge of the door and fired twice. It filled the night with smoke and the smell of gunpowder. I peeked out the door. There was no one there.

"Look out, Pete!" Leo yelled.

I turned around and saw Frank stumbling in through the kitchen door. He must have looped around to catch us by surprise. He fired at Leo, who had started to pick himself up off the floor, and hit him. Leo fell behind the couch with a thud. I fired back at the same time, pulling the trigger three times, although only two bullets fired. The gun was out of ammunition.

But I got lucky. From the fresh wound in Frank's neck, dark blood sprayed the doorframe and across the pink living room wall. Frank managed to stand another couple of seconds before keeling over and landing heavily by the kitchen door, his gun tumbling to the ground.

I ran over and picked it up. Frank was trembling and twitching like a toy whose batteries were about to run out. Blood was pooling on the floor beneath him. He stared right at me. I thought about pulling the trigger again and putting him out of his misery, but I couldn't do it. I turned to Leo. Frank had managed to shoot him in one arm and he winced as he held it.

"Leo!"

"You've got to get out of here. The keys to my car are in my jacket. Run! I'll call the police."

I didn't think twice. Leo's jacket was by the door, and the keys were inside, like he'd said. I ran outside and remembered their car in the garage. I looked down and noticed Frank's walkie-talkie lying on the ground by the door. *Had he had time to tip off Manon?*

I opened the garage and hopped in Leo's four-by-four. I started it up and shot out of there into the stormy night.

NINE

AT THE WHEEL of Leo's SUV, I felt a stab in my abdomen, as if someone had stuck me with a switchblade. I didn't know it then, but Tom had cracked one of my ribs when he kicked me. My shoulder was still pulsating, and I felt dizzy from that fat bastard nearly crushing my head under his foot. But none of it mattered. Not even the fact I'd just killed a man. Maybe some might have reservations about what I did. But not me. It was something that had to be done. I replayed it all: the recoil in my hands, the violent gunshot ringing in my ears, the sight of his body falling to the floor in a heap. *Better you than me, Frank.*

No, the only thing that mattered now was getting to my house in time.

The storm seemed to be reaching its peak. This mother of all storms had come ashore, a titanic thunderhead that seemed miles high and wide. Within its crevices, lightning snaked and crashed into the ocean below and nearby cliffs. The sea roiled beneath it, punished by the devastating wind and rain.

Amid all this, the Land Rover belonging to Leo Kogan—or Leo Blanchard—came barreling over Bill's Peak, took flight, and crashed back down as I kept speeding ahead. At this speed, in the Land Rover's four thousand pounds of steel, I'd have killed anyone that accidentally crossed my path. An unfortunate human being would burst like so many water balloons. Any car coming the other way would turn us both into one mangled block of twisted metal. But none of that crossed my mind at the time, as I kept the steering wheel trained on the road and my foot on the pedal. Still, I couldn't help wishing this was a hallucination, that I'd find the house safe and sound when I got there. That it was just another goddamn trick of the mind. Even if it meant I was crazy after all.

He escaped from the hospital, stole his neighbor's car, and plowed it into a tree. Thank God, his kids are safe. So whatever happened to Peter? Oh, he's living out his days in a nice place surrounded by nurses and beautiful gardens.

As for my head? The pain started again as I rounded Bill's Peak. My old friend was back. I felt the painful pulsing deep in the center of my skull. *Ticktock.* Stronger and stronger.

I was tempted to close my eyes and take my hands off the wheel to rub my temples and scream out in pain. The pain was no longer content in being a dagger deep in my cerebral cortex, no. It grew like it never had before. It blossomed like a flower, like a great white shark opening its maw to devour everything inside my skull.

It bit down.

And just at that moment, I again felt that blinding light envelop me, like another bolt of lightning. Everything blanched to white for a few precious seconds as the pain reached its climax, as if some mad scientist had turned the dial of an electroshock up to the max and kept it there to see how long it would take my head to explode like an egg in a microwave.

I clenched my teeth so hard I thought they'd shatter like glass. But somehow, I managed to hold on to the steering wheel and keep my eyes open—and that's how I finally saw what I saw, like a movie playing out in front of my eyes. It took less than a second for this new vision to unfold in my mind.

Judie and the kids had lingered. They had packed their backpacks with pajamas, towels, and toothbrushes, but now they were in the living room because Beatrice wanted to play something on the piano for Judie. They liked being with one another. Even though they were worried about Dad, it was a comfort to have Judie to care for them. Judie was sweet, pretty, clever. They wanted Judie to be Dad's girlfriend. Judie would be like a big sister to them.

They really had to get going, Judie told them, patiently, as Beatrice fooled around at the piano. But then they heard a noise and saw lights flood in through the living room window. Judie went to take a peek while Beatrice ran to open the front door. Maybe it was Daddy coming home.

But Jip, who stood frozen with his backpack on, yelled out.

"No! Don't open the door! We have to hide!"

It was then that Judie noticed the van turning up the drive—its shape, its particular color, its chromed rims—and felt chills race up her spine.

"C'mon! Out the back door! Quickly!"

The children ran into the kitchen but as Judie opened the back door, she stopped dead in her tracks. Why?

A rumble overhead. The ground shook. Thunder.

My mind snapped back in an instant. I was back in Leo's car. The movie had ended abruptly, and I was back to seeing the world through the rain-covered windshield when I noticed the headlights racing over sandy dunes—and I realized I was driving toward the edge of the ravine.

I slammed on the brakes, but the SUV skidded along the gravel shoulder. The SUV slid and went over the edge. My face crashed into the steering wheel, and I nearly lost a couple of teeth as the truck went down the steep, sandy face of the cliff. I tried to control the SUV but felt two wheels leave the ground, and the truck tipped and tumbled on its right side. I crashed into the door, and my head smashed against the window as the vehicle came to rest on its side, down on the beach, as the rain continued to pour down from above.

It felt like waking from a deep sleep, but maybe I lost consciousness for only a few seconds. Either way, when I came to, the smell of gasoline was everywhere. I was terrified. I thought the SUV was going to blow (Isn't that what happened in the movies?) or at least catch fire.

I stirred and hauled myself across the passenger seat toward the door, which was now a hatch on the roof of this tin can. It unlocked without a problem, and I was able to push myself halfway out of the SUV. Then I remembered Frank's gun. I dropped back down and started to rifle around in the dark for it. It must have gotten wedged under the seat or something. But there was no way to tell in that total darkness. *I have to find it. I have to.*

No luck. The inside of the wrecked truck was pitch black, and the smell of gasoline was only getting stronger. There was nothing to do but get out fast before this thing blew to high hell.

I hopped out and landed on the sand, and if there was a single body part left that didn't hurt, I didn't know what it was. I realized now that everything was repeating itself in a way. Again, I was at the bottom of a ravine after a tumble. All of the events from real life and my visions started to jumble together until they created a new reality.

There was no time to lose. I bolted toward the house.

))))))

IT TOOK five minutes for me to stagger to the house. The front facade was illuminated by the van's headlights. I crouched down and made my way toward it behind the dunes, just as I'd done in my vision. But this time, I couldn't hear any conversations. Instead, I saw a light on in the living room. I couldn't see anyone inside. I came up alongside the wooden stairs, walking on the sandy dune instead of the creaky steps.

When I'd reached the top, I hid behind one of the big pots by the patio, and I could see inside a little better.

Judie was sitting on the couch, her hands tied and a trail of blood streaming down her head. Manon was standing in front of her. She looked like she'd tired of hitting her. Judie's face was swollen and one of her eyebrows was split open. She sat stock-still, neither crying nor pleading.

Manon was speaking into the walkie-talkie—or at least she was trying to. She pulled it away from her mouth and looked at it, as if it weren't functioning. I figured she was trying to reach Frank. She yelled something at Judie, but Judie just shook her head. Manon reached back with the hand holding the walkie-talkie and smashed Judie in the face. She fell over sideways on the couch.

I felt a sudden urge to run and jump through the window and strangle that goddamn bitch. And then I remembered: the shed. There was an ax in the shed.

There was no sign of the burly guy. No sign of my kids or Marie, either. I crouched down and slithered across the sand like an awkward iguana until I was out of sight of the living room. I couldn't stop wondering where Jip and Beatrice were, and my fear became terror because I also couldn't account for that fat bastard, Tom.

I snuck around to the shed and watched the house from my new hiding place. There was a light on in the kids' room. Were they up there? Was Tom with them? Was that son of a bitch having his way with my daughter? The thought was so sickening my mind simply shut it down.

I slipped inside the shed and found the ax. It was small, used to cut firewood, but it was big enough to split a grown man's head in two. With the ax in hand, I went out into the yard and headed toward the kitchen door. But just then, I noticed a shadow flicker nearby, like a spider creeping around the corner of the house.

Amid the rain and shadows, the only thing I could make out was Tom's gleaming knife—coming down toward my unsuspecting throat. I raised my hand instinctively and blocked the knife with my ax handle. That's when I first saw his face. A wide, toothy smile and dead eyes, like a monster.

He was too strong, and I swung the ax around and stepped back to give myself some room. Tom could have called to alert Manon, but he didn't. Instead, he grinned in the silence between us and waved his knife in the air, cutting glimmering figure eights into the night.

"So, you want to fight?" he whispered, moving to my right.

I turned, mirroring his movements. Like the earth and moon. Two bodies in perfect orbit. I thought about something I'd heard or read or seen on television about knife fights: *Rule No. 1, never try to grab the knife hand. Rule No. 2, use a counterattack. Rule No. 3, you won't last long if you just play defense.*

Tom's knife was like a charmed cobra, dancing and hypnotic. This guy was faster than he looked. He zigzagged in short bursts, and I tried to match his movements.

"You've got no shot. Not a shred of a chance," he said. "Just let go. It'll be quick and painless."

"That's the same thing Frank and Randy said," I told him. "They're dead now."

I thought that would intimidate him a bit, but it didn't seem to register at all. He continued wearing that Cheshire cat grin.

"You're lying," he said, advancing toward me. I realized he was trying to back me into the wall.

I sidestepped and swung the ax at head level.

I thought about counterattacking when he lunged, but in near darkness, under a driving rainstorm and with my body bruised and battered, I imagined that gleaming blade eventually sheathed in my liver, kidney, or lung. Tom wouldn't stop smiling.

"Stop struggling, man. You know how this is going to end. You're no match for me. What are you, a lawyer? An engineer? You're not a fighter. Look at your dainty little schoolgirl hands."

He lunged in my direction, and I sprang back. Tom skillfully whipped the knife in the air, and I so clumsily swung the ax down that I nearly drove it into my knee. Tom attacked again, and this time, the tip of his knife drew a hairline across my right cheek. I felt warm blood run down my face.

We'd drifted away from the house and were at the farthest reaches of the backyard, away from the beach. He was trying to corner me against another wall, I realized, the cliff face behind me. Each time I tried to move away, he shepherded me straight back with a swing of his knife. Once he had me backed against the cliff face, it'd be easy to filet me. There was no place left to hide from that eager knife.

As I backed up, my foot bumped against something. It was the septic tank drain cover. It was still sticking out of the ground. I'd made a mental note to fix it, Now I'm glad I forgot. *Looks like the little schoolgirl has a shot, after all.*

I carefully paced backward, like a cat walking along the edge of a fence, until I was standing right on top of the septic tank drain. Tom was focused on my hands and hadn't noticed the dip just ahead of him. I raised the ax to keep his attention up by my hands. And just then, his left foot dropped into the hole. It wasn't more than a seven or eight inch drop, but it was enough. He lost his balance, looked down instinctively, and gave me just enough time to drive the ax down into his head. There was a loud *crack*, a strange moan. And Tom fell to the ground like a rag doll, the ax wedged into his skull. Tom was dead, and I had won a fight I had no right to win.

SUDDENLY, everything went completely silent. Yes, it was still raining and the wind blew in from the ocean and battered the house. Bolts of lightning flashed in the swirling clouds overhead. But for some reason, it felt like the rest of the world had gone perfectly still. And that every step I took resonated for miles around.

I reached for the kitchen door and noticed my hands. To say they were trembling was an understatement. I was barely able to hold on to the doorknob. My legs were shaking, too. I'd killed two men that night, after all. I guess I wasn't doing so bad, all things considered.

I carefully opened the kitchen door remembering the last vision I'd had in this place. But when I stepped inside, the kitchen was empty. There were no children sitting at the table with their hands tied, executed, and my fear subsided a bit. *Thank God*, I muttered.

I opened a kitchen drawer, holding my wrist with my other hand to keep it steady, and drew out a knife as quietly as I could. I didn't grab the big chef's knife, but a sharp, smaller one I could wield dexterously. The same one I'd used a few days back to slice tomatoes while I kissed Judie. I held it tightly in my hand. That night I'd killed with a gun, an ax . . . I guessed it was time to try out a knife.

"Tom?" Manon called from the living room. "Is that you?"

The kitchen and hallway were dark. I steadied myself against the refrigerator and waited. If Manon came through that door, Id grab her by the neck and drive the knife into her kidneys.

"Tom . . . ?" she said again, and then she sighed, almost with a cackle of laughter. "Ah, I see. You're not Tom, are you?"

Two explosions rang out, and the refrigerator door caved in, right by my face. I fell flat on my ass and dragged myself to one corner of the kitchen. I thought this was finally the end, that Manon would come through that door and shoot me where I sat, like a rat. But she didn't come in.

"Who is it? Blanchard? The neighbor? Jesus, Frank and Randy. What a couple of worthless shitheads."

"The cops are on their way!" I yelled. "You're through!"

Manon's response was another blind gunshot through the kitchen door that ricocheted through the kitchen window.

"I have the woman," she said. "And we're leaving together right now. If either of you two even puts his head through that door, I'll kill her."

For some reason, she wouldn't come into the kitchen. From the way she spoke in plurals, she must have thought Leo and I were both here. It stood to reason we had Frank and Randy's guns, too.

I heard a scream—*Judie!*—and Manon ordering her to move. There were footsteps, and then I heard the sliding glass door open. They were going outside. I was just about to slip out the back door, hoping to ambush her while she tried to load Judie into the van, but then I heard a scream, and then another. Someone spit out an insult. I jumped up and hurried down the hall into the living room. There, in the doorway to the patio, three women were tussling: Judie, Manon, and Marie, who'd come out of nowhere.

It turned out that Marie had run down the beach and arrived just ahead of Tom and Manon. She'd hidden in the yard and had watched

THE LAST NIGHT AT TREMORE BEACH

me arrive, but hadn't dared move. She was scared out of her mind. At the sound of the two gunshots, she'd inched closer to the house and run into Manon, trying to escape with Judie. She grabbed Manon by the throat just as I came running into the living room.

I watched as it all unfolded. Manon had let Judie go when Marie grabbed the hand holding the gun. The gun was pointed toward the ceiling, and Marie fought to hold it that way with both her hands. But Manon started punching Marie in the stomach with her free hand. Judie fell to her knees and tried to bear hug Manon to keep her from hitting Marie. But Manon kicked her away, wriggled her gun hand free, and pulled the trigger.

Manon fired right into Marie's chest, whose body shuddered with the gunshot. Her purple pajamas were instantly soaked dark red. Marie stayed on her feet for a brief moment before collapsing into the grass on the patio.

"Marie!" I yelled.

I rushed Manon and felt her body slam against the doorjamb. Still, she managed to squeeze off a shot that disappeared into the night. I grabbed her hands and then felt how strong she was. I managed to grab her gun hand, but with the other, she punched me in the throat. I choked. I instinctively reached for my throat and doubled over as she punched me on the side of the head.

Before I knew it, that bitch had gotten the better of me. She kneed me a couple of times as I dropped to the ground, and she landed on top of my stomach.

We looked each other in the eye. She had blood running down one side of her forehead. Her hair was disheveled. Her dark eyes were furious.

"Say goodnight, you son of a bitch."

I watched the gun barrel come down toward my face, and I turned my head, waiting for the shot through the eye that had

*ended my life in my vision. Peter Harper was found lying dead with
a hole in his skull inside his lovely beach cottage on Tremore Beach.*
Dad would open the newspaper tomorrow and see essentially the
same image I'd seen in my vision. Bodies wrapped in white coro-
ner's blankets, police standing guard. He'd start drinking and smoking again. He wouldn't live long after that. Maybe he'd even find the
resolve to throw himself in front of a train and end it all.

Everything from my visions had come true. The storm. Marie
running down the beach. The broken fence. The killers and their
van. Tom's knife. The tumble by the cliff. The shed. Would my own
death be next?

"How's this, you stupid bitch!" I heard a voice say.

It was Judie. She'd gotten to her feet, grabbed the fireplace poker,
and swung. Manon only had enough time to gasp. She swung
through and bashed Manon with all her might. Manon's face exploded in a burst of blood and bone, and she slumped to the ground
in a heap.

I crawled to my feet and clasped Judie to me. Her body was
shaking. She couldn't stop staring at Manon.

"Did I kill her?" she sobbed.

"I hope so."

Marie was lying prone on the ground with her lips parted, her
eyes open.

Judie ran to call an ambulance, though in the distance, despite
the storm wind, you could already hear sirens wailing.

TEN

AFTER TRAVELING through Turkey's Central Anatolia Region for two days, Clem finally got back into cell phone range and found back-to-back messages on her phone. In the first message, an attaché from the Dutch embassy in Ireland asked her to call as soon as possible; that was the night I'd passed out at home and ended up in the hospital. The second message was from me. It said: "You have to come to Donegal right away. Something terrible has happened."

She and Niels hopped breathlessly on a flight from Istanbul to London to Derry and arrived in Dungloe the next day at about four in the afternoon. Despite my phone calls since—one for every time she changed planes—and the embassy representative who met her at the airport and tried to calm her, Clem arrived white as a ghost.

My father had arrived a few hours earlier. He paid for the most expensive cab ride of his life from Dublin (at least something made him finally leave his house on Liberty Street) and arrived in Dungloe that morning. By that time, dozens of reporters, police officers, and curious onlookers filled the hospital corridors, and my father worried what he might find. When he'd determined his son and grandchildren were safe, he became "the Chief" again and took control of the situation. He took care of the children, spoke to the police and reporters and kept everyone else at bay. When Clem finally arrived, he was the one who gave her an explanation of sorts: "Some men tried to rob Peter's house and there was a shoot-out. But the children slipped out to the beach and hid behind the rocks. They missed the whole thing. They've caught a bit of a chill and a couple of scrapes, but they're fine."

Clem descended on the kids. She hugged them for a long time, examined every inch of them, and showered them in kisses. Only then did it actually hit her that she was in Ireland.

"Jip was the one who told us we had to run, and Judie understood right away. She told us to run out the back door," Beatrice told her mother, as my father and a stupefied Niels looked on. "Jip led the way. He said we had to run toward the rocks and hide in these tiny caves. We stayed there for a long time, and then we heard gunshots. I started to cry. I thought they'd killed Judie, but Jip wouldn't let me leave the cave. Eventually, we saw someone coming for us. It was Dad."

Clem and Niels were tanned from their vacation, but their faces showed the wear of not having slept much the last two days. In a way, I was glad to see them. And I'm glad Niels didn't wait outside the room. Instead, he came in, shook my hand, and asked me how I was doing. I told him I was okay. The last time I saw him, I'd busted his lip. This time, I was the one with the busted lip and broken ribs. When I said it out loud, the three of us laughed.

"I'm still not clear on what happened. The police haven't explained much at all to us. Just that there was a shooting at your neighbor's house, and some men tried to rob the place. Some television reporter was saying there was a shoot-out and your neighbors were hurt. . . ."

Everyone wanted the story. But the real story was hard to explain. Besides, I was still coming to grips with what had happened myself.

Did anyone know anything about Leo and Marie? The last thing I remember in those dizzying minutes after the police and ambulance arrived was Judie applying pressure to Marie's wounds while I rushed out to find the children on the beach. I returned in time to see both loaded into ambulances. Marie was in bad shape. She was as pale as the moon and had an oxygen mask over her face. Before any of us could say anything, the ambulance sped off. In the distance, over the rise on Bill's Peak, I saw another set of ambulances headed toward Leo's house. I'd left him lying on the floor of his living room with two gunshot wounds. Now, no one could tell me whether he was alive or dead.

My dad asked around, but when he came back to the room he informed me that my neighbors were no longer in Dungloe. "They've been taken someplace else. I'm not sure where or why."

More unanswered questions.

"They said you'd been taken to the hospital the day before, that you'd had some kind of nervous breakdown and you left without telling anyone. Is that true?"

That part of the story was especially interesting to the detectives. "Tell us exactly how you ended up in town since you were supposed to spend the night in the hospital for observation."

I didn't lie. I told them I left because I'd gotten a bad feeling that something was about to happen to my family. I told them every detail about my trip from Dungloe to Clenhburran, including the part about the young man and his grandmother who gave me a ride. I told them about my stops at Andy's and at Judie's boarding house, where I borrowed a bike. I told them every verifiable detail, including where I had fallen off the bike, and the criminals had picked me up on the side of the road. How they'd immediately raised my suspicions and, how, luckily, I'd been able to warn Leo and Marie in time. The detectives wrote everything down but kept giving each other sideways glances. "Tell me more about this 'bad feeling' you got."

I saw them talking later with Dr. Ryan and John Levey, the hospital psychiatrist. Both doctors were shaking their heads. I couldn't hear them, but I could make out the gist of the conversation: There was no reason to suspect I'd done anything wrong, but the story didn't completely add up.

Maybe that's why there were two officers posted at my hospital door until late that day. They finally let Judie in, and we were together in the room, along with my dad and Niels. Clem had taken the kids for some fresh air after they gave their statements to the police. She, Niels, and my dad had thanked Judie endlessly for the brave way she whisked the kids out of harm's way but stayed behind to risk her life and face the criminals. But everyone kept asking her the same thing: How did you know they were coming to hurt you? How *could* you know?

"I just . . . got a bad feeling," she said, squeezing my hand. "Besides, we've been hearing a lot of things about robberies lately. They recently ransacked a house near Fortown while the owners slept. Things like that. I just saw that van and something told me there was danger."

"Well," my father said, "thank God for that instinct, Ms. Gallagher."

THE DETECTIVES bought the story. Maybe it was Judie, with her bandaged, angelic face who finally convinced them.

I later learned that doctors Ryan, Levey, and Kauffman issued a joint statement about my so-called "premonitions." They called my visions a "fortunate" coincidence "that was, naturally, completely disconnected from reality." The report also mentioned my visit to the Dungloe police station and the interview with Sgt. Ciara Douglas, who corroborated my testimony: "He was genuinely concerned about the safety of his home. He seemed a little paranoid to me. But maybe that's what helped him survive."

"It's an isolated incident," a neighbor told Ireland's RTE television. "Nothing like this had ever happened here before. Although there's talk of a gang of Eastern Europeans. What I do know is it's not some B.S. story made up by the alarm companies. It's a real threat, apparently, and our small, isolated communities need to be better protected. Or our residents have to be ready to defend themselves the way Mr. Harper did. You want my opinion? I'm glad he did what he did. Four fewer scumbags in the world."

In the evening, other detectives came around and told us Leo and Marie had been transferred to a hospital in Derry. They were alive, though Marie was in intensive care.

"Is she going to make it?"

"We won't know until morning. In the meantime, I'd like to go over a few statements your neighbor Leo made, if you don't mind. . . ."

There were four bodies to account for, after all. The detectives didn't leave until after midnight.

THE NEXT DAY something changed. The police took off, saying they'd had some "new information."

They also told us Marie was out of danger. "She's still in a fragile state, but her condition is improving."

We were allowed to go home the next morning but were told not to leave the country for the next few days. There were still questions to clear up and probably a visit to the courthouse.

Clem and Niels stayed another day, until Judie and I were released from the hospital. I told them they should take the kids and return to Amsterdam. The sooner they put some distance between themselves and this place, that house, the sooner they'd be able to heal. I promised the kids I'd follow them soon.

"You swear, Dad?" Jip said.

"I do, baby. As soon as this whole mess is cleared up, I'll meet you guys in Amsterdam."

It was hard to say goodbye, as the taxi idled in front of Judie's hostel. Half the town had turned out. A few friends Beatrice and Jip had made during their short but intense summer in Donegal came to say goodbye with flowers and other little trinkets. Laura O'Rourke, Mrs. Douglas, and half the regulars from Fagan's had come out, too. No one asked too many questions. At this point, there was an official story—*Thieves meet an untimely end during an armed robbery in Donegal*—and neither Judie nor I were going to contradict it.

Alarm vendors and self-defense courses all of a sudden were getting more business. Even Mr. Durran had started selling motion-sensing outdoor lights. The teenage store clerk from Andy's gave a nervous television interview and said the four criminals had given her the creeps. They had four espressos, and one of them had left his pack of cigarettes on the table. At least her story helped clear up any suspicions about me. She said she remembered me coming in, asking about the four and rushing out again.

On Sunday July 21 the *Irish Times* ran a story in which a police commissioner was quoted as saying that he doubted the four were "common criminals," and that INTERPOL was looking into the case. He was sure they'd have more information soon.

If there was ever new information, it never made it into print.

DAD STAYED A WEEK, spending the night at the hostel with Judie and me. The old curmudgeon was gone. He became another person overnight. He made breakfast every day and forbade Judie from working at the store. "I'll take care of everything, dammit, you're in no condition to be working." Maybe all he needed in life was a reason to care about something. I was glad to see him back to his old self, and I convinced him it was okay for him to go home at the end of the week. I'd be by to visit soon.

Meanwhile, there was no news from Leo or Marie. I called the hospital in Derry and was told they'd been transferred. "The woman was stable, and they left in an ambulance toward Dublin two days ago," the hospital operator said. Destination unknown.

Their cell phones had been disconnected. I tried the detectives, and they told me Leo and Marie had gone to make a statement at the courthouse in Dublin and to meet with members of the US Embassy. The case was in "someone else's hands," he said.

"Whose hands?"

"I don't know, Mr. Harper. But I can tell you two things: The people who tried to kill you were no common criminals, like the newspapers claim. They weren't your average thieves. And your friends? They weren't your average neighbors, either."

A MONTH WENT BY. The town returned to normal. I stayed on with Judie at the hostel. My house, as well as Leo's, were still considered active crime scenes and were off-limits. There was no word from Leo and Marie. None. Not a single phone call.

ON AUGUST 26, police took the crime tape off the doors of both houses. Imogen Fitzgerald went to work and got me out of my lease without any penalty. She also got a cleaning crew in there, and in a couple days, they left it like nothing had ever happened. She set me up with an international moving company and on September 15, I'd hand the keys over and say goodbye to Clenhburran.

Judie hadn't said anything about coming with me to Amsterdam, and I respected her silence. We were both still hurt. Weak. Many a night, I woke up with a shout, in a cold sweat. Tom would show up at the foot of my bed in a dream, intent on revenge, the ax still wedged in his skull, his mouth and eyes twitching from the blow . . . Now, it was Judie who woke me up from my nightmares instead of the other way around. She would hold me and kiss me sweetly on the cheek, and after an hour or two, I could finally get back to sleep.

THE WEEK before I was due to leave Ireland, I finally returned to the house. Judie wanted to come with me, but I told her I'd rather go alone. I needed to go alone.

It was a gray and drizzly morning when I set foot back on Tremore Beach. The sight of the fence, rebuilt and braced while the cement set, sent shivers down my spine.

I went around to the back of the house, where Tom's corpse would have laid before they tagged him and bagged him. Imogen's cleaning crew had painted the drain around the septic tank a brick red, perhaps to hide any blood they hadn't been able to wash away. I stood there, at that de facto tomb, but I didn't say a prayer. I thought back on that night. The sound of his skull cracking resonated in my memory.

The house was still when I finally stepped inside, only the sound of rain pitter-pattering on the roof. The sliding door to the terrace had new glass. The living room furniture and rug had been removed. Imogen said it would be forever before anyone rented this house again, especially now that it had a backstory (not to mention it was expensive and remote). But it was a pretty house. Perfect for an artist looking for a hideaway.

There were a couple of boxes in the attic from when I'd moved in. I brought them downstairs. There wasn't much left to pack besides clothes, some books, and my instruments. I'd have it all sent to my studio in Amsterdam. I'd figure out what to do with it later. Pat had offered to let me stay at his house. He had called me the moment the news went out on the AP wire. Somehow (and I had my theory), the story had made the news back home: *Composer Peter Harper injured in attempted robbery in coastal Ireland.* It had been big news. I'd been described as some kind of hero who had defended his children and neighbors with an ax. Of course, the tabloids ate it up. And now Pat was getting a dozen calls a week about new projects for me. "Free publicity, Pete. (All it cost me was couple of broken ribs.) You can't say no, now. You can smell the money coming in. Everyone wants your music. You have to get back to work. . . ."

An hour later, I was sitting on the floor of the living room, packing up the final items. The rain had let up, and the sun was setting. The house was starting to get chilly, so I decided to get some firewood to start a fire. I came back with the remaining logs from the shed. Despite everything, I'd miss this place. Waking up in the morning and hearing the birds, the waves crashing. Chopping firewood and lighting the fireplace. Hell, even mowing the lawn. And watching Leo run up the beach and calling out to him to come in for a beer.

I started piling the remaining kindling into the fireplace, as well as the stack of magazines next to the couch, a final act of warmth for this old house. Just as I lit the match and was reaching in to light it, something happened. A draft from the chimney blew out the match. And it was immediately followed by three solid knocks at the wooden front door.

Thump, thump, thump. Three quick knocks.

My heart jumped. I couldn't breathe. *This couldn't be . . .*

They knocked again.

I stood up and walked slowly across the room to the front door. I didn't even bother asking who it was. What was the point? I turned the lock and opened the door.

A person was waiting at the door. A person I knew. Soaked through and through. Wearing a smile.

"Harper! Thank goodness you're here," said Teresa Malone, the mail carrier. "I was about to leave."

"Te . . . Teresa?" I said. "What are *you* doing here?"

She was wearing her rain gear, from head to toe. Her scooter, which I hadn't heard with all the wind and rain, was parked out front next to my Volvo.

"Judie told me you were here, and I thought I should, well . . . even though this place gives me the creeps. I don't know how you got the courage up to come back here. Anyway, I got a package for you. I felt I should hand it to you in person."

She gave it to me, wrapped in a plastic bag. It was a small package with nothing but a simple phrase written on it: "Hand deliver to Peter Harper."

"It came inside another box addressed to the local post office. When I opened it, I found this."

I just stared at it.

"Who sent it?"

"There was no return address, but the postmark is British. The address to the post office was handwritten on the side."

"So . . . it must be someone from town. Someone who knows me. And you."

We looked at one another and smiled.

"Have you heard anything from them?" Teresa asked.

I shook my head.

"Two moving trucks arrived at their house yesterday," she said. "They took everything. I know because my cousin Chris knows one of the officers from Dungloe who had to go over there to oversee the move. He asked where the movers were taking all the stuff, and they told him it was going in storage. There was no final destination. But the message was clear: They weren't ever coming back. I can't blame them. After something like that? Still, I thought there would be some kind of goodbye. *Something . . .*"

Her eyes turned to the package.

"Thanks for bringing this over, Teresa."

"I hear you're moving, too. Is that true?" she said, touching my arm. "I was so sorry to hear what happened to you and your children. All of us in town are still horrified. Promise me you'll say goodbye before you go."

"I promise." I said.

I smiled goodbye and watched her walk back to her scooter in the rain. She beeped twice as she turned and headed back toward Bill's Peak.

I closed the door, lit the fire, and opened the package.

There was a letter inside.

I leaned in to the light from the fireplace, unfolded it, and read it.

Peter,

I wish I had more time to write, but I don't know where you'll be in a few months, nor where I will be. And I wanted to make sure you got the explanation you deserve. I'm not allowed to contact you, and I'm writing to you almost in secret, but I feel obliged to do it. I owe you and your family a great debt, and I feel you should at least know the truth.

First, I hope your and Judie's injuries have healed, and I

pray that your children are okay. I hope that one day this whole nightmare for which I feel completely responsible will be nothing more than a distant memory or, at least, one that will make a great story.

Second, I want to say thank you for saving our lives. Marie suffered a serious, nearly fatal, gunshot wound, but the surgery was a success and she's completely out of danger, thank God. She's a strong woman. As for my knee, well, I guess I won't be able to run as fast as I used to, but I'm alive to tell the tale. And that's all thanks to you.

If you hadn't come to our door that night . . . if you hadn't insisted that I carry a gun with me, everything would have turned out very differently. The day I visited you at the hospital, and you warned me the way you did, I went home and tried to shake the idea, but I couldn't let it go. I went into the shed and dusted off an old revolver I'd bought years ago. At first, I thought I'd just keep it nearby, in the living room somewhere or even under my pillow. But that night, the night everything happened, your kids were coming over to spend the night, and I didn't want to leave a gun lying around. Plus, there was that storm. . . . I thought, *is it possible you were right about everything, after all?* Either way, the gun ended up on my ankle, you came through the door . . . and you saved our lives, Peter. You gave Marie just enough time to escape. And sure, we each took a couple of bullets. But we never would have had a chance without you, without your stubbornness, without your craziness, without your *gift*. . . .

Because that's what you have, Pete. A gift. I don't know how you got it, but use it and treat it like gold. I know you've suffered because of it, but I also know it can do a lot of good. Who knows, maybe one day you'll pull the lottery numbers out of the air, and it won't seem so bad. . . . The fact is no one could have stopped this except you. You were right all along. But we lied to you, Peter. We had to. Or rather, we avoided telling you the truth.

I suppose you hate us for having been so stubborn. You knew from the beginning this was going to happen and because we didn't believe you, we put your family at risk. I'm sorry, Peter, deeply sorry. But they don't teach you in school to believe in ghosts and visions . . . especially when they're predicting your own worst nightmare come true. I guess we just didn't *want* to believe it.

I was so close to telling you the whole story that afternoon. The day you asked about Daniel and the painting you'd found . . . I almost ran after you to tell you the truth. I've felt close to you since the day we met, Peter, like you were the first true friend I'd had in a long time. You have a good heart. You can see it from a mile away. That's why I nearly broke my vow of secrecy. I just couldn't will myself to do it. My stupid, old distrustful mind told me it was better not to say anything. "What if you're wrong?" I told myself. "What if you can't trust him?" But Marie never doubted you, of course. She thought maybe you'd picked up something subconsciously, some detail we'd let slip because we confided so much in you. But I was skeptical. That first night when you showed up at our door, I spent the night awake thinking. *Was this all part of some ploy? Is he trying to wheedle information out of us?* I guess it's the residue of being suspicious for a living, always looking out for someone trying to conceal who they really are. Especially when you know someone is trying to find and kill you.

I looked into you. I made some calls to find out who you were, and all I can say now is I'm sorry. If it's any consolation, I did the same thing with the guy who rented the house before you. He must have had his suspicions because he ended up leaving a month later.

By this point, you must already have figured it out. We *are* Leo and Marie Blanchard. Or at least we were. I never really cared

much for the last name Kogan. I like the new one they just assigned
us much better. Actually, we have new first names, too, for added
security. As you can probably guess, I can't tell you what they are,
but rest assured they're good names. They fit our faces.

This is one of the few outright lies I told you. I promise there
aren't many more. Almost everything else I told you is true: that I
worked in hotel security, that Marie painted and traveled with me.
And it's true that I was thinking of retiring in 2004. Like I told you,
I'd been traveling for work for twenty-five years, I'd lived in a dozen
cities and I was tired. Tired of that nomadic life. Tired of always
moving on before we could ever make any friends.

Marie and I had planned to buy some land on the island of
Phi Phi in Thailand, build a bed and breakfast, and spend the rest
of our days there, tanning and sailing. I resigned from the hotel
where I was working, determined to start my new life. But that very
month, out of the blue, I got an offer from a six star resort in Hong
Kong.

It was supposed to be a one-year contract as a consultant to
design the hotel's security and build the security team. *Six stars.*
It was almost four times my previous salary. Looking back, that
should have been a red flag. At a time when hotels were cutting
back on their own private security and outsourcing, where were
they getting all this money? But I was blinded by the prospect.
That money could help fill all the gaps in our retirement plan for
Thailand. I accepted the job, and we moved that summer. I'd pay a
heavy price for my mistake.

I started in May, and it didn't take long to realize something
was fishy. After all those years in the business, you start picking up
on things, especially when something doesn't quite fit. And there
were a lot of things that didn't smell right to me. My new boss, the
director, who was a total newcomer to the business, gave me this

weird "welcome speech" with all kinds of hidden meanings. "We have a very *special* and *distinguished* clientele. Discretion is our number one priority here at the resort, Mr. Blanchard. I hope that's clear. Loyalty and discretion." The amount of money being thrown around compared to how few people actually came to the resort just didn't add up. I'm telling you, the whole thing stunk. I should have resigned that very first day. But I didn't. I guess I figured, "Just mind your own business, stick out the year, and get out."

I could tell you all kinds of stories, things that should have made me run. The clients, first of all, were dirty. That much was clear. You only had to look at their faces. Big limos lining the entrance, hookers and orgies in every suite. The things I saw in those private rooms when I personally had to be called in to carry out some drunk prostitute or troublemaker. After years of trying to do honest work, I'd suddenly walked into a snake pit. And I was in up to my neck. Well, mostly as I was only a consultant. It was my job to set up cameras, install procedures, but they put their own people at the computers and monitoring stations. I paid attention in case I needed an exit strategy.

And, of course, they knew how to deliver a message. With money and gifts. On my six-month anniversary, they bought me a Porsche, to "celebrate a job well done, with dedication and loyalty." Loyalty was the keyword, Pete. They feted Marie with jewelry, almost every month. Gifts she never wanted to accept, but which I told her she couldn't refuse. More mistakes. We were already halfway through my contract, and I realized it would be dangerous to quit at this point. Then, about eight months into my contract, the director of that cesspool called me into his office to offer me a job "in house." They had been pleased with work and wanted to make me "part of the family." You have to hear how those words sound coming out of the mouth of a criminal. And you should

have seen the look on his face when I said thank you, but I have
plans to retire. "Retirement? But you're so young, Mr. Blanchard. It
would be disappointing to see you leave us so soon. It would be . . .
upsetting to our investors."

Everything changed after that. I noticed right away. There
was less work for me to do. Fewer visits with the director. They
started restricting my access, and at first, I was happy about it. I'd
sent a message, and they'd gotten the point. Then one night, on
my drive home, two cars flanked me on the highway. They steered
me toward a detour and down to a secluded area near the port.
Waiting for me was a strange contingent of men in blue suits, led
by a white-haired guy named Howard, who said he was the head of
INTERPOL in China.

"Earlier tonight, in Hong Kong, we detained a suspect who was
carrying this," he said, handing me a folder. In it were pictures of
Marie and me, the address to our house, and the license plate of
our car. "They are going to get rid of you at the end of the year. A
car accident or a gas explosion at home. That's how they do it, to
make it look like an accident, for those who don't 'take the oath.'
You can never go back to your old life, Mr. Blanchard. But you can
help yourselves, right now. INTERPOL can put you into witness
protection and give you a new life. You need to cooperate with us."

The old Leo and Marie were as good as dead, but INTERPOL
could offer to resurrect us into a new life. It was the only option
we had left. They'd give us new names, new passports, and some
money to start over someplace else. In exchange, they needed
something from us. And that "something" was information from
the resort's computers. Names, telephone numbers, dates to which
I had access.

We didn't have much time to think it over. I went home and
told Marie everything. We left the car and went for a walk into

town. We tried to stay in a public place, and we talked for hours, until everything started to close down. Then we slept in a hotel rather than risk going home. At four in the morning, I called Howard and told him we accepted his offer. He sent his agents over to the hotel, and we went over the plan for the following day. One of them spent the night standing guard, drinking coffee, and sitting with his revolver in his lap. Another one watched the door. They told us to stay away from the windows. We'd sleep maybe an hour or two.

I still had access to certain areas of the resort. I had to do it all in one day, before anyone noticed. I showed up at work that day with my stomach in knots, but I tried to act normal. I'd spent my career chasing thieves, and now, I was going to become one of them. I picked out one of the dumber staff at the resort. I told him I had to use the company computers to run some names and needed to get into the surveillance room for a few minutes. I went to work. I downloaded nearly a thousand files onto a tiny drive the size of thumbnail. I hid it under my tongue to get past the security pat down, a procedure I'd initiated. I told them I was going out for lunch—and never came back.

And that's how our lives in witness protection began. More agents arrived at the hotel that day, eight total in a pair of cars with bulletproof windows. They told us they'd take us to a safe house near Dashen Bay, but that turned out to be a lie. We were too valuable to INTERPOL for them to trust even us with the truth. We weren't allowed to go back home. They'd buy us new clothes, whatever we needed, but we couldn't expose ourselves. We left behind our home, our neighbors, our books, our clothes, all of Marie's paintings. . . . It was terrible. We were in shock. Marie asked if we could water the plants before we left. Could we at least leave the cat for the neighbor to watch? No, they told us. Too risky.

Wearing baseball caps and dark sunglasses, we arrived at a safe house on the Chinese border, an old military barracks outfitted with cameras, bars on the windows, and round-the-clock security. They told me to call the resort and tell them I'd had a family member fall ill; I'd be gone for a few days and would call them later with an update.

We spent two weeks locked up there, like criminals. It was terrible. They treated us like livestock. I lost it when they told us not to stand near the windows. Marie couldn't stop crying. It was the one time in my life I was relieved our son, Daniel, hadn't lived long enough to go through that.

Our second week there, they sat us down for some news. First, the "organization" had figured out our play and had sent our names and pictures out to their network. They put a bounty of $100,000 on my head. Not bad, huh? Second, INTERPOL had managed to get a trial date set so we could testify. Only two more months of this. In the meantime, we'd meet once in secret with the judge and the state's attorney handling the case at some other undisclosed location. We'd be transferred to another location, in Laos, while we waited those two months to testify.

We had to sign power of attorney over to an INTERPOL lawyer so he could handle all the details of our disappearance: the sale of our house, transferring our funds to a Swiss bank. We signed away our old lives, all the documents that erased who we had been. Leo and Marie Blanchard were no more.

We lived in the mountains in Laos during those two months, with four INTERPOL agents. The date to testify finally arrived. I flew on a private plane to a Chinese naval airbase in Sai Kung. From there, we took a camouflaged armored van to the courthouse. They brought me in the back door, wearing a ski mask and a bulletproof vest. I sat in a booth, behind bulletproof glass, and swore to tell the truth, the whole truth, and nothing but. I testified to a small group about my one-year contract at the resort and how I'd accessed the information I gave INTERPOL. The questioning lasted close to two hours before they were done with me. "Thank you, and good luck," the judge told me.

Leo and Marie Blanchard died on a beautiful, starry night. The sea was flat and a breeze blew in from the south. The moment we switched vessels, when we stepped off the *Fury* and onto that military powerboat, we left our old lives behind. Our friends and family could never suspect we were still alive. Assassins looking to make good on the bounty had to believe someone else had gotten to us first. We switched boats several miles off the coast of Macau. From there, to a private airplane on the island of Phen-Hou. And from there, to Singapore. Then Europe. And England. Far, far away, to the other side of the globe.

We lived in a house in London for eight months until the final arrangements were made. We got a new last name: Kogan. I even remembered snickering when I read it out loud. We got new passports, birth certificates (we were now born in Salt Lake City, Utah), a pair of Visa credit cards, and the Swiss bank account number that contained the proceeds of the sale of our house, cars, sailboat, and life savings. Sounds simple enough, doesn't it? It's not, believe me. Imagine everyone you've ever known thinking you're dead. You'll never be able to call to wish them a Merry Christmas. You'll never know anything about their lives, ever again. It's like actually being dead. You're a ghost. The relocation program director impressed on us how important it was to never try to contact any family or friends, not even sending a postcard without a return address. Simply knowing we were alive would be enough for the organization to resume their search.

"Your car exploded in Hong Kong yesterday when a tow truck

tried to move it from the spot where it had been parked for four months. The driver was injured, but he'll recover," one agent told me.

In Chelsea, where we lived in London, there was a little newsstand that sold newspapers from around the world, and we'd read them every day, looking for traces of our old lives. There was nothing, except for a small article in a Hong Kong daily about the *Fury*'s disappearance.

Still, it was hard to adapt to this new life. We lived a cloistered existence, without much contact with anyone else. We were scared any little detail would filter out and reach the wrong set of ears. I'm sure our neighbors in Chelsea thought of us as the nice but reclusive old couple of expats. We'd do our groceries, smile at our neighbors, but we always kept our distance. If anyone got too close, we would start to avoid them. We never accepted a single dinner invitation. We were always too busy.

It started to grate on us. It wasn't in our nature to be recluses. We talked it over with the relocation program director, and he was the one who suggested moving to a more isolated area, a rural community. It had worked for others in the past. The chances of our identities coming to light in a small town were much more remote. "Why not try Ireland or Scotland? There's some beautiful countryside there. Cold, but safe. Not too many people around."

And that's how we got to Clenhburran, Peter. From the moment we set foot there, I knew we would put down roots. It wasn't my dream beach in Thailand, but it was a beach nonetheless, a sanctuary, a place we could retire to. For the first time since we escaped from Hong Kong, I felt free. Marie started to make friends again, and I finally felt at liberty to start sharing my own life, always careful not to mention that "minor episode," but never outright lying about my past. That's no way to make real friends.

And that was my plan, more or less. To grow old here with my wife, a warm fireplace and my cup of hot tea. To live out my years here and die in peace, but not before writing one final letter to tell all the people I left behind what really happened—the way I'm writing to you today.

But somehow, the organization found us. INTERPOL still has no idea how. They said we must have broken some kind of security protocol, but I insisted that we'd followed all the rules to the letter. We'd been the most perfect dead couple in history. We had never called or written to anyone from our past. And only God knows how much we'd suffered because of it. The church-going women in town think Marie is a saint, the most devout of them all, but in fact the reason she goes to church to light a candle every day is in memory of some friend or family member she knows we'll never see again.

Maybe, quite simply, our story traveled by word of mouth—farther than anyone thought possible—until that information ended up in the wrong hands. Maybe the international mafia's reach is greater than we ever imagined. Or maybe someone just recognized us on the street. Who knows? The important part is that our friend Peter Harper saved our lives, and that we know for sure.

So now we're on the move again. I'm not sure where we'll end up, but hopefully somewhere warmer, near the ocean, where I can buy another sailboat. You know what? Maybe I'll pool my money and buy myself that dream boat, after all. Marie and I can live on it and maybe I can convince her to go on one last adventure and sail around the world. We'll disappear again on the big blue sea once and for all. One way or another, I'm going to fulfill our dream. I'll keep you posted. You're easy to find, what with being famous and all.

Speaking of which, I've reached the advice portion of this letter. First, the most practical. Now that you know who we were up against, you might be wondering if you have anything to worry

about from the organization. My friends at INTERPOL worked
with the police to clear your name on the official report. Now, it
says only that you killed Tom and Manon in self-defense. That
I killed Randy, and that Frank bled out on our rug as we waited
for the ambulance to arrive. I doubt anyone will miss four evil
bastards in the world. The guys at INTERPOL tell me they were
mercenaries, and it's probably better that none of them survived.
Otherwise, the organization would have killed the survivors for
failing so spectacularly against a little old man and a family man
with his two kids. Then again, they never counted on Peter Harper
and his sixth sense, did they? Either way, you probably have
nothing to worry about, but it never hurts to keep an eye out. Then
again, with your natural instincts, you probably won't have to. Just
listen to that inner voice.

Next piece of advice: about you and Judie. Nowadays, everyone
makes a big deal about their freedom, but I think there's something
people don't understand. I think sometimes people use the word
"freedom" when they mean "I'm scared of taking a chance." Okay,
so I know I'm an old man, and feel free to wipe your ass with this
advice. But if you can see into the future, then I can see into the
hearts of people. And I can tell you that maybe—just maybe—
there's a little bit of that fear inside you. The fear of falling in love
again. The same fear that keeps your father locked away from his
life in Dublin. I know you've been hurt and you're pissed off at the
world and you don't want to let anything or anyone all the way in
again. And maybe that's affecting your music, too. Being creative
is an act of absolute confidence. That's what you told me, wasn't
it? It's about freedom—real freedom. And you've come searching
for that freedom on a desolate beach by the ocean, where you
assume a man can be most free. But you're still trapped in a small,
windowless room of pain and self-doubt. If any good comes out of

this whole nightmare, I hope it's to shake that fear out of you. I pray that it does.

I would have liked to tell you all this in person. To sit on the porch with a couple of Belgian beers and solve the world's problems one last time as the sun set. It's been a pleasure and a privilege to have been your friend, Peter. And I hope this world sees fit to let our paths cross.

Marie sends you a big hug and a kiss, and I know she'll miss you, too. More than likely, one day she'll light a candle for you, for Judie, for Jip and Beatrice, and we'll think of you wherever we are.

Take care of yourself, Peter.

Your friend,
Leo

ELEVEN

AFTER SEEING off the moving van, I put on my best blazer, picked a handful of wildflowers growing near the shore at Tremore Beach, and made my way to the hostel to see Judie.

I found her sitting alone by the window, reading a book in the sunlight that fell softly on her face. Part of me thought perhaps she was destined to spend the rest of her life here in this peaceful place she'd made for herself. And that made me feel a little guilty for what I was about to do.

Judie smiled when she saw me come through the door.

"My, you're dressed so nicely, Peter. Who are those flowers for?"

"Why, for you, Miss Gallagher," I said handing them to her with much ceremony.

"Oh, how kind of you, Mr. Harper," she said, bringing them to her nose. "Flowers to say goodbye," she said, a note of melancholy in her voice.

"Well, my dear señorita," I started to say, a little nervous, "they're not necessarily a goodbye gift. That's exactly what I'm here to clear up. I'd like to ask you a question . . . or rather, to ask you again. Someone once said you have to give a good thing a second chance, or a third or a fourth. And an old friend told me these kinds of things require a measure of formality. So . . ."

I came around the counter and bent down on one knee in front of Judie, who smiled and clasped her hands to her chest.

"Judie Gallagher: Mine is an injured heart, a wary heart, but a loving heart nonetheless. And you are the smartest, sweetest, most sensitive person I could ever have hoped to find on this earth. And I would never ask you this unless I was absolutely certain—and I am. I'm in love with you, Judie. I love you, and I want you to come with me. I want us to start something together. You know I can't stay, I need my kids, to see them grow up and be there for them. And that's why, even though I know it's somewhat selfish, I want you to cross the ocean with me. I know I'm asking a lot. I know you've found a place in the world where you finally feel at peace and I'm asking you to leave it. But I don't want to leave without you. I don't want to leave you behind. You are . . . too important to me."

Judie's eyes sparkled. A single tear ran down her cheek to the edge of her lovely lips. She sniffled and grabbed a handkerchief, flowers still clasped in one hand.

"Peter . . ."

"Yes or no, Judie," I said. "I can take it if it's a 'no.' I'll always love you. But I just need to know."

She slid down off the chair to sit on the floor next to me and took my face in her hands. We kissed. A long, sweet kiss with our eyes closed that transported us, that allowed us to dream together, that took us somewhere beyond where we were . . . until we heard the door and Mrs. Douglas found us kneeling behind the counter.

"Everything all right here, kids?"

"Yes," Judie said, straightening up, and grabbing me by the hand as we both stood up, "everything's perfect, Mrs. Douglas.

"Listen," she told her while squeezing my fingers, "do you know anyone who might be interested in running the store? I think I just gave my two weeks' notice."

A WEEK LATER, a day before flying to Amsterdam, I was in Dublin with my dad. We'd gone to dinner at the pub and sang rousing, drunken renditions of "The Irish Rover," and "Molly Malone" after five pints apiece. We were celebrating life, he said. "Life is *meant* to be celebrated," he said. Judie would be coming to Holland in a couple of months, after settling all her accounts in Donegal, and Dad was coming, too. He said he wanted to start traveling. And to be close to his loved ones.

After the pub, we stumbled along Christ Church to Thomas Street, where we slipped down an alley and took a piss, father and son, partners in crime. We sang as we ambled down the street, waking up the neighbors. When we got home, I helped him to his room and dumped him in bed, where he fell asleep in his clothes, snoring above the covers. I kissed him on the forehead and tried to not tumble down the stairs as I returned to the living room.

I lay down on the couch and fell fast asleep. My headaches were gone, and the nightmares had started to fade. Early on, a full night's sleep was a major victory. Now, little by little, it became the norm. That's what I told Dr. Kauffman a few days back, when I called to cancel my sessions with him. He was happy for me, although he hated saying goodbye to the most interesting case he'd had in a long time. He said he'd like to continue with the hypnosis. To understand where I had gotten that premonition. I told him he should probably forget about it unless he wanted to start publishing papers in pseudoscience psychic journals.

But that night in Dublin, after falling into that happy drunken sleep, it happened again. My eyes opened in the middle of the night. And there, sitting at the dining room table, watching me, was my mother.

This time, there was no trace of her illness. Her skin radiated health. Her hair was lush and thick, just as I remembered it as a child. Her eyes shone, and she smiled.

She gestured to the old upright piano against the wall. She wanted me to play for her one last time, just as I had when I was a boy. I can still hear her humming the pieces I practiced.

I went over and sat down, opened the keyboard, and began to play. A slow, beautiful melody came pouring out of me, one that seemed to always have been there, waiting for me. I played the entire piece, from start to finish.

When I woke up, my mother was gone. But the piece of music was still inside me.

I thanked her, found a sheet of staff paper, and started to write.

ACKNOWLEDGMENTS

The inspiration for this novel was born in a town on the Irish coast of Donegal in 2008. I was living in Dublin at the time and had gone on a brief vacation with some friends to an isolated house near the sea. There was a storm and lightning and countless other adventures, but nothing like what's in this story; all the people and places herein are fictional.

But since then, from that first germ of an idea to the final text, there were several people responsible for bringing *The Last Night at Tremore Beach* to fruition. I want to thank them for helping make this book a reality.

First of all, Ainhoa, my fiancée, who always believed in this book and gave me some great ideas for scenes and characters. She's capable of doing that and cooking dinner, amazingly, while I shuffled back and forth around the house with a pencil and paper, talking to myself about my problems. Thank you for your infinite patience and for being such a great partner and literary consultant.

To my mother, Begoña, and my brother Javi, who were the first ones to read the book, encourage me, and give me valuable comments and suggestions. Their thoughts helped shape the characters Judie and Peter as well as Peter's relationship with his children. My brother Julen gave me wonderful insight into the "sensibilities" of Peter Harper. Plus, he created the magnificent book trailer.

Thanks also to Pedro Varela and Laura Gutierrez, doctors and friends who helped me with the medical aspects in the book. I tried to stay as true as possible to all hospital and psychiatric procedures (as well as the pharmacological terminology) they explained to me, though I took some creative license along the way for which I am solely responsible.

I also want to thank my agent, Bernat Fiol, who bet on me, on the book, and who also shared valuable feedback that helped make the story stronger and more dynamic.

And finally, to all those readers who wrote to me, encouraging me and asking me "what's next." Well, this is what was next. And I hope you enjoyed it.